The Man Who Never Was

A prequel to
The Paladin chronicles

Neil Port

The Man Who Never was
(Prequel to the Paladin Chronicles)

Published by Neil Port Independent Press, Newcastle, Australia

Conversion to e book: ebooksspecialist@gmail.com
Cover design by: Paul Kimber (mule@angelheartdesign.org)

Print Book ISBN 978-0-9873845-8-4

Thank You

I'm delighted you have downloaded or purchased this book. My books aren't perfect, that wouldn't be possible and readers' tastes vary a lot. What one reader likes in a book another doesn't, but I'll try to be worthy of your trust.

The series is Epic (High) Fantasy set in historical settings, often exotic, and combined with a touch of romance. A word of warning: the violence, war, romance (and especially the love making) is not gratuitous but if you have a low tolerance for such, please read no further.

Supporting Charity

My wife and I are retired medical practitioners. When she was working as a medical volunteer she met a writer who funded charitable contributions from her writing. This inspired me to donate all royalties to charity (and pay the expenses out of my own pocket). I don't feel all writers should do this. My financial situation is different from theirs.

As my early books are in part set in what is modern day Syria, I chose "Save the Children Fund, the Syrian Refugee Appeal". It was some years ago now when the tragedy in this country was just starting to unfold.

If you wish to support this worthwhile cause in other ways (as well as, or instead of), it would also help (tremendously!) if you recommend these books to others (who like this genre) and/or give a favourable review wherever you downloaded the book.

The current biggest eBook seller suggests for their star ratings: 5 stars I love it, 4 stars I like it, 3 stars it is OK, 2 stars I don't like it, 1 star I hate it.

Remember by doing this, you are supporting charity.

God Bless and Good Reading.

More Give-aways?

If you haven't yet joined my email list, don't forget to sign up on http://www.neilport.com. You won't be spammed by me, just a few give-aways, news of my next book and maybe a few authors you may be interested in. You may not hear from me for a while as I spend a lot of time on each book before release.

Contents

Notes

I describe this book as a 'prequel' because it refers to events several millennia before the time of 'The Paladin Chronicles', but it was written after book 4. While all my books are designed to be able to be enjoyed on their own, knowledge of the first three books would help place this one in context. Like many prequels, this book is shorter than other books in the main series.

The Elvish Prophecy: Two thousand years before the events described in the Paladin Chronicles, the Western Elves were enjoying a golden age. They had built a mighty and magical kingdom centred on their greatest city, Elvish *Troia* (Troy). They became powerful and fabulously wealthy, with trade that stretched from east to west across their land and the rich bounty from the valleys, plains and seas of their new homeland, *Anatolē* (Turkey).

The civilisation of the Western Elves became so strong that it seemed like it would never end. Yet in the midst of this wondrous splendour *Ælward* ('Elf Guardian') the last and possibly the greatest of elf *Seiðmaðr* (*Sorcerer*), foresaw not only the fall of the elves but their ultimate extinction. The world would face not once, but twice, great deluges, tidal waves of savage barbarians. The second of these would happen at a time when the elves themselves were failing.

By the time of the events of the Paladin Chronicles the elves had lost their magic and scarcely lived longer than the humans they once dominated. Worse, they had very few children and dark storm clouds were gathering for them both to the West and to the East. Ælward's Prophecy, also called 'the Elvish Prophecy', became their only hope.

This prequel goes back almost to the very start of the history of the elves to another place and another time when the elves faced extinction. The written history of this time has been long lost, if it was ever written. All we have is legend and I have used a little known version, with me filling in a few minor gaps.

Seven hundred years before the time of this story the elves had lost a great war against a daimôn army summoned by the *Illvættir*, the 'Ill breed', a group of powerful sorcerers.

Their cities were destroyed and their population slaughtered. Hjørvard, their prince and hero of the war, led the pathetic remnants of his people to the safety of the land of snow and ice. But the Illvættir have not forgotten them.

The elves were welcomed and sheltered by the ancient inhabitants of what was later called *Norge* (Norway). They were a fair race related to the Finns and called themselves *Samit* (Sami).

Now it is the Copper Age, which briefly preceded the Bronze Age. The Sami are being displaced from the south by an invasion of the 'Battle Axe' People, named after their finely wrought stone battle axes.

The 'Battle Axe' People produced some of the finest flint work of the Stone Age and early Bronze Age and are the Stone Age precursors of the Vikings. They originated from the region around Denmark and spread across the sea to southern Norway and Sweden. I have called them 'Norse' in view of their later history. In Hervor's world their arrival and the arrival of copper to Norway came earlier than it did in our own.

The Prehistory of Norway: The prehistory of Norway is confused and open to debate, relying as it does on finds of tools and pottery. Of the current inhabitants of Norway, the nomadic Sami are accepted to be the first to arrive in the North (they probably hunted reindeer more than herded them back then). There is some evidence that challenges a traditional view that the Sami never made it into the south of Norway in any significant way. In Hervor's world, the Sami once occupied all of Norway.

As the ice retreated after the ice age, global thawing proceeded with fits and starts, with large and small fluctuations. Starting about 8,000 years ago there was a relatively warm period (called the 'Atlantic Period') that lasted two or three millennia. Scientists believe that the world was warmer than it is today. This story is set in the early Atlantic period in Hervor's world at a time when the world was warming.

Hervor: Hervor is the name of two famous shield maidens in Norse legend: the original Norse Hervor (who fought disguised as a man and took the name Hjørvard), and her granddaughter. It is also the name of an ancient Elvish Goddess ('her' as in lady, and 'vor' as in 'fore', meaning 'lady of spring'). Even amongst the elves, Hervor was one of their best fighters but she had a different temperament to Jacinta in the main Paladin series. She is a woodland elf who becomes a farm girl; not a young girl training to be a Paladin.

Place of this prequel in the overall story of The Paladin Chronicles: This prequel to the Paladin Chronicles helps explain how the elves ended up in Anatolē (modern day Turkey) all the way from modern day Norway. It also explains the words of the Elvish Prophecy that are especially relevant to book 6:

'When the final time comes God's Warrior must journey into the deepest, that terrible place, to find the weapons and armour that are made for the man who never was, nor ever will be and awaken that which lies within.

Only death will end the one of ancient evil but he will never be killed. He is the one that no one daimôn, no one living, no one dead, no one made or not made and no one of the races of men can possibly defeat.'

It adds some detail about the early history of the Illvættir and their last surviving member Áedán (Æloðulf, meaning 'elf-wolf', hunter of elves). Æloðulf is 'the one of ancient evil' referred to in the Elvish Prophecy. It also touches on the dwarves, just before their fall.

Hjørvard: Hjørvard was also the name of several characters in Norse mythology. It is also the name of the great elf prince and hero of the Illvættir war. It will also be the name of the new hero prophesied to save the ancient elves of Norway. The name means 'sword guard' and of course the elves in this story no longer had the means to make swords (after losing so badly in the Illvættir War and fleeing to Norway).

Prophecy of Gudmund: When the elvish prince Hjørvard finally died of his wounds, the elf Seiðmaðr Gudmund prophesied that when the elves next faced the Illvættir a great hero would arise to save them, a direct descendant of Hjørvard, whose heart would be infused with Hjørvard's courage and love of his people.

'No man will ever replace our beloved prince who has died today, and yet one day when the Illvættir hunt us again, one will be found infused with his love and courage; not a Jarl or King, but nonetheless a true heir who will take the name of Hjørvard

and who will wield a weapon against the daimôns. One who will guard us and keep us safe on the long journey to the new home for the elves.'

Some have said Gudmund was referring to an even older prophecy from before the fall of the elves.

Svartálfar: ('Dark Elves'). They were an elder race of powerful sorcerers, they resembled the elves somewhat in physical appearance and were their original mentors. At the time of our story the svartálfar are assumed to be extinct, apart from a subgroup of them called the Illvættir.

Illvættir: ('Ill breed') were a sect of the svartálfar that chose to summon daimôns. This gave them incredible power and made them almost immortal. The knowledge that one day they would lose their soul to the daimôn they had bonded with caused them to develop a terror of dying. This terrible fear unsettled their minds and led to paranoia, an initially baseless belief that all other beings of power secretly wished to kill them.

Elves: The idea of the Ljósálfar or 'light' elves later became influenced by the Christian idea of angels: they became described as 'fairer than the sun to look at'. Tolkien's elves are closer to humans and mine are even closer still.

The Norse used the term 'elf' ('alfr') in other ways. In its broadest sense it referred to a range of magical creatures (not always benevolent). In one meaning it included dwarves. When compounded in a name it meant inhumanly clever.

In English culture our idea of elves has also become influenced by the Celtic mythology of 'fairies' and 'we-folk' but my elves are human sized; tall, but slender.

Spelling: American readers, please forgive my Australian/ UK spellings.

A native speaker of Old Norse: Well, not me actually, especially pre-Viking Norse. I have cheated and used a very distorted version, ignoring all grammar, often knowingly.

Elvish Languages: Elves are multi-lingual from very young and freely use borrowed words from other languages. If the language of Stone Age Vikings has defeated me I had no hope at all of transliterating ancient Elvish, even if it was available to me. There is no written record dating back to Hervor's time. This version of the legend is taken from an English translation of old Norse. Much of the ancient names and terms are lost or only known to the elves.

Fjord: Originally had a more general meaning of a long thin body of water that was used as a passage, I have used it in the modern sense of a flooded glacial valley.

Metal: After the agricultural revolution sophisticated social organisation became possible in a way that we don't normally think of when we think of a Stone Age. At the time of the Copper Age metals were known about but hard to get, especially tin to make bronze.

The dawn of the Bronze Age relied on vast trade routes stretching far across the known world and the massive social organisation capable of supporting large scale mining, especially of tin.

The dwarves were far in advance of humans. They were the first to use copper rivets in their larger boats and to make bronze, iron and later, steel.

Boats: Humans of the time mostly used canoes of various sorts. For war they used canoes lined by stitched birch bark or giant dugouts, swift and carrying large crews. Old, giant trees were not hard to find back then. Sailing canoes were more an elvish design, the outrigger and the twin hulled. Unlike war canoes they could be sailed, but they were not as fast. The Norse in ancient times did build a small number of *langskips* (longships), precursors of the later Viking ships. They were built of wooden planks and held together with wooden nails, tendon and willow and made waterproof by special moss drenched in pine tar.

Tolkien: Borrowed many names and themes from Scandinavian (and Finnish) lore and history, often using them out of the original context. I have also borrowed from Scandinavian names and language.

Writing and Alphabets: In our world, the western alphabets and written language came from the Phoenicians via the Greeks to Greek colonies in Italy. Runes were adapted from early Italic alphabets so came around 150 AD. In Bjørn and Hervor's world the elves brought svartálfar runes with them.

Some Extra letters in Norse:

ð **(Eth):** *th* as in 'the', so 'broðir' is 'brothir', not 'brodir'. Incidentally Óðinn was said 'Othin' but later became 'Wōden' in Old English.

Þ, þ, **(Thorn):** is virtually the same sound (though softer, th as in "thick"), usually at the start of the word.

æ **('ash'):** so named because the rune that it replaced looks like an ash tree with branches on one side. Say it like it looks. Þræll for example is said 'thra-el' in ancient Nordic, not thrall (like ball), as in modern English.

Ø, ø, **(or ǫ):** represented an original runic character. It is usually said 'er' (occasionally 'ir'). The Norwegian version of Bjørn (meaning 'bear') is pronounced 'BE-ERN'. Björn, the

Swedish version, and Bjorn, the English version, are both pronounced 'BE-ORN'.

Chapter 1: Ālfheimr, Autumn

Ālfheimr, autumn.

There was a great storm brewing, and this was a land of great storms. Air and water currents from the south warmed the narrow coast and then warm moist air had to rise sharply to get over the high central mountains.

They had some good rain and the last two days were hot and dry, so Hervor knew it was a good time for mushrooms. She also remembered a secret spot from last season where she found some white morel, the ones her mother loved most of all, but if she couldn't find them, kantarell, golden and flute-like, were especially good this season.

As soon as she finished her morning chores she hurried to grab her basket. Her mother, Svafa, only gave her a look of mild surprise. She said nothing about the coming storm, nor did she ask her daughter to be careful. They were elves. No warning was needed, and elves are not fond of unnecessary words.

Hervor swung her basket as she hurried up the steep hill, humming a prayer to the Mother Goddess. The elves loved their mushrooms and her contribution was very welcome, but to Hervor a mushroom hunt was more fun than work. She loved exercise and she loved being out in the fresh air. Sometimes she just wanted to run and run, just for the fun of it ... and sometimes she did.

She paused, as she always did at the crest of the hill, to look down on *Ālfheimr* (Elf-home), the village of her birth. The view was shadowed by the coming storm, but to Hervor there was nowhere more beautiful on earth than her home. There was a time when the elves had great cities and numbers beyond counting, but not now. Now there were very few elves, and this was their largest village.

Tens of millennia ago all this land was locked under a titanic sheet of ice but the world grew warmer and the ice cap melted. After that there were glaciers in the valleys. When they in their turn retreated, the rising sea level flooded the glacial valleys and formed fjords: long narrow inlets, flanked by steep cliffs carved by ice long ago and stunning in their beauty.

The fjord that led to Ālfheimr widened into a shallow bay and the main village sat just up from that. The valley beyond was flat and green and fertile. Then came the hills and forest, quickly giving way to the mountains. The mountains were dark, tall and forbidding, naked of trees and white on the peaks, with their sides streaked with snow. The Norse called them the *Dovrefjell* (Dovre Mountains). Only the Sami, the ancient people of this land, knew of ways over them.

For a moment Hervor shuddered. The feeling she was being watched was so strong that she spun around, her free hand clutched into a fist and her elf senses alert. Only another elf could sneak up on her in the forest, but this was no elf, it felt like something dark, brooding and malevolent was watching her.

There was nothing that she could see and the feeling passed quickly, but it still left her feeling unsettled. She tried to calm down, drinking in peace from the view. This was her beloved hills and forests, and down below was her home. She cast her eye over the village again. It was dominated by the great stockade on a rise, surrounded by earthworks and a tall palisade of pine logs, small in the distance now. Inside of the stockade was a wooden watch tower at the harbour end, standing tall. At the other end was her father's great-house; huge and rambling. It had to be big, as it doubled as a meeting house and was home to many of the single men and widowers of the village.

Scattered around were the other houses and sheds: storage sheds, smoke houses, barns, pit houses and a couple of deep dugouts for storing ice from winter or brought down from the mountains, and of course, some precious frozen goods.

Most of the buildings had stone foundations and after the fashion of the elves, were made from wood and gaily decorated; carved and painted with woodland scenes, bright awnings and flowers in small window boxes. Even the canoe houses had plants in pots and wooden lattice windows with herbs and flowers (and 'small magic') to keep insects out.

Trees grew everywhere in the village as the elves loved trees, and the houses and trails through the village were decorated by quartz crystals on strings. At night the elves used their 'small-magic', to make the crystals sing and shine with coloured lights that glowed and twinkled. To live one's life in beauty was one of the highest forms of praise an elf could give to their Goddess, the Great Earth Mother. Ālfheimr was her home. It was a beautiful place, and it was a safe place for the elves.

Hervor shifted the basket more comfortably and jogged effortlessly into the forest, now turning red, gold and brown with autumn. The brief feeling of alarm was forgotten as she used her sharp elf vision to rapidly scan for mushrooms and berries.

While elves do not age like humans, they grow up not too much differently. So at twenty Hervor was the size of a full grown elf-woman. At five foot ten she was taller than many human men of her time but being an elf she was slender, almost delicate looking. She was old enough to bear her own children but elves marry late and Hervor was still considered young for an elf maiden.

Most elves, men and women, shared the inhuman beauty of their kind and Hervor was no exception. She had a pale complexion with a faint dusting of freckles, elfin ears, a heart shaped face and penetrating green eyes that shone in the shadow. She grew her hair barely longer than shoulder length but it was the thing she liked most of all about how she looked. Underneath her blue head scarf it was flaming red, soft and silky.

The mushroom hunt this day was particularly good. She was so absorbed by it that she came as close as an elf could possibly come to forgetting about the storm. By the time she finished dark clouds were boiling over the sky and light was failing under an inky mass of darkness. A last flight of gulls winged for shelter.

The haze in the distance and a chill wind gusting warned her that rain was already on the mountains and moving rapidly closer. Hervor ran now, as only an elf could run, like a bird flying low over the ground. Down the hill and across the valley she raced the wind and storm, barefoot through the grass, moss and sedges. She left the stand of sacred birch behind her; its ivory trunks spotted black like old bones and its autumn leaves trembling and flying in the wind. Nimbly she picked her way bare foot over the stones of the icy stream and then pounded up the slope to the stockade, the air sounding to her tinkling laughter.

By this time the wind had become a hungry, living, animal spirit, howling and clutching at her scarf. The rain had reached the edge of the valley and was sheeting down.

She was barely to the open gate of the stockade when, with a deafening roar, the storm hit. First the hail, stunning her and causing her to put on a burst of speed, half-blinded, her eyes screwed up against the assault.

One hand held down the lid of the basket as she dodged rocks and stunted bushes and then flew, laughing, up the wooden steps of her father's house. She pulled off her scarf to wipe the water from her face and stood for a moment, bent over and panting, in the shelter of the veranda.

"The storm is going to be a big one. Did you run all the way down from the hills, girl?" *Adalwolf* (Noble Wolf) called out from his seat near the wall. "You only just made it, já."

Hervor grinned at him and spun to look back at where she had come. Even with elf vision the visibility was poor, with the storm sleeting and the darkness growing.

She raised her eyes in a prayer of thanks.

"Thank the Mother we got the barley harvest in."

"And thank the Mother that we are safe," Adalwolf replied.

It was the ritual words: we *are safe.*

Elves are a vigilant people and they do not forget easily; and yet it was seven hundred years ago that their last great leader, Prince Hjørvard, led the pathetic remnants of the elves into the lands of snow and ice. Their mentors, the svartálfar, had promised them weapons to fight the daimôns. The dwarves, too, had promised to help. Everyone knew war was coming but when it did come the weapons were never given to them, and the help from the dwarves never came. In the end the free svartálfar, who were so clever and powerful in magic, could do little against a daimôn army.

The elvish warriors kept their courage and they fought ... and they perished. In mere days their great host was lying dead in the fields and their beautiful cities were burnt to the ground. All those who had sheltered within them had been slaughtered and the rest were being mercilessly hunted down. Only the few that Hjørvard led to the cold lands survived.

The cold gave them a way to fight the daimôns. Daimôns are creatures of energy and they cannot abide the cold. Water or snow can banish them, though not forever. Banishing a daimôn gave the elves some respite. It caused a drain on those that summoned them and, without their daimôns, the Illvættir (the daimôn summoners) could be killed.

No one knows the full story of that desperate flight but finally they came to this place, wounded and hungry. It had been a colder, harsher place then, and there had been very few elves.

The world was growing warmer. With the warmth came trees; at first it was snow forest, mainly fir and birch; long lived and slow growing with the short growing season. Since the elves came, there had been more and more deciduous trees. The last of the old animals disappeared and the new animals like reindeer, elk, bears and wolves had become plentiful, along with lots of birds, small animals and fish. The elves fished and hunted and they planted their crops and tended their herds. They had become more numerous and prosperous, at least after a fashion. But still the elves remembered and whenever the cold came, or a great storm, they repeated the grateful words: *thank the Mother, we are safe.*

The older, wiser elves worried that as the world grew warmer their refuge could be breached, but the daimôns did not return. Still, thoughts of safety were never far from the minds of the elves and even a harsh storm was welcome.

A gust of wind blew some rain onto the veranda.

"You may as well come inside." She suggested to the old warrior.

Instead Adalwolf pulled a woollen hood over his head and lifted a pile of blankets onto his lap. "I'll stay and watch while food is made ready. I prefer the company of the storm."

It was not an insult; most older elf men were loners by preference. Adalwolf had been a guard to her grandfather and now he was a guard to her father. No one knew how old he was. His long grey hair signalled that he was nearer the end of his life, but still there were few could match him with a bow in his hand. No human could make the deadly flint arrows or heavy bows to match the craft of the elves, and of course, all elves were inhumanly fast and accurate.

"I hope to see Hjørvard for practice soon." He said.

It was an old joke.

There was a prophecy that whenever the elves were threatened by the Illvættir again the spirit of Hjørvard would return to infuse one of his direct descendants, an elf Prince. The man would be called Hjørvard, 'the man who is Hjørvard returned' or sometimes simply 'the man who is'.

Every small boy-elf (prince or not) dreamed that one day he could become the new Hjørvard. When Hervor was a tiny elf she only had small elf boys as friends. She had once said to her brothers that she wanted to be Hjørvard when she grew up, just like her friends were saying.

From then on her father and older brother, Úlfr, teased her endlessly. When Hervor grew up she wanted to be a man! But she always ran with the boys and when she learnt to shoot, she shot better and used a heavier bow than anyone her age. When she finally became the best pupil Adalwolf had ever seen over his long life he nick-named her his 'Hjørvard', in answer to the teasing.

She nodded in acknowledgement and flashed him a smile as she ducked through the door. A stone weight on a rope pulley pulled it shut, but the wind kept rattling it and worrying at it. Maybe they would have to ask Adalwolf to come inside after all, so they could bar it.

As Hervor entered she saw her father, Angantyr the *Jarl* (Earl) of the elves. Angantyr had dismissed most of his *hirð* (court) to their homes and he was sitting talking with Hákon, the blind elf *seiðmaðr* (sorcerer-man) near the fire.

Hákon was the best of their elf seiðmaðr. Rumour had it that he had voluntarily blinded himself to improve his third sight. Óðinn (the Norse God) was said to have given his left eye to learn the secret of seiðr; perhaps Hákon had gone one better.

The single men: unmarried and widowers had retired to various corners. Sometimes clear silvery elvish voices would be raised in some song, new or old, as they worked, but this evening they were mostly silent: carving, making arrows, repairing or sharpening tools and weapons, or playing games of concentration.

The fashioning of a bow or an arrow were the most difficult of all their tasks. A single arrow could take several nights of careful work to make. It had to be the right weight and balance; the fletching had to be just right and from the same side of the bird, so the arrow would spin properly in flight. The shaft had to be straightened and have the same springiness as the other arrows in the quiver so it would spring back after leaving the bow just in the right way. To be just right, heavier bows needed stiffer arrows and lighter bows needed arrows with more spring. The flint arrow head had to be carefully napped by a special antler tool and a tiny hammer to match the other arrow heads that had been made.

Each single arrow was made for just one bow, one group of arrows, one archer and what he or she would be using it for. Elvish archers, especially in the forest, were devastatingly effective and one of the few things the savage Norse raiders feared.

Brynjar, her other brother, had made her arrows. He had carefully marked them with her individual pattern of colours and feathers, so she could retrieve them. Brynjar was always joking, but not at her expense; not like her father or Úlfr. He was a good brother. He looked after her and their little sister, Alfhildr. Hervor didn't want to say it to anyone in her family but she loved him the best of the men in her family.

Her mother, Svafa, was helping the two cooks, Branda and Helka get ready. Branda's seven year old daughter, Inka, was lighting the fire while Hervor's six year old sister, Alfhildr, helped. As Hervor came in, her mother took the big basket from her and lifted the lid to peek in.

"You found some morel," she exclaimed with delight.

"Not as many as I hoped," Hervor said as she stretched out to accept her mother's kiss.

The wind blew down the smoke hole in the roof. Hákon casually gestured and the fire began to draw properly.

"Stay here tonight Hervor, you too Inka and Branda." Svafa suggested. "No one should go out in that again."

Hervor nodded. She had recently moved into the unmarried women's quarters but often slept on a rug by the fire in her parents' house. She squatted down near the fire and brought out a gift from Brynjar, a whale-bone comb finely carved and decorated. Alfhildr came over and sat on her big sister's lap. It made combing her hair difficult but Hervor couldn't refuse her little sister. Inka saw this and took Hervor's comb and squatted behind her to help.

"I'm not such a lady that you need to comb my hair for me," Hervor laughed.

"Your hair is like silk and fire, sometimes it has highlights of burnished copper. I like its feel, and like combing it." Inka giggled. "When I grow up I would love to have beautiful hair like yours."

"Your hair is blond," Hervor replied, "not red like mine or Alfhildr's, but it is lovely just the way it is."

Inka joined Alfhildr on Hervor's lap and the three sat watching the fire.

"Dómarr asked about you when your brother was up north." Her father said, far too casually.

"Well he can ask all he wants!" She screwed up her face with irritation.

She liked Dómarr, Dómarr the quick. She liked him a lot. His father was a chieftain amongst the elves living far to the north. He was ten years older than Hervor but they had been friends since she was small. He was strong and handsome and fun. Everyone assumed they would marry some day and maybe they would, but right now she didn't want to marry anyone!

"It may be fun for you to tease me but if you keep on about him I won't be able to have a friendship with him, and it would be all your fault because he has done nothing wrong."

It was a long speech for an elf, but her father could be really annoying!

"Leave the girl alone," Svafa called from where she was helping their cook. "She's still half a child."

Hervor hoped he didn't make some joke about Hjørvard next. She loved her father but he didn't seem to know what to do with a daughter when she was born, and so he teased her. Now he didn't know he should stop. Other elf fathers didn't do that to their daughters and he didn't do it to Alfhildr.

Hákon interrupted, talking to her father so softly it was hard to hear even with her elf hearing. "Someone of great power has tried to seek us out. The protection spells held."

Hervor remembered the strange feeling she had had in the forest. She wondered if that was connected to what they were talking about.

"Who?" Angantyr asked softly.

"I don't know but I'm worried, and something is clouding my future sight."

"Illvættir!" Her father almost spat the name.

"It is what I fear, yes. The last of the free svartálfar are dead. Maybe they will turn their attention back to us."

The Illvættir were svartálfar (dark elves) who had bonded with daimôns. Most of the other svartálfar had refused this foul magic, but now the last of the free svartálfar were dead. Hákon was blind but he turned to Hervor as if he could see her.

"Hervor, one day you must leave here and live amongst our enemies."

"I would never do that. I would die first!"

It was so unfair that he would accuse her of such disloyalty! She would never do such a thing!

"Never say never, child. It has just come to me that this will be so. Whatever happens, trust in your heart and the Goddess. A terrible day is coming for us elves. You don't know this, but without you there may be no hope. If that becomes so, you will be asked to give up everything that you love."

"Are we no longer safe here?" Angantyr asked.

Trust her father to be more interested in the people he led than his own daughter!

But could it be true? Was it possible that something terrible might happen, that the elves were no longer safe here? Had one of the Illvættir been watching her?

The shutters on the window were shut but she imagined what it would be like in the storm outside with their tiny coloured lights being tossed violently back and forwards. Their safety suddenly felt very fragile. It was like an illusion, and she felt the darkness and the storm closing in on them.

"We may be hidden from their far sight but if it is them, their eyes are turned this way." Hákon continued. "If they ask the Norse, they will know where we are. I don't know what they can do then but the world is warmer than it was."

They could ask the Norse, Hervor shuddered at the thought.

Not the Sami, the ancient people of this land. They had sent men to fight in the Illvættir wars and they hated the Illvættir with a deep passion. They would remember.

But the Norse, they wouldn't remember, and if they did maybe they wouldn't care.

* * *

Nordheimr (the 'northern home' of the dwarves), Caucasus Mountains.

Sindri left his men below and climbed the stairs alone. This was a secret place deep under the great mountain and for hundreds of years anyone who climbed these stairs had something to hide.

Light filtered down from hidden windows many floors above but it was enough for one of the *dvergr* (dwarves). As Sindri reached the entrance to the secret rooms, the ceiling opened up. Overhead he could make out faded murals of ancient legends and old battles, once inlaid with gold leaf. He didn't recognise any of them and wondered how old they were. This place had been carved out of living rock by a form of magic no dwarf in living memory had ever seen, and dwarves lived a very long time.

It seemed dark and abandoned, rock dust lay heavy on the floor, but it was made to seem this way, he knew. The marks left by his feet in the dust disappeared as he walked.

He chose a door to the left and pushed, incanting a spell. A great stone rolled out of his way and he stepped through into a corridor. To a human's sight the place would be pitch black but to his dwarvish sight a distant lamp threw shadows on the wall. There were no visible guards but if he was unwelcome he would already be dead.

Prince Brokkr's daughter, Dís, stepped out of a solid wall in front of him. Lady dwarves were few and greatly prized by the dwarves, hidden from all other races of men. Dís bore the name of an ancient dwarvish goddess ...and he was hopelessly in love with her.

They had shared lessons in *dweomer* (dwarf magic) from her father until her abilities had far outstripped even his. He was a wealthy noble in his own right but it was scarcely enough to win a dwarf princess, though who can tell which man a dwarf maiden might chose as her life partner?

She smiled at him. "You are expected."

To be attended by the Princess was a great honour, but then her father would want to keep this meeting a secret. King Lofarr, Brokkr's father, had spies everywhere. Brokkr had instructed Sindri to feud with him in public, and join the camp of his enemies. It had proven very useful but this meeting risked everything. Things were becoming dangerous and time was running out.

Brokkr waited in his study, sitting at a stone desk lit only by a small oil lamp.

Dís bowed. "I will make sure no one spies on you."

She gave Sindri a smile meant for him alone. "I have missed you, you know. I have missed you a lot."

Then she turned and walked through a solid stone wall carved with ancient symbols. Her dweomer had become even greater than he remembered. Sindri was flushed with love and overjoyed that Dís would say such a thing to him, but he felt flustered that she would make such a declaration in front of her own father.

"I think my daughter likes you." The Prince said mildly.

He was amused by Sindri's embarrassment. He remembered his own delighted confusion, several hundred years ago, when her mother had chosen him as her life partner. Then he recalled the dream he had, that was more than just a dream. It was only three nights before and he shuddered as his feeling of dread returned.

"I think it is a good thing, because I can no longer protect her."

In his dream it had been early spring and he was searching through Ālfheimr for the elf prince, the one who would be called Hjørvard. He was somehow bearing the armour and weapons he had made for him, even though in waking life they were in part invisible and far too big and heavy for a single dwarf to lift, except by magic.

He couldn't find the elf prince no matter where he searched, all he could find were dead elves everywhere and a burnt out village.

He knew he had failed.

Finally, in the distance, he could see another dwarf. This dwarf had his back to him but he knew it was his father who had come to gloat. He knew his father would kill him once he got close enough. He really should run, but he couldn't stop himself from walking reluctantly towards him.

Brokkr shook himself mentally and brought himself back to the present.

"Our plans have changed. I want you to leave as soon as possible."

Sindri paled noticeably. "But my Prince, soon it will be winter and no one travels across the great frozen land at that time!"

On Brokkr's instructions Sindri had hired two specially designed boats and he was paying a handpicked crew to be ready to be summoned to depart at a moment's notice. The location of the elves was a closely guarded secret but they knew where they were and the boats were designed to be light and able to be carried on specially designed collapsible carriages. From the river port on the Kuban River in the Caucasian Mountains they would travel to the Sea of Azov and then through the strait of Kerch to the Black Sea. There was a way across the known world from there, following multiple waterways with portage (carrying the boats around obstacles and between water ways) till finally they were free to sail across the northern seas to the secret home of the elves.

The humans regularly used shorter sections of the journey for their long distance trading canoes. Similar journeys had been done by dwarves before, though not for a hundred years and no one had ever done it in winter.

"I'm sorry," Brokkr said, "in a dream that was not a dream I saw the elf homeland destroyed by daimôns. It will happen early this coming spring. The Illvættir are already searching for the elves and unless we get the artefacts to them, they will be destroyed."

"Can we send a warning?"

"I think they already know the Illvættir are coming for them, and elvish minds are closed to dwarves. They have no reason to trust us."

The great betrayal had occurred before Brokkr was born. Brokkr's grandfather King Náinn had promised Hjørvard's father that the Northern Dwarves would join the alliance of free peoples. At a critical moment their help never came. The alliance was crushed and elf dead were piled as high as a mountain.

Would the intervention of the Northern Dwarves have turned the tide? It was never known. As the old King was readying his forces, Brokkr's father, Lofarr, used the distraction to rebel. He had the old King imprisoned and Náinn was never heard from again ... except by his grandson, Brokkr.

"Even if we can travel in winter it might take longer," Sindri said, "and we can't be certain to arrive before spring."

"If you don't, Álfheimr will be destroyed."

"Then we will make it, somehow." Sindri said. "Whatever you were working on, is it ready?"

Brokkr nodded. "It only needs one thing."

Brokkr had told him to bring men to carry something. All Sindri knew was that Brokkr had been using some sort of forbidden dark magic. The dwarf prince looked tired, and almost sick. Dwarves lived for millennia and he was still young for a dwarf, but he had aged somehow.

He was one of the most powerful dwarves in dweomer, second only to his father, and the greater weight of whatever had been done must have been borne by him. Whatever it was had drained him visibly.

Involuntarily, Sindri looked around the room. On the desk was a flawless rock crystal, bigger than any Sindri had ever seen, faint lights were moving deep within it. His eyes shifted to the other side of the desk where there were two small gold boxes, shining in the light of the lamp.

When his eyes reached the shadows in the corner, he froze. There were three crates lying on the floor. The waves of evil, hungry, dark power pulsing out of them were unmistakable.

"My Prince!" He said in horror, walking over slowly.

The first was a thin box packed with dark blue silk and on it lay a throwing spear: black and shiny with red highlights. It seemed to be made of stone but Sindri had never seen anything like it, and he was a dwarf. The second box had a rectangular shield of the same material. The name 'Hjørvard' was blazoned across it in golden letters that only a dwarf could see.

Yet it was the main box that caught his attention. It was big enough to carry a full grown elf and it was from this that the dark power was emanating. His eyes told him it was empty and yet there was a sense of something inside, something that didn't reflect light, something that *drank* it with an unnatural thirst. He stared at it, mesmerised, like a small animal watching a snake that was ready to strike.

"It looks empty but it contains the armour." Brokkr said. "The armour is the real weapon that allows the shield and the spear to be used. It hasn't been tamed yet, so don't touch it. It would be the last thing you ever did."

"How did you make this terrible thing?" Sindri asked.

How could you?

"For me to explain that, you must tell me what you think existed before reality was created." Brokkr stared at his former pupil.

Sindri thought for a minute, "why nothingness, I suppose."

He couldn't take his eyes off the empty box.

"As good an answer as any," Brokkr agreed. "There was nothingness, but a nothingness that was, and still is, alive in a way that is beyond our comprehension. And it is hungry. We took part of it and caused it to bond with reality. Not our reality, so it is trapped in this plane."

"It is thirsty for more of that reality, but cannot find it here." Sindri said in slow understanding, "It is alive, yet trapped and cut off from the rest of itself. You have created a monster, something truly evil."

"Not to mention angry," Brokkr added, "apart from my daughter, you were always one of my better students."

"But how are you going to control it? You would need an unbelievable amount of power."

"Do you have any idea how much power each one of us carries inside, if only we could find a way to use it?"

"NO!" Sindri cried as he grabbed his dweomer master by the shoulders as if to shake him. "Not an immortal soul!"

You cannot mean using that!

"Nothing else has the power." Brokkr said simply. "It will drain the soul of whoever joins with it but not destroy it, not even it can do that. What is left will be bound to it forever."

"In endless torment."

"Perhaps in torment, I don't really know, but sometimes to fight evil, you have to create an even greater evil."

"Even preserving the elves is not worth this," Sindri said.

"No, but stopping the Illvættir is. It will be partly up to the elves themselves, or at least one elf. They have a prophecy that when the Illvættir come for them the second time the spirit of Hjørvard will return to infuse a great elvish warrior, a prince of the elves. He will take the name Hjørvard. I think one of the sons of the current Jarl is destined to be that man."

Brokkr paused. "I felt myself guided as if I was fulfilling that prophecy. It says he will be given the means to fight daimôns and lead the elves to safety. Safety would normally be further north but I want you to convince them to go to *Hatti* (Cappadocia, Turkey)."

"Hatti?" Sindri looked at him in surprise.

It was the home of two of the only three dwarvish cities, they were called the *Sundriheimr* (Southern Homes).

"Why not here? We are stronger here."

"The Southern Homes are very old but above and below ground they are vast. There are many places to hide and feed the elves. It is because we are stronger here that I think the attack will come to Hatti first. Return the armour to the resistance here for the magic that will preserve its power and then take it back to the Sundriheimr where it will be stored permanently, until it is needed."

"But will the southern dwarves help? They stood aside when your grandfather offered to help the free svartálfar."

"I think their kings no longer believe that the Illvættir are no threat to dwarves. For them to say that the Illvættir were a problem for the elves and the svartálfar to deal with was one thing, but to see both of them so utterly destroyed has been something else again. They have already offered sanctuary to any surviving elves.

"I do know my father would close the gates against the elves and in truth we don't have the space for them in the Caucasus Mountains. I don't think even my father has the power to destroy these artefacts but if he lays his hands on them, I'm sure he will hide them. Something was made to fight the daimôns at the start of the Illvættir Wars but it disappeared and he has forbidden anyone fashioning weapons against daimôns ever since."

"Why would he do such a thing?"

Brokkr paused and closed his eyes with old remembered pain.

"I don't really know." He said slowly. "He has made himself the most popular king we have had in all our long history. He has proven very clever in all other things but, it seems, in this. What he *says* is that if we don't attract the attention of the Illvættir, they will let us be. Dwarves want to believe him, and so most of them do. Most of us do not give much thought to the wider world; most believe we can hide away in our underground cities forever. Maybe even my father believes it himself, or maybe he remains popular by telling people what they want to hear. I just know that if you cross him he will stop at nothing to have you silenced, even one of his own kin."

"Alright, but how will *an elf* bind this armour to his will? It has been created by dark *dweomer* (dwarf magic)."

"Ah for that it needs to be tamed, and that sacrifice will be mine. I have already explained to my wife and daughter ... they weren't happy. Long have I had to bear their anger at me."

"My Prince!" Sindri repeated, appalled. "No! Let it be me! I will bind this terrible thing with my soul."

"Sindri my dear, dear, friend!" Brokkr looked at his former pupil with tears in his eyes.

"You can't comprehend what you are offering, but thank you. You don't have the power, nor I am sorry to say, the ability. I will meet you at the river and then bind this weapon with my soul. Are you ready?"

Sindri hesitated, and then he nodded.

"My daughter will join us there, but in disguise. It is the only way to keep her safe. You have the blessing of myself and my wife for the two of you. It may be the only gift that we can give you."

The boxes were surprisingly heavy and even though Sindri's men had brought special trollies that could travel over stairs, Sindri had to use lifting magic. After they had removed the real boxes they put new boxes in the corner that looked the same, including one that looked empty but was heavy and pulsing with dark magic.

After Sindri finally left, Brokkr sat for a while deep in thought, with Dís waiting by his side. He needed to make his final goodbyes, including to his wife, but after years of planning he was reluctant to start. He started to say something, but Dís caught something out of the corner of her eye and shadows started to dance quickly back and forwards across the walls.

"Father!" She screamed. "We are under attack!"

Chapter 2: The Illvættir

As Hervor had been running from the storm, someone in the Norse kingdom of Vest-Agdir had been watching her with his far sight.

"Did you find the elves?" Aranwen asked Brice as she came through the door she had been guarding. The Norse did not believe in privacy, so they had to make use of one of the pit houses, one of those storage houses whose floor is a sunken pit. This one was used for storing onions hanging on strings, and the primitive type of wheat the humans grew.

"I saw an elf girl running from a storm, but it doesn't tell me where she or the other elves are." Brice replied. He swung his feet over the pallet he had been resting on and massaged his face.

"The elves will be exactly where these humans say they are, love. Don't worry; we have waited seven hundred years. Waiting till spring won't kill us."

Then she paused, puzzled. "If you saw just one elf it means she is significant to you, do you know in what way?"

Brice shook his head. He remembered the vision of the elf running over the meadow like a bird in flight. Her pale elfin features touched with a faint blush on her cheeks and the tips of her ears. Her eyes were a startling green and she had red silky hair tied by a simple blue scarf. He felt warm in his chest, a quickening of his pulse and a stirring in his loins. She was so lovely!

It was a shame he would have to kill her.

He had not had many women in his life. The first was Ailla, the one everyone called 'Silver' for the colour of her hair. She was a powerful sorceress, far more gifted than he was, until he had bonded with his daimôn that is. The same was true of no few of the Illvættir, apart of course from Áedán and his handpicked central council. Many other Illvættir had only been mediocre in their powers until they bonded with their daimôn.

Silver had chosen the wrong side in the war. He remembered they had such a bitter argument when she found out he was joining Áedán (Æloðulf), the powerful and charismatic leader of the Illvættir. He was sorry because it was the last time he had seen her. Not much later he had met Aranwen and convinced her to join the Illvættir with him.

Silver would be long dead. Most likely she had been killed by one of his friends. If not, svartálfar rarely lived for more than five hundred years. He and Aranwen were amongst the youngest of the Illvættir, and they were already a thousand years old. Daimôns didn't age and bonding with them conferred immortality, almost.

Almost, but not quite; slowly he *would* age and ultimately die. Each time he summoned his daimôn brought that day just a little bit closer. And then of course he could be killed...

Brice's only other lover had been Aranwen and she was beautiful still. Her hair was golden like butter, with startling grey eyes and pretty elfin features. Svartálfar men, unlike elves, had sparse beards but svartálfar women were physically hard to distinguish from elves if the colour of their hair or eyes didn't give them away.

Aranwen was good for him. Did he love her still? It was hard to know, it had been such a long time. She was easy to be around and she always made him feel *comfortable, fulfilled.*

"What are you thinking?" She put her hands around his neck and slid into his lap.

"Just how mad all this is." He smiled as she reached up to kiss him. "We have driven them back to the Stone Age and in all this time the elves haven't sought us out. Yet somehow we still see them as a threat."

When he did die, his daimôn would absorb his soul. He almost had immortality, almost infinite power. There was a time when it had seemed worth the cost. Brice now wearied of his long life but the thought of death and what it meant was absolutely terrifying.

He had given up the true immortality of an eternal soul for a false immortality in this life. When he died he would cease to exist. His soul would be stolen into the daimôn he had bonded to.

Does the immortal soul have a voice? Now he knew that it did. Ever since he bonded with his daimôn somewhere deep inside him it was whimpering its fear. It was true of all the Illvættir; lurking not far below the surface, was an overwhelming terror of death.

The mind demanded an explanation for such overwhelming terror, something within its power to fight, lest it fall into ever greater madness.

It led to the paranoia of the Illvættir, the belief that any others with power wanted to murder them, or were destined to give birth to children who would kill them. That must be why they were so afraid of dying! They were no longer helpless in the face of overwhelming terror. It was no longer bottomless and endless and if they could (and would) do something about it, it was easier to bear.

It was madness, of course, but once the seed of the idea was planted, they could not take the terrible chance that it might be true.

At first the paranoia was focused on the free svartálfar. The easiest thing to do was to kill them first, starting with the most powerful. As it became obvious what was happening, it forced their enemies to band together for protection.

As their enemies began to fear them then they really did want to kill them. The paranoia born out of feverish imaginings turned to hostility towards others and this created the very reality they had feared, as hostile paranoia often does.

For millennia there was an uneasy standoff, but both sides knew what was coming.

Now they had won that war and they had finished hunting down and killing the last of the free svartálfar. The terror seemed to lessen for a short while as their mind told them they had dealt with it.

The lessened fear told them they were on the right track and yet it still remained, hidden in the darker recesses of their soul … so they must not have finished the task! They must look around for a remaining threat.

It was time to turn their attention back to the elves.

Elves were magical and fast. They had been numerous once. They didn't breed as quickly as humans but they bred more quickly than svartálfar and lived almost as long. They were superb fighters, but who can fight a daimôn? Even so, they were too dangerous to be allowed to live.

But when the elves were gone, and maybe even the dwarves, how long would it be before the Illvættir began turning against each other?

Eiríkr put his head through the door.

"*Heil* (good health to you)!" he said cheerfully.

He was the third member of their group. It was getting harder and harder to get the Illvættir to co-operate with one another. More and more of them were disappearing. They were getting ready, each in their own way.

If Brice completed this mission for the central council he and Aranwen would be seen as useful and that would buy them protection for a time, but he worried what would happen after that.

Fear of an eventual purge by their own people was the reason that Eiríkr was living the life of a semi recluse surrounded by savages. It was how he had found where the last of the elves were hiding. And, as he had hidden amongst the Norse, Eiríkr had fallen in love with them. He dressed like them, talked like them and had adopted one of their names.

He would probably move on after this, change his name and disguise who he was.

Just for the moment though, Brice wished he would leave the two of them alone, but Aranwen smiled and invited him to join them. Join a couple while they were kissing in a pit- house amongst the onions!

"I have just talked to *Alrik Konungr* (King Alrik)." Eiríkr said excitedly. "He *segja* (said) one more raid this *ar* (year) and then he will be ready to join with the Vest-Fold to attack the alfir."

Brice made a sound of disgust. It was so frustrating! They couldn't summon their daimôns *every time* they wanted to kill a single elf or a small group, it would only kill them in the end. And they couldn't chase the elves if they hid in the far north or amongst the snow and ice of the mountains, so they needed human allies.

They had initially approached the new petty king of Vest-fold, Ragnarr. Ragnarr was young, ambitious and brash. Surely he would help them kill a few elves in exchange for their help, but Ragnarr was too cunning for that. He would not take his army against the elves with their famous archers unless he had help.

Alrik the old and powerful leader of Vest-Agdir was the obvious choice. Besides this, his kingdom with his ships and large army lay between Ragnarr and the elves. Alrik agreed readily enough but he had a vendetta of his own to finish first. It meant they would be delayed till spring.

"Can we winter at your farm?" Aranwen asked.

Eiríkr looked uncomfortable. "I'm sure Alrik Konungr will insist you stay as his house guests."

No Illvættir would want another Illvættir, or worse two, staying under his roof to sniff out his or her magical defences or murder them while they slept. Brice and Aranwen were unusual amongst the Illvættir in still sleeping in the same bed together. According to the council that was one of the reasons why once Eiríkr had found the elves, Aranwen and Brice had been chosen to help him exterminate them.

Brice and Aranwen were still young enough to recognise the paranoia for what it was, but it wouldn't help them when the others decided to come for them. Brice wanted to get rid of the elves quickly, so they could get ready themselves.

Had it already started? Had some Illvættir decided to act in advance of the others; had some of the Illvættir who had disappeared really been killed? Brice felt a familiar gnawing anxiety in the pit of his stomach and shook his head to banish it.

None of the Illvættir had any children anymore and they had killed the rest of the svartálfar. Soon they would exterminate themselves and that would be the end of their race.

Áedán (Æloðulf) had always managed to get them to work together but he had disappeared before the last great battle against the elves. No one knew what had happened to him, or at least no one who was talking about it.

Some said he had been killed by a group of the Illvættir acting together. It couldn't be anything less because Áedán, if he still lived, would be the most powerful of all the Illvættir.

Maybe it was true. Maybe the killing had started. If not, it was probably too late for Áedán, even if he could be found, to fix what was happening to the Illvættir.

"You have to tell Alrik what you intend to do to the elves." Eiríkr warned him. "He is not like Ragnarr. These Farsund men are stiff with their honour. They won't want you attacking the elves unless the elves use magic against them first. They will insist the elves be given a fair chance to fight."

"Give the elves a fair chance?" Brice sneered. "How stupid can they be?"

He was fed up of dealing with these mad primitive humans. They had no conception just how dangerous the elves were.

"These Agdir men have a code," Aranwen said, agreeing with Eiríkr. "It is manly and brutal just like the savages they are, but it is a code."

"That is why I'm not telling them!" Brice snapped. "They will change their tune when their blood is up and they see all the plunder we will get for them. And once they see what our daimôns can do they won't dare oppose us."

"One more petty conquest for Alrik and he will be ready," Aranwen soothed him. "Have patience, my love, in spring the killing will start."

Spring, he only had to wait till then.

Spring was the killing season for the Norse.

* * *

Nordheimr, home of the Northern Dwarves.

Brokkr looked up as the captain of his guards, Falr, stepped through a solid stone wall. Falr looked at him in surprise and then at the spreading blood stain on the front of his shirt, before dropping to his knees. There was the sound of a second body hitting the floor. Brokkr's own heart almost stopped as he saw his wife lying motionless, dead on the floor with a dagger sticking out of her back.

"Run, Dís!" Brokkr's voice, heavy with panic and anguish, came loudly in her mind. "Find Sindri and get him to leave immediately. I will try to get there, but don't wait for me."

Dís glanced back at her father before she stepped into the wall. They both knew it would be the last time she would ever see him.

Brokkr put his hand on the crystal that waited on his desk. It allowed him to see the figure concealed in the room.

"They didn't expect their king to kill them." Lofarr smiled at him.

"This time you have gone too far, father. You will never get away with this!"

His father wouldn't care but he wanted to delay him.

"Oh, I think I will. Very few of you dwarves would suspect me."

You dwarves!

Then Brokkr knew.

"You're not my father!" He said in shocked realisation.

The dwarf king fell to the ground in a dead faint, behind him a shadowy figure straightened up, tall and powerful and radiating menace. He carried a knife dripping with blood. It was Áedán, the missing leader of the Illvættir!

"In a manner of speaking I am your father," he said. "I have been sharing his mind for so long I sometimes forget who I am. At first I was helpful to him; he thought he could use me. He thought he was too strong for me to take him over, but eventually I did."

"It was you that killed my grandfather."

"Yes, it was a mistake to keep him alive for so long, but I was draining his memories you see. I never expected him to reach into your mind and teach you all he knew." Áedán shrugged and stepped forward. "I have been waiting to kill you for some time. I had planned to let you bind yourself to this weapon first. I could have shown others and the horror of it would have strengthened my hand, but you decided to wait until you had moved it."

"How did you know?" Brokkr wanted to turn and run ... or cast a spell.

He found he couldn't move. He stood frozen, helpless.

"Your thoughts are well guarded but I have your father's blood."

Brokkr grunted as Áedán punched the knife into him.

Áedán smiled as he looked into his eyes. "It was very slow but while you slept I was able to touch your thoughts, a little at a time. Your daughter won't be able to hide from me forever."

Brokkr fell to his knees, his life force draining from him. Áedán followed him down to whisper in his ear so Dís couldn't hear. "Oh and I know all about the resistance."

"You have doomed us all." Brokkr said.

"Yes, I have." Áedán agreed. "The dwarves are doomed."

* * *

Kuban River, the Greater Caucasus Mountains

A small figure wrapped in a dark cloak and hood was riding hard, leading two spare ponies. Few marked her passing and if they did, they would have only seen a twelve year old human girl, maybe stouter than many twelve year olds. But this was no child, nor was she human.

Dís was driving her animals to the limit, and using every trick she knew to keep hidden and to travel swiftly, trying to staunch the tears that kept falling. An Illvættir sorcerer of great power had taken control of her grandfather, the King. He had murdered her great grandfather and now he had killed her mother and father, along with their most loyal servants.

Áedán thought he had taken control of the weapons and armour her father had made. She had to stop him finding the truth. He believed she had not heard that he had infiltrated the rebellion. The artefacts must never fall into his hands.

She burst in on Sindri as he waited by the river for her father. He held her in his strong arms and when her sobbing finally settled he got the rest of the story.

"We will have to flee to Ālfheimr." He agreed, if they stayed now they would only be killed. "Maybe the elves can help us. Maybe we can get a message back to the members of the resistance. I'm not sure what the elves can do now that the armour hasn't been tamed by a dwarf wizard. We might take it all the way there and find it is useless."

They would follow the Kuban River that drained the Greater Caucasus Mountains into the Sea of Azov, then across it into the Black Sea and then on to the mouth of the Dnieper River. There they would go upstream, travelling many lakes and rivers and carrying the boats over land till they had crossed half the known world. When they finally reached the Neva River that drained Lake Ladoga they would follow it into the Gulf of Finland and then brave the stormy northern seas that led them to the refuge of the elves.

"Give me a moment to myself." Dís asked him. "My father gave me something that he wanted me to hide within the armour."

When Sindri had left Dís turned to what seemed an empty box. There was only one thing she needed to hide within the armour. Áedán would take her thoughts slowly, bit by bit. One night he would look into her mind and see that Sindri carried the real armour and he would see exactly where they were. After that, there would be no place to hide.

She carefully took off her clothes and folded them in a neat pile on the floor. On top she left a note.

"Oh my love, I'm sorry," she whispered.

Standing naked, she turned to what seemed to be an empty box. She had felt its evil before but was not prepared for the power and hunger of the thing. As she placed her hand inside she found herself being sucked in, spinning faster and faster till the world was a blur and her screams rent the air. Sindri came running when he heard her cries, but it was too late.

He looked wildly around but Dís was nowhere to be seen. Her clothes were in a neat pile on the floor with a note on top. And then he saw it, the armour had become visible.

Chapter 3: The Dnieper River

The Dnieper River, north of the Black Sea.

Báfurr sat in the bow of one of his boats and patiently studied the village. It lay on the southern-most tip of the largest island in the Dnieper River; marking the start of a very long section of the river dotted with islands, rocky outcrops and rapids. It was impassable for big boats or for large travelling canoes.

Sindri had moved the lid of the box that contained the armour so he could whisper to it. It showed no response, staring balefully out of the box. The feeling of evil became almost overpowering once he opened the lid, and the other men hated him doing it. To them the armour was cursed. Yet Sindri had to believe that somewhere deep inside Dís was still there and could hear him.

"What do you think?" He asked after he replaced the lid and crawled closer to join Báfurr.

"What I think is that this trip is dangerous enough without travelling so bloody late in the season," Báfurr replied, "and I wish you wouldn't keep opening that 'thing'. None of us like it, though we promised we would carry it."

"I know," Sindri tried to say as gently as possible. He glanced back at the box that contained the armour. "People I loved gave their lives to get this cargo to us and the woman I loved gave her soul."

"I'm sorry about your woman," Váli, one of Báfurr's scouts said. "But Allatu have mercy she must be dead. Why can't we just throw that thing over board?"

Sindri's hand flew to his axe. "Maybe you should try."

"Váli, hold your peace! We have given our oaths and we will take this thing to the elves," Báfurr growled. "You too, Lord Sindri. I'll have no fighting."

"I was just saying, is all," Váli grumbled.

The village they were staring at was a collection of single roomed clay and brushwood huts, roofed by thatch made of reeds. Like most human dwellings they had a door way and a single covered smoke-hole in the roof but no windows.

There was a fine haze of smoke in the afternoon sun. Some of the dogs had spotted the boats and were barking half-heartedly. A few small children were playing and some women walked around the village. After an initial inspection, they hardly glanced at the boats.

"They don't seem too concerned about us." Sindri commented.

"They get this every few weeks, and they can see we are dwarves," Andvari, Báfurr's second in charge said. He was from a tribe of the wandering dwarves, one of those few groups of dwarves that didn't live in or around one of the three great underground cities.

He spat over the side into the river and watched the current take the spittle away. "If you look more closely you will see archers hidden in the trees."

The humans living on the river were fishers and hunters, raising a few cattle and goats and planting some primitive wheat, rye and peas. They traded and made extra from portage: mostly cargo canoes plying up and down the river. They were handy with their bows, they had to be; outside the river valley was dry steppe, the home of savage nomads.

It was still hot; perhaps the last of the truly warm weather but some of the deciduous trees had already started putting on their autumn colours. They were still being attacked by clouds of midges and had to rub grease and herbs on any exposed skin. It was maybe the only thing that the dwarves wouldn't miss once the weather turned colder.

Four men trotted out of a hut, pushed a canoe into the water and began paddling towards the waiting dwarves. They seemed to take slow, rhythmic strokes and yet the canoe knifed quickly towards the waiting boats.

"They will take salt, flint or obsidian but give the best value for copper." Báfurr advised Sindri as he watched them approach. "They use it mostly for jewellery and trade. And they are known to drive a hard bargain."

This section would be the longest section of portage they would face. The village turned out forty human men to help. To add to that the dwarves had themselves and two short but sturdy ponies. Váli grumbled to any who would listen that they should have used dugout canoes, not boats. Of course canoes would not carry all their cargo and the ponies.

He also said that they didn't need to hire so many men to carry the boats. He said the humans were using it as an excuse to charge more. The humans were certainly earning a handy bit of copper out of it, but even the first boat took three full days of struggling, straining and hauling, and they had to rest the human and dwarvish men in shifts.

By the time they arrived back to collect the second boat the heat was intolerable. There seemed no breath of air and both man and beast were in torment from clouds of biting insects. There was only time for a quick swim before they set out again, the humans said it would storm later, and they wanted to hurry. The day had an air of heavy expectancy but the dwarves looked at the clear, cloudless sky and wondered what they meant. By the late afternoon heavy grey clouds began roiling over the sky and the daylight rapidly failed.

The humans called a halt barely minutes before the storm broke and sent everyone running for the shelter of a grove of trees. The dwarves didn't manage to get their ponies under cover before lightning lit up the sky and thunder cracked almost on top of them. The rain hit in a torrent as the dwarf ponies bucked and squealed, almost enough to break free. Both humans and dwarves had to run to help get them under shelter.

It teemed most of the night, slowing to a drizzle by the morning. When the sun rose, the path had turned into a quagmire. The carriages kept getting bogged, both dwarf and human slipping in the muddy conditions and a few of the dwarves lost boots to the mud. Váli didn't repeat his earlier remarks that they had hired too many humans.

Finally, after almost eight full days of struggling they were able to farewell their human helpers. Man and beast were exhausted; Báfurr decided not to go on for two whole days.

"The men need to recover," He insisted. "And you need to recover, my lord, after working all that lifting-magic."

Sindri couldn't argue. Most dwarves had a little dweomer, enough to hide themselves. Those that didn't carried charms, but to hide the whole party or to use lifting magic mostly fell to Sindri with a little help from a few of the others, one of whom was Andvari. Sindri could barely keep his eyes open and was so tired he felt physically sick.

When they finally set out they made good time paddling upstream. The cool sunny days floating on the river with the trees decked in their autumn beauty was deceptively peaceful. Soon they would have to face the full fury of winter.

They saw bands of mounted warriors patrolling near the river, going south. The dwarves couldn't be seen but they had to proceed in silence and sleep on their boats mid-stream. They also had to keep their distance from anyone on the river or they would be seen.

Once they came upon a whole village on the move and couldn't avoid them. Fortunately, they were not only friendly, they were delighted to meet other travellers, especially dwarves. Their leaders earnestly tried to convince them to turn around and head south. They couldn't understand why they would be travelling this late in the season and of course the dwarves couldn't tell them the real reason.

Finally, the sightings of humans became rare, and then they stopped. Not only were the seasons changing, they were heading further north into colder country. By the time the steppe and deciduous trees gave way to pine autumn was well and truly over. The days were short and the winds bitterly cold with frequent snow storms. There were no human settlements to help with portage but fortunately the distances were not long. Also Sindri and the ones who could help found it easier to float their boats over the snow than over mud.

* * *

Nordheimr, sometimes called 'the Deepest'.

Nýr didn't need to be summoned to light a lamp and offer King Lofarr a cup of his favourite wine at the usual hour. He had served as Lofarr's Master of the Household for almost five hundred years.

With him in charge, everything worked with seamless efficiency. Guests were shown in, refreshments and meals appeared, beds were made, baths were made ready and fresh linen was on each bed, always exactly on time.

He remained so much in the background that it was tempting to ignore him and think of him as deaf and blind. Whenever he was called upon, he was such a respectful and helpful confidant that it would be possible to think of him as a friend.

Not that Lofarr would make those sorts of mistakes.

He, like most of the other dwarvish nobles, chose his house servants to have little dweomer ... so they couldn't spy on him. And Lofarr was careful in every other way.

Still, it is part of the job of every servant to anticipate the needs of their master or mistress. It became part of a servant to be curious, which meant a good servant had to snoop, discretely.

Nýr was very far from stupid and no less curious than most servants. He knew far more than he was supposed to know, far more than was good for him. What he didn't know, couldn't know, was that Lofarr already knew about him and had decided to do something about it tonight.

Lofarr seemed the perfect ruler in all areas except one. He insisted that the Illvættir would not be a threat unless the dwarves provoked them. It was a highly popular view. That he secretly went to brutal lengths to supress anyone who opposed his view was not at all unusual in a king. That he didn't tell the truth to his subjects where he thought he could get away with it was fairly normal in a leader of any sort.

That he wouldn't allow spying on the Illvættir or allow the dwarves to get ready in secret was ... disturbing. It defied common sense and screamed of folly ... or something else. But Nýr continued to wear a mask to hide his concerns, and kept his silence.

It was not long after Lofarr killed his own father that Nýr's suspicions were shockingly confirmed. Something was far, far, wrong.

Of course, no one told Nýr that the old king was held prisoner and he was too careful to openly question anyone. A body was removed in secret from a forbidden section of the palace. After that there was no need for guards on doors, nor was there need for certain special meals.

When the section was re-opened Nýr made sure he did a solitary inspection. Likely the whole section had been cleansed of any magical interference from the old king but sometimes the lack of magic can be an advantage. You don't overlook normal ways of hiding, something as simple as a hidden compartment behind a garderobe. It contained King Náinn's diary.

The contents were terrifying, including the old king's fears that his son might be being taken over by an evil force. Nýr approached Skáviðr, the previous king's old war-chief and that was when Nýr joined the secret resistance.

"Nýr, do you remember the artefacts that I recovered from my son, after which my granddaughter disappeared." Lofarr asked as Nýr poured his wine.

After you murdered your only son, your daughter in law and their whole household.

"Yes my king."

He had never been told what the artefacts were for, neither by the King, nor for that matter by his resistance contacts. He knew the resistance were working on a weapon that would take both an elf and a dwarf to activate, something to fight the Illvættir.

"Well, I haven't been able to locate my granddaughter and Lord Sindri has disappeared too. Sindri had been very close to Brokkr and Dís but then he publically denounced them. I'm starting to think that was a little too convenient."

Nýr was careful not to show any reaction beyond polite interest. Lofarr was playing with an odd shaped key. Holes cut in it glowed with a sickly green light shining out from inside it. Lofarr seemed to come to a decision and strode to a wall and opened a door Nýr hadn't known existed.

Nýr felt a thrill. The king was finally becoming careless around him. He went as far as the door but no farther, best not to appear too curious. Lofarr bent over three boxes in the corner, a long one seemed empty. Lofarr held his hand over it and a flash of power lit the room.

"It is empty!" He said in surprise.

He stormed out of the room, pausing only to lock the door and then he settled back on his chair ... and laughed.

"Clever, very clever; with her father dead Dís is the only one that can bind the armour and tame it. That is why I can't find her. Sindri is taking the true artefacts to the elves!"

"Do you need ..." Nýr started and then stopped himself.

"Do I need what, my dear Nýr?" Lofarr had his knife out as he stood up.

It was bronze but shined like gold in the lamp light.

Nýr tried to take a step back but found he couldn't move.

"I didn't catch you directly Nýr; you were far too clever for that. I have a source within the resistance. Bad luck for you, I suppose. Since then you have been very useful to me; passing false information to Skáviðr.

"You and I both know that Illvættir are on their way to deal with the elves once and for all. You want to know if I want to warn anyone that the elves may be given a weapon. Now, that would be telling, wouldn't it?"

Lofarr was under the control of Áedán, the missing leader of the Illvættir and Áedán had no intention of doing anything of the sort. If dwarves found that out it would provide irrefutable evidence of a connection between himself and the Illvættir. Not only that, the last thing he wanted to do was to advertise where he was to any but the very few Illvættir who already knew.

This place was not only the best place to attack the dwarves from; it was far too good a hiding place for when the Illvættir turned on one another.

He placed the point of his knife on Nýr's throat.

"You think I am going to kill you? I might, but not just you. If I kill you, I will kill your parents, your brothers, your sister and her husband and that little niece you are so fond of."

Nýr couldn't move, he couldn't speak and he had to fight for every breath. He started to sweat and his heart raced.

"Or, we could take our relationship to a new level. I need some information about the resistance and after you give that to me I have some tasks for you. I will let you stand here for a while to consider whether you are willing to help me or not. You are looking a little pale but of course the spell I used is rather unpleasant.

"I know you have feared me, but it seems that you did not fear me enough."

There was one thing Áedán *could* do. He couldn't track the artefacts Brokkr made, they were protected from that. He couldn't track a dwarf, not normally, but wherever Sindri was now there was one spot he would have to pass, carrying the boats over land. That would take all his power and he would become visible for a day and more.

Áedán planned to have friends waiting. That would stop the artefacts falling into the hands of the elves, which was one problem, but he was also running out of time.

He would kill Nýr as soon as he had finished with him, but it still wouldn't be enough. Dís knew that he had control of the King, so Sindri and his men would know by now. Would his allies be able to kill them all? Probably, but even if they did it was likely that other dwarves already knew. It would not be believed of course, but it would plant a seed of suspicion. Over time that would wear down the trust he had so painfully built up.

He would have to bring the attack on the Southern Dwarves forward he decided, even before they had finished with the elves. Paradoxically, it would strengthen his position with the Northern Dwarves. They would turn to their King in a time of fear and crisis.

He just had to appear decisive while secretly sabotaging their defences. He would use the daimôns of his Illvættir brothers and sisters to attack the Southern Dwarves but he planned to try something rather new when he turned his attention to the Northern Dwarves, something they wouldn't know how to fight.

He walked away, deep in thought, leaving Nýr fighting for breath.

* * *

Vest-Agdir, Southern Norge, late autumn.

"I suppose we should congratulate our brave ally." Brice said in disgust.

"I really don't know why he bothered." Aranwen laughed as they surveyed Harald Vikarson's lump of a turf house. It was a fifth the size of Alrik's *langhús* (long house) at Farsund, the roof and walls were still green with the autumn rains and it had yellow weeds flowering all over it.

The only wood that could be seen from outside was a drift wood fence, a narrow entrance door and a single covered smoke hole poking out of the roof.

Nearby was an outdoor shed covering a pit latrine with room for several people to relieve themselves at once; then there were stables, a smoke house, and a number of pit houses. There weren't many animals; they would be brought back from the high pasture for the winter soon.

Harald Vikarson had been *Herbrand Konungr's* (King Herbrand's) brutal lieutenant. A freeman, he had been rewarded by his king with this small strip of coastal land. It made him a petty *Yfirmathur* (chieftain) in his own right. He had no shortage of *þrællr* (slaves) but his *dróttin* (war band) only numbered two hundred, even with his *húskarlar* (house-carls).

It was why Alrik had decided to attack with only three hundred men. Harald had an enviable reputation and it was a point of honour for Alrik to show he could win with fair numbers.

"If we have to stay here the night, I hope the walls are lined with wood. I hate sleeping inside damp earth walls." Aranwen said.

"What about the last one that didn't have an antechamber, every time the outside door opened and the wind blew, the room would fill with smoke," Brice screwed up his face in recollection.

"I just hope it doesn't have an internal latrine." Aranwen added, wrinkling her nose.

Brice laughed. Alrik's langhús had a partly separated area with a channel lined with stone leading to the outside and poles so the habitants could perch along it and relieve themselves like birds on a fence. He must have thought it was a great convenience, but the smell inside the house was appalling.

Alrik would put one of his own men in charge of the *stadhr* (steading) and the *þrællr* (thralls). The few of Harald's men who had survived could join Alrik, most as lower status warriors. If they didn't want this, they had fought well and would be allowed a clean death.

Harald's wife had submitted. As her husband had died bravely she would become a þræll in Alrik's household without any further indignities, but not so her daughters. Astrid, thirteen and Helga, fifteen, had resisted and offered insult to the men. They would be humbled, in the traditional way.

"Why *are* we here?" Aranwen asked, turning to Eiríkr. "Why don't we wait in comfort till these stupid humans finish their silly games? You have us following them around like dogs."

"I have already told you." Eiríkr explained, once again. "These men have no love for sorcerers and witches. They don't see sorcery as men's work. They value physical courage above all else. So we are making a point by being here."

"That's ridiculous. I could kill all of these humans just by myself." She snorted.

"No you can't." Eiríkr reminded her. "Even daimôns have their own code."

Surprisingly, it was true. Daimôns would not attack allies, even former allies, unless of course the former allies threatened their master first. When the Illvættir finally decided to attack each other their daimôns would stand aside. Unlike when they killed the svartálfar and the elves, when the Illvættir killed each other they would have to do it in the old fashioned way.

"We need these humans." Brice reminded her. "We can't use our daimôns to hunt down individual elves or small bands, the cost for us to summon our daimôns each time would destroy us."

"I'm warning you both," Eiríkr switched to speaking mind to mind, "these Norse may seem to be savages and in many ways they are, but they have their own ideas of right and wrong. They admire the elves. That is why they want to be the ones to beat them in battle. They will be outraged when they find out we want to eliminate them. To them it is the height of cowardice to fear an enemy so much that you want to kill their women and children. They already see sorcerers as womanly."

"Ah, Eiríkr and his noble savages; you have dwelt amongst them too long." Brice laughed. "It is the price of our help. You Norse will just have to get used to it."

"But you haven't even told them!" Eiríkr reminded him.

"I've told you before, they only have to see what our daimôns can do and these primitives won't give us any trouble."

As they made their way to the door of the long house they were interrupted by terrified screams. Ritualistic gang rape, with a pagan religious twist to it: something about the two young girls carrying the seed of great warriors.

It would break the girl's spirits forever and prepare them for a life of slavery. It might be highly effective but it was another of the less than attractive habits of the Norse.

* * *

Toropa River, Western Russia, winter

The shortest day passed with driving snow, coming down fast. It was hard to see more than a few feet in front and the river they were travelling on was narrow and dotted with floating ice. They were forced to slow in case they ran aground or hit a concealed log.

The cold was so intense that the dwarves were chilled to the bone, even huddled under their furs. In the open air their breath froze on their beards. At least the rivers now drained north and they were being carried along by the currents, rather than fighting against them.

They had run out of meat. All they had left was water and barley broth cooked on earthenware braziers and there were no human settlements to buy more supplies. This was a region of nomadic hunters and herdsmen, long gone for the winter.

Báfurr and Andvari climbed forward to the bow of the lead boat to stare through the driving snow for landmarks. Finally Báfurr shouted out his satisfaction and pointed to a great rock slide, much of it hidden by the snow. At some time in the distant past a great slab had broken off high up on an overhanging cliff and diverted the river. Over time mud and sand had built up in the bend. At a sign from him, the two boats made for a shallow sandy bay.

"Now we wait for the weather," Andvari told Sindri. "But don't worry. This is the last section of portage. We will be visiting the elves well before winter breaks."

After months of worry Sindri's face broke into a wide grin. "We made it, we really did. We are really going to get there in time."

From here they had to carry the boats to the start of the Kunya River (South West modern day Russia). It was the last section of portage and a short one.

Further down the Kunya River they would find fishing villages and finally be able to replenish their supplies. From the Kunya River they could keep to the water ways: travelling downstream all the way to Lake Ladoga ... and Lake Ladoga, the largest lake in Europe, drained into the Gulf of Finland where they would find the *Østersøen* (Baltic Sea) at last.

"You know," Sindri laughed, "I will miss carrying these dam boats across land. It will feel strange to hoist a sail and let the wind do the work for a change, but from what I have heard it is too soon to dismiss the northern seas in winter."

Andvari said nothing about the northern seas in winter; he just gave a knowing smile.

Their luck seemed to hold now and by the afternoon of the second day after their arrival the skies cleared, enough for them to unload their boats. Now all they had to do was find the upper reaches of the Kunya River and then transfer their boats.

The winter sun didn't reach directly over-head but followed an arc closer to the south. The days were still short so the next morning they set out in darkness, but darkness didn't bother the dwarves.

The path was concealed with snow. Sindri, Báfurr, Andvari and the three other scouts went on ahead. The main party dragged the artefacts and their dwindling supplies on sleds just behind them. Everyone kept their axes loose in their belts and shields over their shoulders, but the forest seemed deserted.

Finally they found an ambling snow-covered clearing lined by deciduous trees, dark and naked in winter. They could hear the water rushing beneath their feet and it got louder as they followed it downstream.

They had found the Kunya River.

"Careful you don't go through this ice." Báfurr warned them as they got further down-stream.

He finally got them to stop and climb the bank into a clearing; not far ahead the ice and snow was breaking up into patches of open water. When the rest of the party arrived with the sleds, they finished setting up camp and then the main group trudged back to collect the first of their boats.

The sun had woken to a clear, fresh, magical world. The ground was blanketed in crisp new snow and the pine trees were heavily laden with white against a light blue sky and patchy cotton clouds. The temperature was still far below freezing but there was little wind and it was enough to put the dwarfs in a good mood.

When they got back to the boats some of the dwarves had built some snow sculptures: a giant caterpillar, a great sturgeon and a dwarf family with two children. The dwarf father was wearing Báfurr's spare hat and scarf.

Someone started a snow fight and even Báfurr joined in, leading an assault on a laughing group of defenders led by Andvari. Someone else was dragging one of the sleds up a small knoll and a small group were waiting their turn to ride down on their bellies. One of the dwarves had snared two snow rabbits, so to celebrate they all had a little barley broth with rabbit added. Each dwarf only got a mouthful but after only barley broth for weeks it felt like a great feast.

They may be low on supplies but they had beaten this frozen land and its dreaded winter and they had no serious injuries apart from some minor frost bite.

Chapter 4: Death at Kunya River

Kunya River (modern day western Russia), winter

They had docked both boats for unloading. The rear boat would have been safer if they took it back mid-stream, but everyone was in a hurry now. So they left it under guard, dumped their shields, tools and spare weapons in the first boat and set out to winch, drag and float it along the path.

They were using magic to help, so were unable to use a concealment spell. They had almost got the first boat to the Kunya when Andvari gave a cry of anguish.

Somewhere, nearby, dwarves were dying.

"Put the boat down over there and grab your weapons!" Báfurr shouted.

They wedged the boat against a stand of larch and snow drift and gathered behind it. Through the trees they could see a column of smoke. Their other boat and camp was already on fire.

Andvari exchanged a wordless glance with Sindri as they waited behind the makeshift barrier. Coming closer were many voices screaming and yipping like wolves.

A *shaman* appeared first, swinging a great stone axe. His only garment was a cloak sewn from wolf pelts; his face and body coated in white clay and painted with dripping blood. The heads of two dwarves swung from his belt.

A huge war band of howling, snarling humans thundered just behind him. Their dirty bodies and faces covered in woad tattoos with hair in dreadlocks; faces red with battle rage and twisted in hate.

The dwarves wore no armour but they had thick shields and bronze axes. They were deadly underground or in ambush but out in the open and visible they were at a serious disadvantage against humans, and they were about to be overwhelmed.

Four wild-looking men tried to bash through the sheltering trees and the snow drift behind them while another dozen circled around to come at them head on. Ten concentrated on bashing holes in their boat but luckily for the dwarves the rest ignored them and raced on to capture their supplies.

There was no time to count their numbers, maybe another fifty or sixty. Sindri was too depleted to use his magic. He spared a thought for their guards and then he was too busy.

"Charge them!" Báfurr screamed. The dwarves surged forward to bring the men in range but holding their shields above their heads, they struck downwards, not upwards. Moccasins and trousers gave little protection against dwarf axes. The men collapsed with broken and crushed bones and came in easy reach. The dwarves had won free, but the remaining human men saw what was happening and ran on, to tell the others.

"Let them go!" Báfurr ordered, gasping.

"They'll kill our guards." Sindri shouted at him.

"Our guards are already dead," Báfurr told him tiredly. "We can't catch running humans and we can't fight that many. If they come back for us we are dead men. If we keep together maybe, just maybe, we can put up some sort of fight."

Just then, in the distance, a human screamed in horror and agony. Then a great number of humans began shouting and screaming all at once.

"What was that?" Andvari asked, looking pale.

"They tried to steal the armour." Sindri whispered in fear.

"What is happening?" Andvari asked.

"I don't know," Sindri shook his head. "I think it is protecting itself."

They had four dwarves badly wounded. They made stretchers and crept back towards the Kunya River. Keeping a fearful watch for a return of the raiders, but they were gone. What was left was a scene of utter devastation.

Their guards had formed a small knot to defend themselves but they hadn't had a chance. All that was left were naked headless bodies, hacked and trampled into the blood stained snow.

Their modest supply of food, even food for their ponies, was completely gone and the little bit of hay they had had been dumped into the icy water. The rest was scattered around but only half their metal was stolen, as if the raiders were interrupted.

They had smashed the boxes that held the artefacts. The armour was lying some distance away clutching the spear and shield across its chest as if it was a warrior resting on its back. There was blood on both the spear and shield and the snow was all churned up. Nearby there were seven dead humans, including the human shaman, all with enormous gaping wounds.

"This is what they were after all right," Báfurr said, looking stunned. "But it fought them. I think the rest ran when it came to life."

"As I would have, look at the size of those wounds." Andvari shuddered. He couldn't take his eyes off the armour. "If they had orders to steal it, they probably had orders to kill us once they had it. I think it saved our lives."

"We are alive for the moment," Báfurr countered, "but we are in a bad way. We have no food and we only have one boat left, with nothing to fix it with. We will bury what we can in a snow cave and travel light. We will follow the river, trying to find a path where the snow is not too deep. The village of Kholm used to be where the Lovat and Kunya rivers join. It is a long way on foot but it is our only hope. I hope it is still there and the people are still friendly."

"I can't leave Dís!" Sindri protested.

"Then you can stay here and bloody die with that cursed woman of yours!" Báfurr shouted, colouring. "It's that thing that brought this on us. Whatever it is, it looked after itself once and it can bloody well do it again."

* * *

Kunya River, winter

Their luck turned evil now; the weather closed in with driving snow and howling winds. Sindri could hardly see the next dwarf in front of him. Dwarf night vision was of no use in a blizzard. The snow kept finding its way under his clothing, leaving him cold, wet and numb.

Maybe they shouldn't be going on like this; maybe they should search for shelter. He tried to shout that out to Andvari just behind him but the wailing storm drowned out his voice.

Andvari had seen him turn and closed the distance between them to shout in his ear.

"We have to go on while we have the strength," he said, almost reading Sindri's mind. "We don't know how long this will last and we don't have any food. I really doubt we can make it."

Dwarves are a tough people but most are not used to being outside of shelter in bad weather. By the fourth morning they had lost the last of their wounded. No one had seen him take his turn but Váli still muttered that, as sad as it was, at least they didn't have to carry them. Báfurr had to stop a couple of the other dwarves from attacking him.

When the first of the ponies died there was a break in the storm so Andvari directed them to slaughter the other one as well and cut the meat up.

The other dwarves were angry at him for what had happened so Sindri made sure he did his share and more. All the exertion so soon after using his magic made him feel hot and tired. He bent down to grab a handful of fresh snow to suck. Andvari lurched towards him and nocked it from his hand.

"That will kill you. Here, you need to thaw it first." He took Sindri's water skin and bent down to pack it with snow and then got him to tuck it under his outer clothing. "If your body temperature drops you won't be able to walk or think. You will feel warm and sleepy, but if you sleep then you will die."

You would feel warm when you were cold? But Sindri was far too tired to ask.

Two days later that he got his chance to see it for himself as the first of the dwarves become dull and clumsy. It looked like the exhaustion but much worse. Sleep beckoned seductively; if only they could rest, it whispered, they would feel better.

Andvari got them to shake any sleepy dwarves and get them moving again, but after a few days of it, no one had the energy to spare.

Váli was the first to be lost. He refused to get up no matter what Sindri did or said to him.

"We are all going to die *Lord* Sindri. You and that bitch in the box have killed us. Now go away and let me rest, just for a little bit."

Sindri lost track of the days as their numbers began to dwindle. He began to forget why they were walking. He only knew he was doing it for Dís. It was for Dís that he kept stumbling on, and for Dís he kept picking himself up when he fell.

He didn't notice the storm had stopped. All he could do was put one foot doggedly in front of the other. He heard dogs barking but his foggy mind couldn't understand what it might mean. He smelt smoke and wondered if it was the raiders burning the boats again. Something told him he should be fleeing from the raiders but he couldn't seem to figure out how to stop or change direction. All he could do was to keep stumbling slowly forward.

When he came to any sense of himself, he was lying on a bed of straw and rushes on a dirt floor. He felt a weight of furs on top of him and a small fire was burning nearby. He glanced around and realised he was in a single roomed hut.

A grey haired, wizened human woman was sitting spinning wool and watching him closely. She gave him a toothless smile when she saw he was awake.

"I can't feel my left foot."

It was a silly thing to say the first thing after waking with all the questions he should have had, but his mind wasn't working yet.

The old woman shuffled sideways like a crab. She gave him water and then brought a bowl of warm chicken broth, which she began rhythmically spooning into his mouth.

"Wrapped it in rabbit fur, I did. Frost bite kills the skin before it gets its teeth into the deep meat. It won't be as bad as it looks."

Not as bad as it looks... He wondered how bad it looked.

"Worst thing is to thaw it in front of a fire and then refreeze it the next day. The heat wakes it up, see, and then it needs a lot of blood as it tries to heal, see? If you freeze it after that will lose your toes faster than you can count. Thaw it yes, but keep it thawed at all costs."

The old lady obviously knew a lot about frostbite but Sindri had no idea what she was talking about.

"None of us could build a fire towards the end. What is your name? I need to thank you."

The old lady grunted and shuffled back to dump the wooden bowl and spoon into a wooden bucket of water. She tended to do things before answering questions, he realised.

"I'm Morana. Tell me what were eight half-lings doing out in that storm?"

"Only eight?" Sindri struggled to sit up. "We started out with thirty. We were travelling to find the elves, but we were attacked and our supplies stolen. We had two boats but one is burnt and they punched holes in the other."

"Attacked?" Morana whistled. "Our chief Václav will want to make sure that whoever attacked you is gone from here."

"It wasn't near here. I'm not sure how long ago it was, maybe two weeks."

"If you lasted two weeks in that storm without supplies you did well. We can help you fix your boat but none of you are fit to travel and there are no elves near here."

"I have failed, then." Sindri whispered.

So many of his companions were dead and they wouldn't reach the elves in time.

Chapter 5: The Fall of Ālfheimr

(Remember: ð, Þ and þ, are all 'th', Bjørn is Be-ern)

The days were lengthening quickly now. The snow storms had finally stopped, and the snow was gone from the lowlands. There had been cold winds, grey skies and rain, but not today; today was bright and sunny and Hervor rushed through her morning chores as fast as she could.

She had promised to teach Alfhildr how to forage and her little sister was bursting with excitement. She had kept following Hervor around as she did her chores, asking questions and talking about what they would do when they reached the hills. Alfhildr had been in the hills before, of course, but had never done any serious foraging. Hervor was known to be the best of the young elves at foraging and Alfhildr kept saying how lucky she was to have her as a sister, and how much she loved her.

In truth, this early in the season was a lean time for foraging.

It was too soon for the greater harvest of mushrooms or even the earliest berries and fruit. If Hervor saw new bramble bushes or desirable plants she would note where they were for later, but it would only be herbs, fresh greens for salads and maybe some roots, where the ground wasn't too frozen.

All the plants and trees were in a rush to push out their green tips, so the fresh shoots were the sweetest and freshest at this time: chickweed, saxifrage, wood sorrel, dandelion before it flowered, nettles, goosegrass, and bittercress. And it was the best time for fern and fir shoots, which were delicious if lightly fried. She had spied burdock and sweet cicely the other day and wild garlic (onion grass) was always plentiful.

Being elves of the water, hills and forest they would only take part of what the Mother offered from each spot. They allowed the rest to grow and prosper for future harvests. They were also careful to plant any useful seeds and sow mushroom spores in good spots and thank the Great Earth Mother for her bounty.

She lifted Alfhildr; even young elves were good at climbing and running but Hervor felt too impatient to wait for her sister's short legs. Another day would be soon enough for that.

Hervor's mind idly asked her which season she loved best as she trotted lightly up the hill, her sister was on her back and two baskets were clutched in one of Hervor's hands, one big and one small.

It certainly was not mørketiden, no, no; not mørketiden in the heart of winter when the sun didn't shine. Mørketiden was the dark time with its frigid arctic winds. It was the time for indoors and old stories and songs and handicrafts.

Hervor did her share of handicrafts with the other elves but she was not like some elf-maids who didn't mind sitting all day just sewing, spinning, knitting, mending, singing and chatting. The long confinement was almost enough to drive her mad.

She would rather look after the animals, shovel snow, bring wood in from outside or even muck out the stables. She was strong for a young slender elf maid and she loved outdoors and exercise.

Once she could get out and put on her snow shoes and join her friends riding their sleds, making snow sculptures, having mock snow-fights and joining in the endless outdoor competitions against the other elves, winter was not so bad for her. But it still wasn't her favourite.

Was spring her favourite then? After all, that was the meaning of her name; 'her' (lady) and 'vor' (fore, the first season). 'Our Lady of Spring', the name of an ancient elf Goddess no longer worshipped by the elves. Now the old spring Goddess was said to be just another aspect of the Great Earth Mother.

Spring in this, Hervor's land, was so beautiful; the trees and plants waking into life and then hurrying to deck the meadows and trees in flowers and blossoms. It made her want to sing with joy. There were the endless colours of spring: greens and all the colours of the flowers, the warming sun, the white of the snow against the dark of the mountains and the blue-green of the fjords.

Spring had its smells, everything fresh and new.

And spring in the meadows and forests had its sounds as well: the melt water swelling the rivers and waterfalls into a rush; animals emerging from hibernation and skies crowded with birds arriving back to their breeding grounds. There was the honking of whooper swans, the drumming sound of a common snipe, the tapping of woodpeckers and too many bird songs and calls to mention.

She loved the spring equinox festival, Eostre, when young elf girls would paint their faces, put on scarves and long skirts, and roam from house to house collecting candy and cakes. Everyone would put exquisitely painted hollowed out hen's eggs on graves to symbolise rebirth into the next life. At night elf women would wear their long white dresses in honour of the Earth Goddess and the elf men would light great bonfires so they could all gather for feasting and hymns.

Was it summer that she loved best: summer with its hours and hours of glorious sunshine and short nights? Summer was the time of plenty; the meadows were still covered in wild flowers: like poppies, bluets and marguerite. There was a lot of work, of course, but still time to get out into the forest to walk, hike, fish and paddle the small skin boats on quiet lakes with her friends. Elves just love to get out into the beauty of nature.

The berry and fruit season started in midsummer in earnest: bilberries, raspberries and summer stone fruit. In mid-summer was the festival of the Great World Tree. The elves erected tall poles with long dangling ribbons. They put garlands in their hair and grabbed a ribbon each to dance around the pole: elf men and women, elf boys and girls together or separate. A favourite pole dance was the one where they had to mimic various animals like frogs and bears, or do actions like washing clothes or digging in the garden.

And then there were the summer fun games like egg and wooden spoon races, tug of war and novelty throwing contests.

As each season came to mind she thought, maybe she liked it the best.

There was autumn with the forest ablaze with red and gold. It was so beautiful, but gone far too soon. Autumn was the last chance for a swim, ignoring the chilly water. It was the time of the harvest festival. The meadows, forests and rivers would still have the Mother's bounty in autumn. It was a great time for angling or baited traps because fish became voracious in preparation for winter. It was still a good time for mushrooms and many of the berries were at their sweetest in autumn, especially up in the hills: lingonberries, blueberries and the delicate honey coloured cloudberries that the elves prized so much.

Elves love berries and fruit. There was great competition amongst the younger elves to be the best at berry picking but everyone knew Hervor was the best. No elf would gather berries before they were ready, but a young elf had to know where the best bushes grew and keep the location a secret. Hervor tried to make sure no one followed her when she checked on her ripening berries but the elves were very good at watching in secret and the other young elves saw it a great game to spy out Hervor's secret places while she tried to hide them.

As her thoughts went to autumn, she remembered last autumn when she had gotten a very special surprise that marked her transition into a lady.

Dómarr came to visit with three of his friends. Her parents had known he was coming but they had never told her. And Dómarr did something he had never done before. He had come all the way from his far northern home ... just to visit Hervor.

Even though it was late in the season they were having fine weather and her heart was thundering when he invited her to travel the hills and forest with him; just him, no chaperones.

Her parents stood proudly, their eyes shining with tears when he asked her and she stuttered her reply. Then he gave the ritual promises to her father that he would care for his daughter ... and Hervor was officially being courted.

They had spent three nights kissing under the stars and chasing each other through the forest in the moonlight. Their steps so light, few could notice their passing. Dómarr had brought his pan flute and Hervor sang for him. And at the end, he gave her a ring, intricately carved from a walrus tusk.

She was almost to the top of the slope now and ready to turn back to look over Ālfheimr as she always did when, faint on the breeze, she heard a distant horn from the entrance to the fjord.

"What is it?" Alfhildr asked as she set her down so they could both listen.

"I don't know, sweetling," Hervor said. "Maybe an attack on our Sami allies, but we had better head back."

The Sami looked much like the Norse, fair skin and hair but with rounder faces. They were known for their especially beautiful clothing made from animal skins. They were a very ancient people. They once owned all this land, well before the elves and the Norse came. Since the Norse came, the Sami had been driven out of the southern lands by the Norse with their kings and farmers. They now lived in the north and the central upplænd (back country) and worked at what they had done for a millennium: reindeer hunting and herding, fishing and trapping.

The elves would never forget the help the Sami gave them when they came to this land, cold and starving. It would be foolish to mount a serious attack on the Southern Sami with the elvish archers protecting them, but it wouldn't be the first time for a lightening swift raid. It wouldn't involve Hervor directly but she had better get back in case her father needed her.

The lookout tower in the stockade took up the call, this time with a long and drawn out note. The pair paused, frozen in disbelief. Straining her eyes, Hervor saw them coming in the distance. Alfhildr hissed, her small body rigid.

Canoes, hundreds of them in two great fleets, partly separate but side by side and timed to arrive together. There were lots of smaller birch bark canoes which had up to a score of warriors but there were also great war canoes: dugouts with up to eighty men paddling, two to steer and one man to beat a drum. Towards the rear would be the cargo canoes with simple triangular sails made of two poles making a 'V' pointing downwards. Most of them were built in the elvish fashion with a platform across double hulls, or with an outrigger.

This would be two armies combined; four thousand or more warriors!

She saw her father's own men struggling to launch their own canoes. It would be her brothers Úlfr and Brynjar in charge of them. The elves had more fishing and cargo canoes but the only advantage of the great war canoes was in their speed. Any fighting from canoes was by bows and throwing spears and cargo canoes were better for that. They couldn't prevent a landing against these sorts of numbers even with elvish archers shooting from the shore, but they would make it cost them.

Her father's wooden stockade had its gates wide open and they were herding townsfolk inside: old men, women and children. The humans would be able to plunder the houses but the elf bowmen in the fort would make them pay dearly. Who were the human petty-kings foolish enough to think they could attack the elves?

She dropped the baskets and swept Alfhildr into her arms to fly, running and leaping down the hillside. Her elfin ears could already hear the pulse of pounding drums, still faint in the distance but they were coming fast.

She was half way down to the valley when the horn in the stockade began to blow a different note. The enemy ships had diverted to unload at either extreme of the shoreline. They would approach overland and attack the village from either side. If they could bottle most of the elves up in the stockade, they could loot the village.

Let them loot! Most of the villagers would be safe in the stockade.

Hervor reached the valley. She splashed through the shallow river that was her town's water supply and pounded up the slope to the stockade, her sides heaving. The enemy were already leaping off their boats into the water and her father's men were trying to close the door to the stockade. Her mother, Svafa, stood in the gap, her face a mask of anguish and her head darting back and forward looking frantically through the milling crowd for Hervor and Alfhildr. The air was full of the screams of women and children and men shouting. Hervor slung Alfhildr off her shoulder and straight into her mother's waiting arms.

"I need my bow!" she screamed over the rising clamour.

"Hervor, it's too late!" Svafa tried to keep the gate to the stockade open but she was grabbed and roughly pulled inside.

There was no time to say goodbye and tell them that she loved them. It would be something Hervor would always remember because it was the last time she was to see them alive.

The two enemy forces coming from either side were not far from the village. With most of the village in the stockade, they wouldn't face any resistance until they got in range. At least then, with the elves under cover of the stockade it would become a very uneven fight even though the elves were badly outnumbered.

All Hervor had was a belt knife made from sharpened antler bone and some flint cutting tools.

Foolish, foolish, foolish Hervor! You have become too used to peace.

Yes, she could make it to the women's quarters in time to get her bow, but only just!

BANG! BANG!

Hervor screamed. Two daimôns had materialised in the middle of the village! One was dark red and in the shape of a giant wolf. It immediately began running for the warriors on the shore. The other, shaped like an orange dragon with agate eyes, scurried across the ground towards the stockade. With a clap of power it blasted a hole in the earth works. Mud and dust sprayed everywhere and a cloud of smoke billowed into the air.

The elvish defenders began firing desperately, raining down arrows on it, but it was having no effect! It stood up to its full height and played a long jet of fire along the wall of the palisade. It had cut Hervor off from the women's quarters. She bent to grab a short heavy stick from a pile of wood as a makeshift weapon. By the time she looked up again one wall of the stockade was already alight.

There were shouts and screams of terror. All resistance from the stockade had collapsed. Elves were leaping from the wall at the back and throwing children to the waiting arms below. The daimôn was running round to cut them off. She had to help them somehow but she didn't have a bow!

The elves by the shore had stripped off their clothes and were soaking pieces of cloth in the cold sea water and wrapping them, dripping, around their arrows. The red daimôn began to cower under the hail of arrows ... and then it disappeared.

At that a stranger who looked like an elf with silvery hair turned to run away.

He was an Illvættir!

He waved and his back was protected by a green shield of power but an elf appeared in front of him, drawing back and loosing his arrow all in one movement. The daimôn-summoner sent a burst of power at the elf and stumbled a few paces before collapsing.

Another group of elves had made it to the icehouse and began pelting the second daimôn with ice, even tying small bags of ice to arrows. It staggered aside, trying to flee ... and then it too disappeared.

But just then the human raiders hit the village with cries of "Óðinn! Óðinn! Óðinn!" after their God, and "Alrik! Alrik! Alrik! and Ragnarr! Ragnarr! Ragnarr!" after their two kings. Most were armed with tall spears tipped with flint or bone, with wicker shields. Many had clubs or stone axes thrust into their waist bands.

The stockade and her father's house was a single inferno. There were dead elves lying everywhere and the stench of burning flesh. Hervor wiped tears from her eyes so she could see. She was cut off behind the body of the attackers coming from the south.

A warrior seemed to spring out of nowhere aiming a great two handed stone club at her. She ducked to one side and swung her improvised club hard across his shins with a hard 'crack!' As he stumbled, she hit him over the back of his head with all her strength. Someone grabbed her from behind, she ducked down and rammed her stick back behind her and twisted around to jab him in the face as he doubled over.

She almost stumbled over an elf body, it was Adalwolf who had shot the Illvættir sorcerer! There was no time to grieve his death but she greedily clutched for his bow and quiver. A third of the arrows were already gone. At least today one elf had sold his life dearly!

A man with an undyed woollen coat went running past, screaming a war cry and she drew and shot. He seemed to trip and skid on his face but lay unmoving, the arrow sticking from his back. Two men turned to run at her, screaming the name of their God. She shot one not four yards away and the other just as he reached her. He was tall, covered with woad tattoos, heavy set and with curly brown hair and blue eyes wild with battle fever.

Despite the arrow in his chest, he raised his club and swung at her head. She ducked, dropping her bow and snatching at her belt knife. As he stumbled forward, her hand clutched at his shirt, grabbing a silver necklace instead and spilling crystal beads on the ground. She didn't know if he was dead or not but she stabbed him in the throat as he went down.

The few remaining elves were hard pressed. A group of children who had escaped the inferno that had become the stockade and were being shepherded into the hills; Hervor grabbed the bow and quiver and circled around behind the humans to give them cover. She shot as fast as she could until she had no arrows left.

The last of the survivors were a group of warriors trapped down by the beach. They had hastily thrown a barricade of brush and timber between a boat shed and the rotting hulk of an old dugout canoe. Their enemies had formed a wedge and were pressing in with shields held in front.

Hervor was casting around for another quiver of arrows when there was a bright flash near the boatshed followed by a shining blue light. Hákon, the elf seiðmaðr, had produced a shield of power.

"Let them go, father!" A great giant of a man shouted nearby.

He had blond hair and beard and light blue eyes and was standing in a cluster of human men. He must have been one of the human king's sons and this must be the king's body guard. They were not more than a few paces away from her!

Hervor had lost her belt knife and was out of arrows. She lifted a small throwing spear with a bone point off a dead human.

Throwing one of these can't be too hard.

It had a leather thong near the point of balance but she ignored it. She pulled back and threw as hard as she could at the king, giving a short 'huh!' as she strained with the effort.

At that very moment the son looked up and their eyes met across the battle field. The spear sailed up into the air trailing the leather thong and arced down to strike him in the thigh with a soft 'thunk!' The shaft dropped off, leaving the tip of the bone point lodged in his thigh, not as deep as she had hoped. He grunted and bent over almost casually to work the point out; all the time he looked straight at her with those blue eyes of his. And then he gave a smile.

"Don't kill her, she's minn!" He yelled out to the surrounding men.

A couple of the king's body guards began to move in her direction, Hervor spun and almost ran into a man coming up behind her. He had slung his shield over his back so he could fight two handed with his spear. He had been about to stab her in the back but deftly spun the spear around and cracked her hard across her shins.

Hervor screamed in pain and almost fell. Limping and desperately hopping, she tried to get away but he was on her in a couple of strides. He hit her hard over the back of her head ... and darkness claimed her.

She couldn't have been out for long. She woke being carried over the man's shoulder and felt herself dumped none too gently onto the ground. The breath was driven from her with an 'oomph!'

For a few seconds she couldn't breathe and all she could do was to make faint whooping noises. The blond giant limped closer to grin down at her. He had his great hairy arms crossed, showing a woad tattoo of Thor's hammer on his forearm.

"You're supposed to use the thong." He told her. "That's what gives it its power, many times that of your elvish long bows, but that was a good shot. *Hvot* (what) es your *nafn* (name), alfr?"

I was aiming at your father.

"Hervor Angantyrdotter, I'm the Jarl's daughter," she managed, gasping.

He had been watching her from a distance during the fighting as she ran between patches of shadow and sunlight.

He couldn't help but notice her. *Hervor, Lady of Spring; it is such a beautiful name and you are impossibly beautiful, my elf lady.* Flaming red hair, shining silky in the sun, inhumanly fair skin and penetrating green eyes filled with hatred.

"Þú (thou) fought well, Hervor. Minn nafn is Bjørn Alriksson. I am the youngest son of our king and þú are now my prisoner. Do þú claim warrior right or will þú become minn þræll?"

Bjørn means bear, Hervor thought. He was such a big bear of a human with curly blond hair and beard and a wide toothy grin. She spat her defiance at his feet.

"Elves do not steal, murder or rape like you dirty savages do. I would never fight for you, and I will never be your þræll. You had better kill me now, *human*! It is my warrior right!"

"Bravely said, alfr." Bjørn said nodding. "But what about these?"

He pointed to the four very young elf children sitting nearby. Three were unusual in being from the one elf family: identical twin five year olds, Niall and Nori, and their three year old sister, Brenda. The other was Inka, the cook's seven year old daughter.

They looked so young and so frightened. They were dry eyed, but the girls had been crying. There were maybe two dozen other elf captives, men and women, but they were all badly wounded or burnt. Some wouldn't survive and none were in a fit state to look after children.

The Norse were checking for more elf wounded and treating them very gently, but the daimôns had not left many.

She looked back at him with agony written all over her face.

"No raping, Bjørn, já?"

"Agreed, alfr." He nodded. "*Vilja* þú (you) submit, já?"

"Já, I will." Hervor nodded to him, her shoulders slumped in defeat.

She held her hands up to him to be bound and the children copied the gesture but he just shook his head angrily and turned to limp away. He was angry, but it didn't seem to be with her.

"Faðir minn!" He shouted as he moved closer to the king. "Did þú *kenna* (know)?"

He gestured to the terrible slaughter.

"Neinn Bjørn, to *minn eiginn skømm* (my own shame). Minn *rad* (bargain) with that lying witch-man was for him to stop the alfir using *þierra* own *seiðr* (magic) against oss, neinn more, enn he would share the plunder."

Bjørn spat. "Þar is no *heiðr* (honour) in the use of bol wights!"

"Neinn, nor the murder af *wifr* (women) enn *bairnr* (children)." Alrik agreed. "Þessi will *surr* (sour) minn *nafn* (name)."

"Did the Vest-Fold menn kenna, do yor *þekkja* (think)?"

"Já mayhap, ver will see."

Elves were good at languages, and Hervor had been taught Norse (and Southern Sámi) from young, but she was out of practice and was having trouble understanding their dialect.

She realised they were unhappy about something, but what? They had won hadn't they? And they were taking rich plunder, but there was no laughter or smiles. They all looked grim, why was that?

"They sent monsters against us," Niall informed her, as if she didn't know.

"Our Mødre and Fader tried to shield us but they killed them."

She leant her back against a stump and arranged her dress on the ground.

"Why don't you children come and sit on my lap?"

Nori wasn't sure he was allowed to do that. He had to look after his little sister now, so he had to be grown up.

"It's alright, Nori," Hervor coaxed as the other children came across to her. "You can come too."

Hervor studied their captors as she worked out how she would escape with the children. Most of them were dressed in wool: woven woollen trousers with *kyrtills* (shirts) down to their upper thighs: most undyed, some *madder* (red) or *woad* (blue). Their long hair looked woolly and unkempt from the battle, either braided or roughly tied. A lot of them were blond but some were brunette, red or dark haired; with light, ruddy, complexions. Unlike elves, they had lots of body hair on their arms.

They seemed to be taking no chances with the prisoners but apart from Hervor and the children, none were in any condition to escape. Why did they need such a large guard over them?

Then she noticed it was only one army gathering prisoners, even cautiously removing them under the eyes of the other army. Their guards spent more time eyeing the other army than watching their own prisoners.

They are protecting the injured elves against the other humans!

Something strange was going on and it was important, but Hervor felt almost too dull to care. Her world had been destroyed. The Southern Elves had had not much more than five thousand elves in all the world. In only moments something like fourteen hundred elves had been killed, most of the population of Ālfheimr.

She stared, dry eyed, over the burning stockade and thought of her mother, her father and her little sister Alfhildr. She regretted all the fights she had had with her father. It seemed so petty now. Did he know that she really loved him?

* * *

Ālfheimr, after the defeat of the elves

When Brice managed to stagger over, Aranwen was kneeling over Eiríkr's body. She looked up, tears staining her cheeks.

"He got too close." She whispered.

Brice fell to his knees beside her and vomited on the grass. After that he felt a bit better. He wondered how Eiríkr could not only run but also cast a spell after having his daimôn banished.

"He must have thought he was one of his beloved savages, running into the middle of a battle like that." He muttered in disgust.

Whatever Brice felt about Eiríkr as a person, this was a terrible blow. They would have to finish the elves with just the two of them or be forced to ask for help. It made Brice feel angry at the man ... and frightened.

He never expected the elves to be able to banish both their daimôns, let alone kill Eiríkr. Not to mention that it happened when he was sure the elves were finished. There had never been that many Illvættir, perhaps the elves really could become a threat to them. It was lucky that he had kept Aranwen's daimôn in reserve.

But he needed to talk to the humans. There weren't all that many elves left but the humans had stopped attacking the survivors!

As he walked through the village he felt cheered by the devastation. There were elf bodies everywhere; the stockade where most of them had fled was still burning fiercely. The smoke was thick all around and heavy with the smell of burning flesh. A building inside the stockade collapsed, sending sparks shooting high into the morning air.

He found the two kings were waiting in a clearing in the village. They had agreed to divide the plunder from the elf village and one of the men had drawn a furrow in the dirt with the butt of a spear. The Vest-Agdir men were facing the Vest-Fold men across it with their weapons drawn. The Norse had brought their canoes closer but they were keeping the two fleets separate.

Alrik gave him a sour look when he approached.

Brice was becoming heartily sick of him. He deliberately ignored the dividing line, dragging his foot as he stepped across it.

"What's wrong with you, now? We fought the battle for you and you are letting the rest of the elves get away!"

The small elf fleet had evacuated the few remaining elves and had withdrawn to the far side of the inlet. It looked like they were abandoning the boats for the moment and escaping into the hills.

One of the Vest-Agdir men held a flaming brand up and asked a question of the king. Torgny, Alrik's eldest son, simply shook his head; his face expressionless. The man dropped it on the ground and kicked dirt over it.

"This *skítkarl* (shit man) knew *hvat* yor were going to do!" Alrik said. "Yet minn fight is neinn viðr him, it es viðr yor."

"We can argue about it later. Get after those elves!"

"*Enn hverr* (and who) be *þú* (thou) to give mik orders, witch-man?" Alrik said coldly.

The men around Alrik began to murmur, gripping their spears tightly. Sveinn, Alrik's middle son, was bouncing the head of a heavy stone axe from one hand to the other as if in thought.

"Who am I? I'm the man who gave you this village! We had a deal!"

"Já, witch-man," Alrik said bitterly. "Þú (thou) said neinn about killing bairnr and unarmed wifr. Þú said neinn about killing for its own sake. And Þú used your foul seiðr *before* the alfir used any magic of their own."

"Don't you understand?" Brice screamed at him. "Alfir are too dangerous! They would have slaughtered you and your stupid men." He pointed to the captives. "Kill all of these, now!"

"Fear *af* (of) an enemy be a coward's mark." Alrik said, staring at him unblinking.

"Þes don't look dangerous to mik, witch-man." Torgny, the eldest son, moved closer to his father's shoulder.

"Don't be fools!" Brice spat. "You can't enslave them. If you don't kill them, they will kill you one day."

"Mayhap þeir will kill *yor*, einn *dagr* (day) witch-man." Sveinn, the second son suggested. "If þeir can, þeir have the right."

The men from both armies were stopping what they were doing and beginning to drift over, lining up behind their leaders, but there were more Vest-Agdir men.

Just then Brice saw the red haired elf girl he had seen in a vision. She was sitting amongst the captives, clutching four elf children to her as she glared at him, her green eyes full of loathing.

"Kill that one and the children!" He demanded, pointing, "Kill her now!"

"Careful," Aranwen's voice sounded loudly in his mind.

"Þeir have submitted." Alrik said quietly. "Þeir be ours to do with as *ver* (we) please but þú (thou) have koma to kill all alfir, haven't þú *witch-man*? Þú never wanted plunder. Þú are full of lies and womanly ways. At least Eiríkr died glikr (like) a *maðr* (man)."

"Þú can be killed *níðingr* (nothing man, perverted man)." Torgny added in a low, dangerous voice.

"Only if you get rid of our daimôns." Brice reminded him. "And Aranwen still has hers. We can still take your whole army with Ragnarr here to help."

Aranwen felt something cold hit the back of her neck and spun around. The Vest-Agdir men behind her were grinning broadly. They parted to show her a wooden barrow filled with crushed ice from the elvish ice house; each of the men were taking balls of ice and slush into their hands.

Alrik pointed to a small canoe. She could see some barrels lashed to the floor. "Þú are neinn velkomin amidst *oss* (us), join viðr the Vest-fold. Ver kenna Þú can neinn use your daimôns over water."

Brice's face darkened, he took a deep breath.

"They'll kill us!" Aranwen's voice came urgently in his mind. "We have to leave while we can."

Brice looked at her a bit wildly.

"We have broken the elves. It's not worth dying for these few." She said aloud.

Brice turned and walked stiffly to the waiting canoe, his face like thunder. A snowball hit the back of his neck, and behind him was the sound of laughter.

Even Ragnarr was laughing as he watched him go.

"You're making a big mistake." He said to Alrik, gesturing at the devastation the Illvættir had caused.

"Mayhap," Alrik nodded. "But when I *deyja* (die), I vilja deyja a *maðr* (man)."

Ragnarr smiled at that. "Then yor vilja deyja, old man."

When they next met one would kill the other. They both knew that, but Ragnarr would have powerful sorcery on his side. He had seen what daimôns could do. It was said to be cowardly, but he didn't care. He turned to follow the Illvættir. The witch-woman was paddling the canoe.

A shadow fell across Hervor and the children where they waited. Two large men leered down at her. She recognised them as Bjørn's older brothers.

"Little *broðir*!" Torgny bellowed out. "*Ver* (we) have taken a fancy to your she-þræll, ver have never *hafa* (had) an alfr."

Hervor was unarmed and a captive, she was surrounded by savage Norse men. She tightened her grip on the children. She would fight if they forced her to, but they would only take what they wanted and then they would kill her and the children.

Bjørn limped over as fast as his leg would let him.

"þú cannot hafa, she beð (be) minn."

"She is a certain *fagr* (fair) thing." Sveinn, said. "þú (thou) can have her, *broðir*. We just want our *skør (share)*. Those cockless seiðr-menn murdered or burnt all the alfir maids. Surely þú wouldn't refuse *yðvarr* (your) future *Konungr* (king) and yðvarr beloved middle broðir the use of yðvarr þræll."

Hervor had no real expectation Bjørn would protect her from his brothers. They were both as big as he was. The middle one took out his stone axe and began spinning it in his hand.

"She be a *skjoldmøy* (shield maid) and she caused this *und* (wound) þú see. I promised her no rape in exchange for her surrender."

"Ho, Ho." Torgny laughed and clapped his youngest brother cheerfully on the shoulder. "Mayhap it should be þú wearing the dress and her the trousers, then. Do þú claim the kynder *auk* (also)? They be nothing more than *fjórir* (four) hungry *muthr* (mouths)."

"Já," Bjørn nodded. "I taka *bairnr* (children) *auk* (also)."

His two older brothers snorted in amusement. "Then they beon yours broðir minn. In troth they beon all wights, make sure þú neinn sleep, já."

Hervor looked at them, astounded.

They would honour their youngest brother's promise not to rape her! And Bjørn had spoken up for her. It was something she certainly didn't expect from savages like these.

A voice inside her said he was only protecting his property, but he had also agreed to take the children. She could continue to care for them now, just like he had suggested.

He didn't have to do that. The children would be a burden. She felt relief and gratitude flowing through her. "Þakka, Bjørn."

"Velbekomme, alfr." As he smiled down at her she realised how handsome he was.

She scolded herself for noticing. The man was a savage and a monster, he might show a little kindness on occasion, but she and the children were at his mercy now.

Hervor hoped the humans would spend a few nights drinking and feasting at the site of their great victory. At night she could get away, even with the children. Humans see poorly in the dark and even young elves were good at sneaking and hiding.

Instead, the humans seemed in a hurry to leave!

Bjørn and Harald had two canoes. One was a small war canoe with space for eight men paddling and four resting. The other was a cargo canoe, an out rigger with a singular triangular sail pointing down. She watched in dismay as their men pushed them both out and started to clamber on board. Bjørn told her and the children to go towards the out rigger.

"Aren't you going to stay and celebrate?" She asked.

"What, so you can escape?" Bjørn laughed.

She coloured as he laughed at her. She really hated him then.

"The wind is favourable. Besides if we stay near the Vest-Fold men we will fall to fighting."

"That's all you Norse ever do, isn't it? Fight!"

"Hervor, this time the fight will be over you. They wanted to kill all you alfir."

"Of course they did, they are led by the Illvættir!" Hervor replied angrily. "But you cannot allow that, can you, because we are your *property* now? I'll have you know, we are people, no matter what you savages think."

Bjørn could think of no suitable reply to that, so he just shook his head.

Hervor was surprised when Harald waded out and Bjørn passed him the children, one by one. They were placed gently in the boat, their feet dry, after which Harald climbed in. They were treating the children with kindness.

Bjørn offered her his hand and gave her one of his superior smiles.

Her lip curled in disgust. "I don't need your help, *human!*"

She lifted her dress and leapt lightly onto the gunwale. Harald looked at Bjørn and grinned. Bjørn gave him a wry smile and shrugged, then followed her aboard.

"Neither of our boats is considered proper war ships," Bjørn confided to her while he checked that she and the children were properly seated. "We will have to travel in the middle with the rest of the cargo ships. It will only take a couple of days if the following wind holds. Do þú want to eat?"

The children started to say they weren't hungry, but Hervor snapped at them in Elvish.

Bjørn tossed them an old bun each.

"Stale bread, that's *all slaves get*." Hervor mumbled to herself as she nibbled at the rock hard bread.

Bjørn gave her that smile of his, his eyes twinkling with amusement as he and his men shared out the remainder of the stale bread and ate with exaggerated enjoyment.

It made her feel angry, and maybe a bit ashamed. Then she reminded herself that she owed these monsters nothing.

The Vest-Fold fleet followed behind but slower, allowing more space to form between the two fleets. Whoever was in command of the Vest Agdir fleet kept the fleet together and got most of the war canoes to hang back between the cargo canoes and the following Vest-Fold boats. The two fleets moved slowly, warily, like two fighters moving around each other before a fight.

"Is our master a bad man?" Niall asked her softly. "These humans came to kill us, steal from us and make us their slaves, are they all bad, then?"

The children didn't need to hear how bad their situation was, at least not just yet. She tried to think of something reassuring.

"I don't know sweetling. They don't think the same way elves do. They came to do all those things but in the end the worst was done by the daimôns. It sounds like they aren't happy about the terrible things that were done to us. His family saved us and a lot of our wounded from the Illvættir and our master stopped his older broðiren from hurting me."

"Then he is not a bad man." Niall said confidently.

"I hope you are right, Niall." She said softly.

Because if he is, we are going to find out soon enough.

Hervor sat in silence with the elf children looking back at the column of smoke until it was out of sight. Her mind was crowded by the faces of those who had died. There were very few elves left now. A race of powerful sorcerers was determined to exterminate the last of her people and she and the children were being carried away to a strange land to become the slaves of their enemies. There didn't seem a lot to say.

Chapter 6: The Sami, Dwarves and Hervor's Journey to Vest- Agdir

Finmark, Land of the Sami.

A great evil had awoken. The future was clouded and their ancient magic was blocked even in this, the northern lands of the Sami.

The old *noaidi* (shaman) Juoksa sang to his drum, tapping it as he held it close to his ear. He held it over the heat and smoke of the sacred fire and then tested it again and again. He was very patient. This step was critical for the magic he had to perform.

More than two hundred years ago the frame of the drum was made from a special *burl* (rounded growth) of a pine tree. It was hollowed out, intricately carved and then painted with arcane symbols of power by the great noaidi Gáktu.

Gáktu was a man that Juoksa had come to know very well. When Juoksa first met him he was a young man: weakened by fasting, smoke and sacred mushrooms and Gáktu had been dead for a hundred and fifty years.

This drum could only have one use. It was only for the most powerful of all magics and Juoksa was the only man alive now who could properly drum with it.

The timber, resonance, tempo and rhythm of the drum were critical to the spirit that was to be called, the strength of the connection and the questions to be asked. Inside were sticks on rawhide strings to tap on the underside of the drum head in a very special way.

Its head was made from green rawhide and only the dreaming magic told Juoksa how it would sound when it dried and stretched. Even so, he had to heat the drum and hit a certain part of it just right, and sing into it the right way so it would sing back, just as it had to.

The man assisting him, Mohkku, was also a powerful noaidi (shaman). He had travelled from the north and east in search of Juoksa and he led *Samit* (Sami) warriors that were camped some way away. There were too few, of course, but they were all that could be spared. The other person in the *lavvu* (tepee) was Nilse, a wandering noaidi from the south; he was a famous seer who had come following a great vision.

Finally Juoksa smiled, satisfied. He began his *joik* (chant).

"Ohowohowwowow."

He was calling on Tornassuk, the great spirit of the polar bear. Tornassuk was known for his wisdom and was a powerful noaidi in his own right. Only he had the power to break the spell the Illvættir had put on this land but it was dangerous to call him, he could be angry if he felt he was disturbed for reasons that he didn't see as important.

Outside the *lavvu* (tepee) the three men could already hear the river and the wind talking to them and as Juoksa fell into a trance, a great shadow entered the lavvu.

* * *

Nordlándda, the lands to the north

Not all the Vest-Fold men had followed the Vest Agdir fleet south.

It would be too much to hope that they could catch any more of the Southern Elves so easily, but there were some elves far to the north, maybe they would not be ready.

If Ragnarr wished to attack the Northern Elves he would have to sneak a sizable force past Alrik's fleet for the long journey north. But for now he already had a large fleet more than a quarter of the way there and he wasn't at war with Alrik, at least not yet. If he wanted to surprise the Northern Elves, this was his best chance.

He selected twelve of his best war canoes under *Garðr* (Garth) bearing six hundred of his finest warriors. The greatest elf village in the far north was the small fishing village of Vágar with maybe four hundred men, women and children. They would hit there first, killing all they could and then work their way south. Garðr would have plenty of men to attack the Northern Elves, but maybe they would face more than just elves. The elvish village lay deep within the lands of the *Fenni* (Finns), the ancient people of Norge who called themselves *Samit* (Sami).

As they journeyed up the coast, even in the far north every fisherman's hut or small settlement seemed deserted. Small canoes could be seen watching them in the distance, whether they were Fenni or elves, Garðr couldn't tell. It seemed they would not be able to surprise their enemies after all.

* * *

Úlfr, Jarl of the elves

Úlfr (wolf), Brynjar and a few of the elves that had managed to escape looked over the smoking ruins of Álfheimr for a long time in silence. The bodies in what had been the stockade had been burnt beyond recognition.

"We should have run," Úlfr eventually said. "As soon as we knew the Illvættir were looking for us, we should have run."

"It had been our home for seven hundred years, brother." Brynjar replied softly. "It had kept us safe until now."

"The world has grown warmer, we should have known that." Úlfr insisted, looking over the ruins. "And as soon as I saw the enemy canoes, *I* should have known that Illvættir would be in the fleet. It is the only reason why the humans dared attack us. And it is why far-sight gave us no warning. I should have been evacuating the town, not defending it."

"The decision was our father's, for good or for ill, and when the enemy was upon us there was no time. We were straight away fighting for our lives. We made mistakes ..."

"Like herding everyone into the fort?" Úlfr spat on the ground. "We cannot afford a second mistake, not like that one. It would finish us."

It occurred to him he might be the last jarl of the elves.

Dear Goddess, no! He had to find a way to save his people.

* * *

North Sea, off the coast of the Norge, sailing south

Hervor tried to keep the children out of the way of the human sailors. They were jammed into a small corner between furs, sacks of various elvish handicrafts, precious metals and other plunder. It seemed Bjørn was in charge of the war party but Harald was the better sailor and in charge of the ship.

As the daughter of the Jarl she had met Norse before. They had always seemed loud and brash and endlessly curious about elves. These men weren't like that at all. Apart from Harald and Bjørn they tried to avoid her and the children and Harald was always busy with the boat. She had to admit Bjørn seemed attentive and kind but then she kept reminding herself what he had done and she felt her heart harden once again.

He seemed to watch her whenever he could, but pretend he wasn't doing it when she looked at him.

He owned her. Why did he need to play such games? It felt like he was planning something for her when he got her back to his home, maybe away from all these witnesses.

The idea made her shudder and feel unclean, but what was she going to do? If she got herself killed fighting him, who would protect the children? How would she protect the children anyway from these savages? She felt so helpless.

It was a rough night but at least elves do not get sea sick. Hervor couldn't remember much of it, she felt too miserable, fearful and sad. Her heart kept going over and over what would happen to the children and wondering what she could do to help them.

She didn't get much sleep. The men sailed by the light of the moon and took turns manning the boat while they had a following wind. The children slept fitfully at first and then little Brenda woke and began crying and wouldn't be comforted. Hervor hugged her, patted her and sang to her but nothing worked till Hervor's body ached with fatigue, her throat was hoarse and it felt like sand had been poured into her eyes.

The night had passed in misery, the sea was calmer and the sun was a pinkish glow on the horizon when Bjørn finally approached her. She blinked up at him as the sun started to peep at the new day, forging a rippling golden road over the water stretching from the horizon towards the boat.

She feared he would be angry and may strike her, or even the child. She clutched at the little girl defensively but he only looked down at her and gave her a sympathetic smile. She realised what a mess she must look.

"Give the *lyt wei* (small-weight) bairn *her* (here)." He ordered gruffly, reaching out and bracing himself against the mast.

She reluctantly stood and passed the elf to him. Her little body was still wracked by sobs. Brenda was so small and defenceless and he was a great bear of a man. He could hit her or even throw her overboard in his anger. She tensed herself, ready to spring up in defence of the little girl, but instead he held her tenderly over his shoulder and made soothing sounds. He patted her gently and massaged her back with circular motions. Hervor watched, incredulous, as the little elf stopped crying.

Bjørn remained standing, somehow keeping his footing in the rocking boat and patting her. He began murmuring a song. To Hervor it sounded excruciatingly mournful, but Brenda seemed to like it. Her eyes glazed over as she lay across the big man's shoulder and gave a sigh. Eventually her eyes shut and her breathing became regular.

Hervor looked up at the big man, disbelieving.

He winked at her, looking very smug and superior.

For a moment, her heart surged with gratitude and relief. And it also seemed just a little comical and heart warming: the big man and the tiny elf girl he carried as he moved around, attending to his morning tasks, but she couldn't keep her own eyes open any longer.

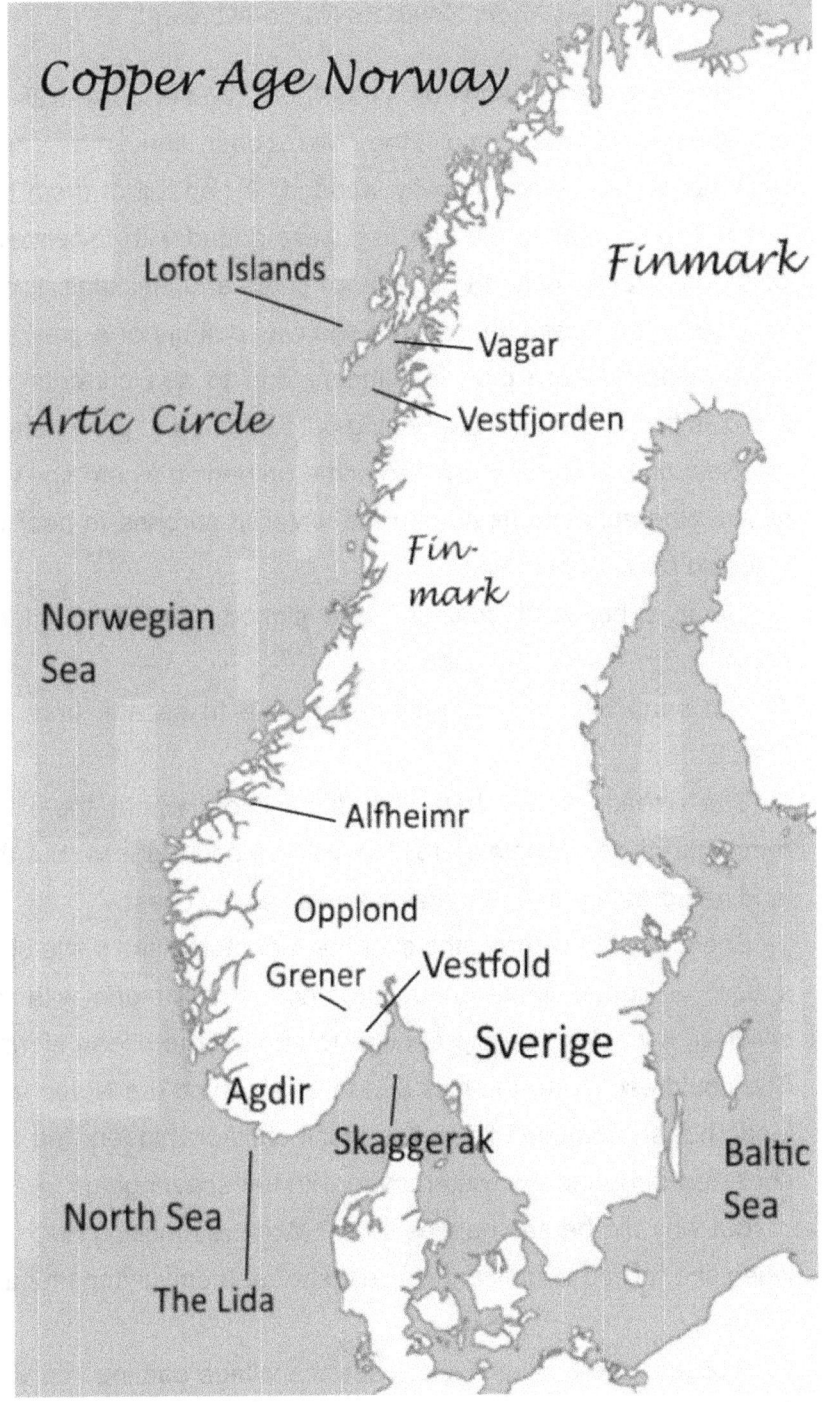

Copper Age Norway

Lofot Islands

Finmark

Artic Circle

Vagar

Vestfjorden

Fin-
mark

Norwegian
Sea

Alfheimr

Opplond

Grener   Vestfold

Sverige

Agdir

Skaggerak

Baltic
Sea

North Sea

The Lida

Vest-Agdir, Southern Norge *(Norway)*

The first Hervor saw of *Vest-Agdir* (West-Agdir) was an archipelago of islands off the wild coast line, most were uninhabited, rocky and heavily wooded. A handful of them had been cleared near to the sea and were dotted with fishermen's cottages, with a scattering of sheep, goats and chickens. It was very green and fresh, though the sea was dull under a grey sky. It was warmer here than in Álfheimr due to sea currents and breezes from the south. Everything here seemed to grow better.

"Beautiful, isn't it?" Bjørn had come up behind where she was sitting. She almost jumped into the water in surprise to hear his voice so close behind her.

"Já it is beautiful, master." She sighed, "But it is not my home."

"I'm sorry Hervor. You'll neinn be able to escape from *her* (here)."

She already knew that. She didn't know where the pitiful remnants of her people were. Maybe she could guess, but this land had great central mountains and a narrow coast.

She didn't know the paths over the mountains and if she stole a boat or canoe small enough for her to sail alone with the children, it wouldn't be big enough to survive the ocean storms. She could escape to the hills and forests behind the Norse farm lands but she couldn't keep five small children hidden, fed and sheltered throughout a winter, even with her scavenging.

But why did he say he was sorry? Was he mocking her? Yet when she turned to look in his eyes, she read only sympathy and concern.

Puzzled, she looked back to see the village coming into view in the distance.

Farsund meant 'deep sound' and the village lay on a peninsula that formed one side of the entrance to a great and narrow inlet. As the ships rounded the headland and entered the fjord the wind died.

"Ver hafa had a good *vindr* (wind) but now *ver roa* (we paddle)." Bjørn sighed. "It would be a mikill thing if we could arrive *viðr* (with) the rest of minn kynr, just this once."

Hervor looked up. "All alfir have 'little-magic', Lord. We may not catch them but we can certainly surprise them if you wish. It is at the limit of what little magic can do but shouldn't make me too tired. I was always good with little magic."

"What's 'little-magic', Hervor?" Bjørn asked.

Hervor didn't reply, she just gently blew on the sail.

The little cargo boat began picking up speed as Hervor puffed harder, her forehead wrinkled in concentration. Bjørn watched, laughing with delight.

"Takka, Hervor, by minn trú, yor folk are *kynligr* (wondrous kin)."

While the men in other boats shouted and cheered them, he only had eyes for her. Hervor, his beautiful lady of the forest; her red hair the colour of autumn leaves, her deep green eyes the bright green of spring reflected in deep pools, her skin fair like summer sunshine and her lips red as fresh cherries.

Her elfin features were so finely shaped, her body was tall and slender and her fingers long and thin. It made her look thin and delicate, but he knew that was misleading in an elf.

She was the most beautiful woman he had ever seen, he felt dizzy and breathless even to be near her. She was as wary as a wild animal caught in a trap. Her heart was filled with fury and horror about what happened and she had no reason to love him, he understood that.

It made her cold and aloof, but then she would smile in gratitude at some small kindness. It was then that she looked even more beautiful than seemed possible. All he wanted to do was look at her and be near her and have her smile. Could he ever win her love?

Was she blushing now? Her cheeks, the tips of her ears, and her neck had a faint redness, or was it the strain of casting her magic? She was so beautiful it made his heart ache. He wondered what it would be like to kiss her.

Hervor had to concentrate on her magic working but it was hard *not* to be aware of the big handsome man standing so close besides her. She had pleased him, and that was good but the way he examined her so closely made her feel shy.

She wondered if he would touch her, it seemed like he might. She didn't want him to and he had never tried, and yet part of her imagined his tender touch and wondered what it would be like. Her head was a whirl of confusion as the boat sped to the harbour.

* * *

Entry into Farsund

As Bjørn and Harald's canoe landed at Farsund it felt like the jaws of a trap had closed on Hervor. She felt a surge of panic to see humans swarming everywhere, crowding, running and shouting as they welcomed the returning fleet. She made sure the children and especially Bjørn didn't see her fear.

The harbour was in a shallow bay to one side of the entrance to the sound. The town was on a low flat rise set back from the harbour, surrounded by a defensive ring of trenches and earth walls broken only by four pathways to the top. It was dominated by Alrik Konungr's great langhús surrounded by its own wooden palisade, but the gates lay open and welcoming for the returning fleet.

Bjørn lived another day's journey by canoe east. He lived on a *stadhr* (steading) belonging to Harald's father and it lay in the hinterland of the small fishing village of Líðandi. All his men came from around there.

Hervor wondered at this, Bjørn was the son of a king, why didn't he have his own place? And why were his boats smaller than those given to his older brothers, and why was his war band so small? He was a third son, maybe that was it.

Most of Bjørn's men left for their homes immediately, leaving only the cargo canoe with a four man crew to come later with Harald and Bjørn. Hervor wondered at that too. There would be celebrations. These humans had defeated the legendary elves, yet it seemed surprisingly subdued for a victorious home coming.

After they trudged up the hill to Alrik Konungr's fortified langhús with some spare bedding, Bjørn and Harald took Hervor and the children to the king's stables.

"I suppose we are nothing but animals to you, now." She muttered darkly. "May as well keep us in the stables."

"Are Alfir too fine to stay in a barn now?" Bjørn laughed. "You'll be a damn sight more comfortable her than in the house of my father. It will be I that will be envious of you. And Hervor," he turned to face her, "don't think to run away, you will be found and brought back and it will go hard with you."

"If I ran, human," Hervor raised her chin to stare at him, "you wouldn't catch me."

She sighed. "But where would I go? I can't get home, it's all gone."

She was trapped, but it was worse than that. She couldn't keep the children alive and fed by herself and they were too small to do a lot of work for their human masters. If Bjørn or those he lived with found them a burden (as Bjørn's brothers said they would) they might sell them, or worse, cast them out!

How could the children stay alive without adults to look after them?

She and they were totally at the mercy of Bjørn and the other humans. Hervor had already explained to the children just how desperate their situation would be as soon as they arrived in the land of their enemies. She told them to be polite at all times and always willing to work and not cause any trouble.

Bjørn stared at her for a long while and then nodded, as if satisfied. She felt her hatred boiling up inside her.

"I will see that Knut looks after you." He said gently, leading the way into the stables.

Knut (knot), to Hervor's relief, was a kindly old man. He was Alrik's horse master and shorthanded with all the King's wars and raiding. Working with animals was something elves understood very well. Hervor couldn't match the brute strength of a human man or even some of the really strong human farm girls, but she was fit and strong for an elf. She could do any skilled work quickly and for anything within her strength she didn't tire easily. The three older children were also anxious to help. Knut was surprised at how quick and nimble they were.

"Yor alfir look slender and graceful but þu are stronger than yor look." He said. "Þu are willing workers and are good with your heads, not just your hands; even your young-lings."

It was good to be able to relax around at least one of these humans. Knut liked to talk whenever he took a break from the work and he was one of the family's oldest retainers. He was a mine of useful information.

"Your lord doesn't get on so well with his broðiren." He explained. "The older one, Torgny is the *Erling* (heir) so will be the *Konungr* (king) einn dagr. He used to ride Bjørn hard when he *vesa* (was) smali but all three brothers ran wild when they were young without a mother, and their father wasn't always around. They are broðiren stilla and would stick together ef it ever came to it."

Hervor knew about being teased when she was small, she supressed the memories of her father and brothers that came crowding in on her.

"I don't think he is happy with what happened at Ālfheimr." She offered. It puzzled her.

"None of us are!" Knut's voice sounded loud in the barn; the children looked up in alarm.

"I'm sorry," he calmed himself down somewhat. He paused to make the protective sign of Thor's hammer with his closed right fist: forehead, centre of chest and left then right breast. "Those seiðmenn ..."

"Illvættir," Hervor supplied automatically.

"Evil breed, es that hvat yor call þeim? That is *góðr nafn* (good name), já. Þeir came and offered the Konungr *hjalpa* (help) handling the seiðr af yor alfir. But Þeir played oss false and brought forth unnatural *vættir* (wights). Our warriors hardly struck an honourable blow. It made oss worse than thieves and scavengers, at least those vermin do neinn pretend to be real menn."

"I don't understand." Hervor shook her head. "You can raid but you can't steal?"

"Of course not! A *maðr kanna* (man can) use strength, cunning and luck to defeat an enemy. Ef yðvarr enemy allows himself to be weak or unwary it is his fault after all. But þú (thou) neinn taka by stealth or magic. That is womanly. What þú taka, you must earn, fight for. And þú cannot kill unarmed women and young children, such acts are *níðingsverk* (work of a perverted man, a nothing man, someone without honour)."

Hervor felt more than a little dizzy as she tried to understand these crazy Norse.

"You can rape and enslave girls and women, but you cannot kill them."

"Já that is rettr." Knut nodded in agreement. "*Þú* need to put yðvarr claim on þeim of course, but if they submit þú mustn't mistreat them. This slaughter, this *illr dað* (ill deed) has cast *fúll reykr* (foul smoke) over all the great things our men have ever done. We will be remembered for this, not for our victories. The mood of the menn is *uggligr* (ugly), and there have been fights already. Keep close to here, the sight of an alfr is a reminder of what happened. The sooner *þú gan* (thou go) to Líðandi the better."

Hervor wondered if she could ever understand these savages now that she was at their mercy. Firstly, it was hardly the fault of the elves and secondly she had no choice as to when she could leave. She had to wait on her new lord.

She decided not to say what would have happened to the Norse if they met with the elves in a fair fight, even though the elves were outnumbered.

"What about the wounded elves?"

"They will be safe here if they cause neinn trouble, will they linger?"

"Neinn," she admitted. "No matter what you do, you can bind them or cage them. As soon as they are well enough, they will be gone."

"And what about you, Hervor?"

"Me?" she sighed deeply, for a moment overwhelmed by a feeling of helplessness. "I don't know. I have the children to look after and I have given my word to submit. That means something as long as Bjørn does not treat us too badly."

"Bjørn won't," Knut said. "He is a good man."

"I certainly hope so," Hervor said softly. "I certainly hope so."

* * *

Sleeping in the barn, Farsund

"Arghh!" Hervor cried out.

For a moment she didn't know where she was. Then a horse snorted and she saw the nearby shapes of children sleeping; good, she hadn't woken them.

She realised she had been dreaming. Her parents and Alfhildr had been trapped in a burning house. They were desperately calling out for her to help them. She had been frantically struggling to reach them but was being dragged helplessly away. It had been a giant blond man with no face: no eyes, mouth or nose. No matter how hard she struggled she couldn't get loose.

Sitting up in the darkness for a moment she couldn't breath and her heart was on fire.

Tears came to her then and soft sobbing, all alone in the darkness.

* * *

Farsund, the next morning

Bjørn came to see them the next morning. Hervor saw him coming in the distance and told the children not to bother him. He would be too busy to worry about slaves. But they were too excited to listen, especially Brenda who ran up and asked to be carried.

He had been drinking and she could smell it on him. Some men became irritable in drink but he seemed in a good mood at least. He had brought cloth dolls for the girls and toy canoes for the boys.

"Þakka, Bjørn." Hervor said softly, feeling the heat flood to her face. "You didn't need to, we are slaves."

He coloured and made a dismissive gesture, casually lifting Brenda up onto his hip and kissing her cheek. "I need to stay at least four days or *minn gan* (my going) will be talked upon." He said. "The sooner I'm gone the better I will like it."

She nodded, surprised that he felt any need to explain himself to her.

"More drinking and feasting then?"

"And boasting and bad poetry. I'll see that þú and the kynder get *matr (*meat). Þú can't koma, but then I suppose þú wouldn't want to."

She stiffened. "Neinn!"

Celebrate what happened to her people? Did he really need to ask?

He gave her a hurt look and for some reason it made her feel sorry.

"Not if you are going to sing," she offered, trying to smile.

"Hervor, don't þú like minn singing?" He grinned and pretended to be shocked.

She laughed a little, still uncertain of him. "Is that what you call it Bjørn? We thought it was a dirge, only Brenda seemed to like it."

He flashed her a smile that for some reason made her feel hot and breathless. What was wrong with her reacting like a silly young girl? After he was gone she plonked herself down on a stump, her mind was whirling in confusion.

It was only last autumn that Hákon had told her that she would have to go to live amongst her enemies, these brutal humans. At that time she thought it would be impossible, she would have rather died. And yet here she was, trying to cope with a harsh new life and a clouded future.

What else had Hákon said? He warned of something terrible coming for the elves. Well that was easy. It had already come, though it was far from over.

Hákon had said that she might be the only hope for her people. How could that be? She was a slave to her enemies and she had four children to protect. Even protecting the children seemed impossible and made her feel almost mad with fear and desperation, and what could one slave girl possibly do to help the remains of her people? Who could fight daimôns?

Hákon had given her a piece of advice. She sat for a while trying to recall what it was. Ah, that was it! Trust the Goddess and follow her heart. Well her heart was telling her that Bjørn was a good man. Her head was telling her he was a bitter enemy and a brutal human.

The way he secretly watched her angered and frightened her. She couldn't shake a feeling that he had further plans for her when he got her back to his home and she was helpless in his power ... and yet, so far, he had seemed kind.

* * *

Bjørn brought the meat himself from the feast and a large jug of mead for Knut. As he left the feasting hall, his brothers and their friends teased him loudly, saying that he was more interested in what lay between the legs of his new þræll than in the welfare of Knut and the rest of his new slaves.

He couldn't argue about his attraction for his new slave but reminded them that he had promised he would never force her. They found that hilarious, a pretty female Þræll he couldn't make use of! They warned him she would become his mistress soon enough, and he her slave.

As he entered with his gifts Hervor bowed her head low to accept them and place them on a work table. As she did so, he saw the ring Dómarr had given her.

"Hervor, you have a man friend. Are you spoken for?"

He touched the ring.

She snarled, whipping the knife off the table and sprang up. Her eyes were flashing with rage as she backed away from him. Her body was crouched as if ready for an attack.

"Careful girl!" Knut barked out. "You can be killed for drawing a weapon on your master."

"Hervor, please!" Bjørn shouted. "I'm sorry! I meant no harm."

Hervor looked at him in confusion, and then looked at the bone knife in her hand as if wondering where it came from.

"You couldn't have known." She said, carefully putting the knife back. "Dómarr is a childhood friend and I love him. We are not betrothed, no, but it is expected one day we will be. And you, a man, shouldn't touch the ring though you wouldn't have known that."

* * *

Finmark, land of the Sami and a stone siedi

Mohkku bowed to the siedi. It was a pyramid of granite, as tall as a man and split off from the surrounding rock. It was a very special siedi and had guided the soul-journey of countless noaidi for over a thousand years.

Siedi connect the waking world with the spirit world. They can be instantly recognised by how they stand out from their surroundings and how they bring focus to the soul. They can be built, like an altar, but the best and most powerful ones were formed by nature itself.

After the drumming of Juoksa and the help from the polar bear spirit, the land of the Sami had been cleansed. Mohkku could once again travel in the spirit world and the veil had dropped from his sight. Not in the south though, there the influence of the two dark sorcerers was too strong even for the polar bear sprit.

He carefully placed his offering of carved reindeer horn and sang his welcome, asking for its help. Then he built a small fire. He sprinkled pine needles around the rock as an additional offering and then on the fire to give off sacred smoke.

When everything was ready he took out his drum and began his chant. In his mind an image of twelve war canoes formed; a raiding party coming from the south.

* * *

Entering Líðandi

Líðandi was named after *the Líða* ('the end'). The Líða was a finger of land poking into the sea and marked the southern-most part of the coast of *Norge*. It also marked the border between the North Sea and the 'Skagerrak', that triangular wedge of a strait between the coasts of Norge and *Sverige* (Sweden). The western side as they approached was rocky and wild, the surging seas dotted with lonely, brooding islands of rock.

As the point came in sight, Hervor had a dull sinking feeling. She and the children were approaching the place where they would be slaves in the homes of the humans.

Then this feeling gave way to a rising fear of the sea and rocks. The wind, as they made for the point, was high, causing the waves to crash many paces above, with spray high in the air. As the sea sucked back, it revealed jagged reefs lurking just below. It seemed to Hervor that they were waiting hungrily to rip the bottom out of any boat that was foolish enough to dare the crossing.

It was here that Hervor learnt why Harald was captain of their small ship.

He stepped across to the right hand side to take the steering oar from Bjørn.

"Down sail!" He yelled as the men scurried to do his bidding.

"Positions!" As they scurried to grab paddles. "Now pull you bastards! Pull as if yðvarr lives depended on it!

"Bjørn, the tide vilja shove oss on those rocks if we are not mindful. I want you pulling on the side opposite mik."

The men grabbed deep with their paddles, muscles bunching, red in the face, backs arched and grunting, racing and paddling for all they were worth. Hervor would have offered to help but she was too frozen with terror. She could hardly do more than grip the children and rattle off a prayer.

The canoe was tossed sideways and down. She clutched the children hard, waiting for the jolt and the crack of tortured timbers that would end their lives.

Harald stood like a titan, one arm wrapped around the steering oar, his hair tossed in all directions and a wide grin on his face.

"I don't suppose you alfir have magic for this!" He called out, laughing.

Five elvish faces stared up at him, pale and frightened.

"Don't worry, almost there." He seemed to be enjoying himself.

The boat shot forward like a horse out of a gate and swung quickly to the left as it hit a tidal race.

"I have sailed this section of coast since I was wei bairn."

Such a thing was clearly impossible but nonetheless they suddenly surged forward into calm water, paddling gently towards a small harbour.

As soon as they arrived Harald and the men helped Hervor and the children out. They were all grinning at them.

"I hear the alfir are great sailors too." Harald said cheerfully.

Hervor didn't reply. She only made it a few yards up the beach before her legs gave way. She was forced to sit on the grey pebbly sand, the children around her, watching the men draw the boat up. The village was little more than a collection of fishermen's cottages, smoke houses, woodpiles and pit houses around the pebbly beach and up against the side of a hill. It stunk of fish and rotten sea weed. There was the constant mournful cry of gulls.

Four dugouts and a bark canoe were already pulled up on the shore and fishing nets were strung between trees to dry.

As soon as their canoe was first sighted, people had started to crowd onto the beach. Some of the fishing canoes were still out but there were still more than enough men and women to make a fair crowd, with more people spilling out of the houses as she watched. It seemed as if everyone was shouting at once.

This was something Hervor had been dreading. She had grown up knowing everyone in her village. She was an elf, and elves looked and acted differently. They didn't talk like this, not so quickly and so loudly. And they didn't crowd in like this!

She wasn't ready to be surrounded by a whole jostling crowd of human strangers. On the boat she had been isolated from most of the crew and at Farsund the focus had been on the King's return. She and the children had been kept out of sight and out of trouble.

Here there was nothing to protect her. She tried to stay calm for the children's sake. After all, what were they going to do, kill her? It felt like they might.

She didn't tell Bjørn or Harald how frightened she was. Would they even care? They would be proud to show off what he had caught. It was worse in a way than being a caged animal. At least a cage could keep crowds away.

Several people surged forward to greet the men but at least they held back from the side where the elves were. Still, they stared and shouted and pointed as she and the elf children stood up in a small cluster, holding on to each other and moving slowly closer to Bjørn for safety. Hervor's heart was racing, her breath coming fast; she felt so frightened she felt dizzy.

"Don't crowd þeim!"

The crowd parted and a grey haired lady limped forward. She was plump, and only five foot tall or even shorter, she was the shortest human Hervor had ever seen. For a moment Hervor wondered if she was a dwarf living amongst humans, until she heard them calling her "Amma" (Grandma).

"Who's that?" She hissed at Bjørn.

"She's the hæfuð (head man), everyone calls her Amma."

The head man was a woman, and she was named Grandma?

She couldn't really be everyone's grandmother could she?

But Amma was getting people organised.

"Everyone, stop crowding around and staring; haven't you seen alfir before?"

No they haven't, Hervor thought fearfully as she looked around at the sea of alien faces, her heart was fluttering like a trapped bird. At Amma's direction a wedge of women surrounded Hervor and the children and brought them safely inside a small langhús and set them up by the fire. She settled down gratefully and began to warm up.

"I heard what happened to your home, and I'm sorry." Amma said, "That was an awful crime. I want you to know you are amongst friends here."

So, we are amongst friends here ... Hervor wondered if the old woman had gone totally mad.

They offered her and the children *skyr* (thin yoghurt) with pickled cabbage and onion, and salted salmon served with fresh flat bread. It made Hervor realise just how cold and hungry she was from the sea voyage.

Brenda was already sitting on the lap of one of the older human girls and chatting away as if she had known her all her life. The human girl was as tall as an elf, with blond hair. She was big boned, with muscles almost like a man and yet she had a kind and pleasant face.

Hervor insisted that the children only spoke Norse amongst themselves to practice and pick up the accent. Brenda was already beginning to talk like one of the Norse: her 'Ws' were becoming 'Vs' and her voice had an upward inflection at the end of each sentence.

"Ve kanna stay," Harald was saying. "I just vant minn cart and horses. Ver will camp on the way. After all this time away, I'm in a hurry to get back home."

Hervor had been terrified of meeting a large number of humans but now she was warm, fed and surrounded by people being kind, she didn't want to leave.

"You're neinn taking the kynder to camp out this early in the season!" Amma said in a tone that was not to be argued with.

"You can stay the night and leave early in the morning like normal decent folk. Did you bring a change of clothes for the alfir?"

Harald and Bjørn exchanged a puzzled glance, it hadn't occurred to them.

Hervor and the children only had the clothes they were captured in and they were looking very much the worse for wear already. She had to clean her dress the best she could, while still wearing it, because of the constant presence of men. She had a knitted jumper but it wasn't warm enough for the cold nights. None of the children were any better off.

"By the *Alfodr* (all father, Odin) are you both daft? Þú brought back plunder but no clothes for the kynder. Do you think clothes grow on trees?"

"Don't worry," she said to Hervor. "I *hafa* (I have) a big family *her* (here). Tell me child, does Bjørn treat *yor* (you) kindly? Has he forced yor?"

"Nothing like that mam, he promised not to." She said shyly. "He seems kind. He has been very good with the children."

She nodded to Brenda who had fallen asleep on the human girl's lap.

Hervor's fears of this place were melting away.

"Well, he had better treat you right," Amma said firmly as if that settled it, "or I will hear of it."

They had asked the men who normally lived in the langhús to sleep somewhere else for the night and for that Hervor was grateful. Bjørn and Harald left as soon as they saw her settled in, to join the main welcome party outside, so she didn't see them till the morning. She could hear singing and loud laughter outside and some of the women were coming and going.

She and the children were exhausted by sea voyage and she asked permission to sleep early. Somehow she felt safe here. She had one of the best sleeps she had had since she was captured, no bad dreams despite being surrounded by all these human women. The women stayed up late gossiping and there was a loud party around a fire on the beach but Hervor hardly heard them.

In the morning they were offered a generous breakfast of bread, skyr and fried fish. When they got ready to leave Hervor and the children had a coat each, moccasins (though elves more usually went bare foot) and spare clothing; it was coarse home spun but nearly new.

Harald and Bjørn busied themselves with hitching up two short but heavily muscled ponies (Askr and Embla after the first man and woman) to what looked like a small hay wagon: every bit of the frame was made from wood, including the axles. It was going to be a slow trip to the farm. There was a large pot of thick animal fat and Harold gave a generous dab along the axle with a cloth and wiped his hand on some grass.

Hervor waited with the children as Bjørn and Harald loaded the cart with their property; *their stolen property*, she reminded herself.

Just before getting in Bjørn lifted Brenda up and kissed her face.

"Koma," He said "Lyt wei, þú (you) riða the kartr."

Hervor looked at him in surprise; she had been resigned to carrying the child. The other children wouldn't be so bad, elf children were better than human children for walking and running but Brenda was too small.

"Your beard tickles!" Brenda announced loudly.

The humans started to laugh.

"Ho, what?" Bjørn cried with glee. "Tickles, does it? What about this, then?"

He lifted her up and bared her stomach to tickle it with his beard, to her squeals of delight. Soon the pair had everyone laughing, even Hervor.

"Put the lyt bairn here," Harald called patting the seat next to him.

Bjørn spun the laughing child around and plonked her on the seat and leapt up to sit next to her. She immediately climbed into his lap.

"Lyt wei." He murmured, hugging her, as Harold took up the reins.

"Weigh little, that's not my name Bjørn. It's Brenda!" She declared loudly.

"Why sure it is, þú don't wei much at all, just look at you! You must be lyt wei!"

"Neinn," she laughed with glee. "My name is Brenda, silly."

"No, it's not," Bjørn tickled her gently, "it's lyt wei."

Brenda leaned back and arranged Bjørn's thick hairy arms around her waist.

The girl misses her father, Hervor realised with a pang. Her eyes grew moist and she felt a single tear run down her cheek. Her new master seemed to be kind to the children but now she feared that they were starting to love him. He was their slave master after all; he was sure to disappoint them.

"Thank you mam," she bowed to Amma.

"Come here, alfr." Amma moved forward and used her apron to wipe the tear from Hervor's cheek. "Give an old lady a hug."

Suddenly the old lady's kindness, everyone's kindness, was too much. Hervor was surprised to find her eyes were leaking tears. An elf should have more control than that!

"I'm sorry," she whispered hoarsely.

The old lady held her tight and soothed her. "I know, I know. There, there."

It was just nonsense words but it caused Hervor to lose the last bit of control she had.

She dropped to her knees, sobbing and clutching at the old lady; burying her head in her ample bosom. She didn't want to do this in front of all these humans, she didn't want the children to see, nor Bjørn nor Harald, but she just couldn't help herself.

Ashamed and blinded by tears she stumbled back over to the cart. No one moved to stop her or touch her.

Her head bowed, she murmured gruffly. "If it pleases my lord, I am ready."

"You look after that girl and those bairnr!" Amma called out a warning, wiping her own tears. "Or yor will answer to mer!"

Hervor felt angry with herself and ashamed. It seemed the slightest hint of kindness from these humans, especially towards the children, and she lost all control. She knew she was only young for an elf but she had once been strong and confident, how had she become so weak?

* * *

Nordlándda, home of the Northern Elves

The village of Vágar was in the land of the midnight sun. It lay on an island in the northern part of the *Lófót* (lynx foot)

Archipelago, really a flooded chain of dark granite mountains just off the far north coast of *Norge* (Norway).

The sea between the Lófót and the mainland was a rough body of water called the Vestfjorden, using the old meaning of fjord, which was a passage. As the small Vest-Fold fleet entered Vestfjorden, the Archipelago appeared to the left, looking like a continuous mountainous wall, long, dark and brooding. The locals called it the *Lofotveggen* (the Lofoten wall).

The storm came out of nowhere; one minute the sky was clear, next minute the winds began to gust, getting rapidly stronger as inky clouds rushed to cover the sky.

"This is no natural storm," Rúgálfr, his second in charge yelled over the growing roar. "In Ragnarr's father's time we tried to raid the Fenni with some Vest-Agdir men and they sent a great storm against us."

"Those foreign witch-men were supposed to protect us against this." Garðr shouted back.

Rúgálfr didn't bother to reply. Soon they were facing howling winds and ten foot waves. The canoe 'Afkárr' capsized and was lost with all hands. Fighting against strong cross tides and cross winds, Garðr gave the order to run for shelter. Somewhere halfway to safety the small canoe 'Sigrún' got separated from the rest and was never seen of again.

* * *

Village of Kholm, where Lovat and Kunya rivers join

At first the dwarves could do very little. They were weak and tired easily. Báfurr and two others had lost toes and would be left with permanent limps. Andvari was the oldest dwarf and amongst the survivors had been the sickest. He was still plagued by coughing and he was short of breath with the slightest exertion. For a dwarf, he looked positively gaunt.

It fell to the men of Kholm to make temporary patches for their boat and float it back to the village with the remains of their cargo. Once they had it there, the dwarves insisted on making the repairs themselves. Dwarves were fussy tradesmen and in any case they would be the ones inside the boat as it faced a pounding from the North Sea.

For Sindri it was a very uncomfortable time. Andvari was the only one still being civil to him. The attitudes of the others varied from frosty through to barely concealed hostility.

"They blame me for what happened." He said to Andvari when he could finally get him alone.

"They do." The old dwarf was overcome with a bout of coughing. "Not for the journey, we knew it was dangerous but the pay was good and there was adventure to be had. Going in winter was more dangerous. In summer that little walk of yours wouldn't have killed us like it did, but we almost made the crossing in winter and in record time. That would have been a grand thing. So they don't blame you for travelling in winter, not completely anyway."

Dwarves were a tough people and they could accept hardship once they had agreed to it.

"The attack of those raiders," Sindri suggested. "They came after my cargo, the armour and weapons."

"That was bad enough but it was the action of an enemy." Andvari gave a wry smile. "And we chased them off. No, it's not for any of those reasons, as bad as they all seem. They are sailors and they believe you have done something that is completely unforgivable."

Andvari was overcome with coughing and couldn't go on for several moments.

"They believe you brought a curse upon us, both man and ship. Brave men can fight all manner of things and accept all sorts of risks but who can fight a curse? It brings a special type of ill luck that can defeat even the strongest man. To them, you knew you were bringing a curse upon your companions, and yet you did it anyway, and that is a terrible crime."

Sindri sighed. "What about you?"

"A new born child can tell you that thing is evil and you wouldn't deny it." Andvari jerked his thumb to the hut where their cargo was stored, even from a distance they could sense the armour and its malice, "but I don't think it was a curse that got us. Have you worked out why we got attacked where we were?"

"They were waiting for us." Sindri said as he worked through it slowly, thinking. "They knew roughly the way we would have to go and they were after what we were carrying. They stayed in the north waiting for us and that was no small thing, so they knew its importance."

"Perhaps, but why there?"

"That's it!" Sindri looked at him in amazement. "We were moving the boat and we couldn't stay hidden!"

"And who would know that? Certainly not that unwashed shaman."

"Áedán!" Sindri said, bunching his fists as if looking to hit something.

"Yes," Andvari paused for a long time to let it sink in. "This wasn't bad luck brought on by a curse. A powerful enemy sent those men after us. We were lucky to survive. So no bad luck, no curse."

Despite himself Sindri laughed, "did you tell the others this?"

"Yes I did but they are still too afraid to think clearly, it's why I didn't tell them the other thing."

"What's that?"

"Áedán, at least as Lofarr, has met you many times before, so it is easiest for him to track you." Andvari said simply. "You were near dying, I think that he would have been able to see you then. Now that you are better you have disappeared again."

It took a few moments for that to sink in. They were being hunted by the leader of the Illvættir, the most powerful wizard in the known world, and while he couldn't see them at the moment he knew where they were!

"It is not all bad news." Andvari added with a small smile. "Your mind was clouded, it made it harder for him to know where you were, even you didn't know."

He paused when he saw Sindri's expression.

"All right, it is likely he is powerful enough to track you to this place, but we are far away and surrounded by a tribe of humans. I doubt he has another mob of nomads to send after us. He can't see you now, so we might have moved on by land or water, which would make us hard to find.

"He has vast power but his power is not unlimited. Even if he could, say, send his daimôn after us, it is unlikely he would wish to expend so much of his resources just to track us down and kill us. What he really wants are the artefacts but he can't track them, they are protected from that, and the last time he saw us we didn't have them."

He paused and Sindri nodded.

"Still, without the proper intelligence it is dangerous to try to read the mind of an enemy and assume what he knows, what he doesn't know and what he can or cannot do. The wise commander simply assesses threats and takes precautions."

"You have a slippery mind, my friend."

"I come from a tribe of dwarves who live in the wide world rather than you dwarves that live under ground in safety. I have fought battles and led men. All I can tell you is that I think we are safe, but it is by no means certain."

"That is not completely reassuring."

"No, I suppose not."

* * *

Vágar, largest village of the Northern Elves

The storm did not reach nearby Vágar. Some of the older elves had been feeling uneasy for many days now but they had no way to know why. None of them had true far-sight so they had no knowledge of the disaster that had struck Álfheimr.

This was the busiest time of the year for the Northern Elves. They were far, far to the north; up in the land of the midnight sun, but warm sea currents from the south made the winters tolerable.

Now, in the spring, the skies were crowded with flocks of migratory sea birds returning to nest. More importantly for them and their Sami friends, fish also came in great numbers to spawn: in spring cod came to the deeper waters and herring closer to shore. In summer, salmon crowded the rivers and the streams.

The herring they netted when they could but cod were too deep for handmade nets so these they caught with great fishing lines, each bearing many hooks; the whole village going out and coming back to dry and smoke their catch.

There was still plenty of time for fun. Dómarr, his older brother Hagbarðr and their friends Jossur and Gyrd were just back from hunting on the mainland where Dómarr had missed a stag. Everyone teased him that it was because he was day-dreaming of Hervor. There was more than a little truth in that. He promised himself, yet again, that he would visit her this spring.

One of the villagers had just reported a colony of harp seals resting on their way north to their summer feeding grounds, so the four friends were no sooner back than they had gathered at Dómarr's father's house to coil their ropes and sharpen whale bone harpoons, cutting deep notches in them so they would stick in flesh.

They were there when they heard the signal horn. Jossur and Gyrd grabbed for the harpoons as the only weapons they had handy while Dómarr and Hagbarðr reached for their heavy hunting bows before running to the water front. Elves from the village were already gathering and they paused in shock as they saw four great war canoes knifing quickly through the water towards the village. They must have contained two hundred human men in all, racing to reach their harbour.

Then they relaxed.

The sides of the canoes were painted in bright red patterns made from the juice of alder bark. The men wore red leather hats, lined with fur, with trousers and brightly decorated *gákti* (smocks). One of them sang out a friendly "Bures!" greeting.

These were Sami, but most were not from near here. They came armed with harpoons, spears and the heavy bows. They had come for war, but not for war against the elves.

Dómarr saw his old Sami friend Onela in the front of the first canoe and waved at him excitedly, but the look on his friend's face was enough to still his heart.

"What under the Goddess's heaven is wrong?" He called out as his friend walked up the beach. The human simply shook his head in despair and moved over to greet Dómarr's father, Ansgar, the head man of the village.

"This is Mohkku of the Northern Sami," he introduced a burly human in colourful leathers to the elf chief, "and this is Nilse from the south."

Nilse was dressed in shabby reindeer leathers. His face was weather beaten and he had started to grey but he moved like a much younger man.

"They are noaidi (shamans) and they have brought us terrible news, Ālfheimr has fallen."

Dómarr felt like a great weight of metal had been dumped into his chest. Many of the other elves stood rigid, their eyes reflected their pain, some moaned. Hagbarðr shook his head in disbelief. This could not be real!

"Nilse is our greatest seer and I will ask him to speak for all of us."

The human's face was expressionless as he raised his voice. "Elves of Vágar, hear me. Ālfheimr has been attacked by daimôns and is all but wiped out. There are over five hundred Vest-Fold warriors headed this way in war canoes. There had been more," he gestured to Mohkku, "but thanks to Mohkku here they ran into a bad storm. Still five hundred is more than enough to kill all of you here. You will need to get your warriors ready and evacuate everyone else."

A crowd of elves was far quieter than a similar group of humans, even in the face of dreadful news, but this was too much even for elves. All the adults began shouting at once.

"What of the Jarl's family?" Someone asked loudly.

"They had fled into the fort and it was set alight around them. The Jarl, his wife, most of his people and his young daughter all died." Nilse told them. "Within moments more than fourteen hundred elves were dead, more died in the days after of terrible burns and other injuries. Only his two sons and handfuls of other elves managed to escape."

Dómarr couldn't breathe; there was a hollow feeling in his chest. "What happened to Hervor, the Jarl's other daughter?"

Mohkku answered for Nilse. "It was I who concentrated on the search for the Jarl's family. Living or dead, no other daughter of the Jarl remains in the northern lands. If I knew Hervor maybe I could use that knowledge to search the south for you. My guess is she has been taken to the Norse Lands as a þræll."

A groan escaped Dómarr's lips. So many were dead, and his brave and loving Hervor held captive by their murderers. It felt like his world had ended between one breath and the next. Anguish burned inside him like a fire.

But there were more immediate problems.

"How many warriors do you elves have?" Nilse asked them.

"We are peaceful folk." Dómarr's father Ansgar looked unbearably weary. "I never prepared my people for war. I never expected it to come this far north."

"The Illvættir have destroyed Álfheimr and now their allies are coming for Vágar and they plan to raid isolated settlements throughout this whole region. In one blow they will finish much of the world's remaining elves."

"Father, lead our people to safety and let Hagbarðr and I handle these Norse." Dómarr told his father.

"We are elves, father." Hagbarðr agreed. "There are seventy men or more, and a couple of dozen women who are quick and accurate with a bow and I have fought with the Jarl against Norse before. They have no answer to elf bows, it will be enough."

Chapter 7: Olaf's Farm

Journey to Olaf's farm

Hervor wanted to protect the children, but she was almost as helpless as they were.

From the first moment she was captured she had kept her muscles tight, as if bracing for a blow. She had expected the Norse to be savages in everything, but she was finding no few of those she met could be surprisingly friendly and welcoming; especially considering she and the children were slaves.

Today was a lovely sunny spring day and her first chance to be out walking in the open air and sunshine. It was hard for her to resist. She decided to put her fears out of her mind and live in the moment. For now she would simply enjoy the green shoots of spring, the warm sun, the light blue sky and being out of doors and exercising.

"Hey Alfir!" Bjørn called out to her, laughing. "Stop running! Our horses neinn can keep up with yor."

The wagon was thumping and creaking as if it would rattle apart as it rolled down a small hill. As she suspected, it was hardly making a walking pace on the flat and was only creeping up the hills. Hervor turned around to run backwards for a while and laughed.

"Elves love to run, especially on a day like today, but we are not really running like we could."

It was lovely to see her laugh and smile, Bjørn thought. Despite her fear and anger she was always so beautiful, but when she smiled it seemed like the sun had burst out through the clouds. And he was enjoying the children too, especially Brenda. It felt like something had been missing in his life but he had never even known it.

By late afternoon they were not far from the end of the journey and the children were tired. Bjørn and Harald lifted the twins, one after the other on top of some furs where they fell instantly asleep despite the rocking and jarring and creaking. Bjørn climbed down to walk with Hervor; he was only limping a little now.

Inka's small shoulders were slumped with weariness but she had refused to let Hervor pick her up earlier. She stumbled so Hervor grabbed her and lifted her over one shoulder. Bjørn offered to take her.

"I can manage!" She snapped, scowling.

"Neinn, wif (woman) *yor* have been walking allr *dagr* (day)."

Hervor felt a hot surge of anger. He had made her into his slave and he had brought her to this far place. Why would he care how she felt now?

But as he stood there waiting patiently, with a look of concern on his face, she felt ashamed of herself. She sheepishly passed the child over and Inka settled comfortably on her new lord's broad shoulders and, with a sigh, closed her eyes.

"See that's not so hard."

Hervor flushed crimson. Was he was laughing at her now?

"You have nice broad shoulders, not bony like mine." She admitted with a wry smile.

Why did her new master have the power to confuse her so much? One minute she hated him with a deep hatred. The next minute she felt ashamed because he was trying to be nice when he didn't have to be. And sometimes her heart felt like bursting with gratitude for his kindness towards the children.

She was starting to feel safer around him at times and was beginning to see him as a possible protector of her and the children ... at least of sorts. And, although she hated that he had enslaved her, he was big and strong and nice to look upon, especially when he smiled.

"Bjørn, I'm sorry about what happened in Líðandi. I shamed you as my lord and I shamed myself. I'll try not to let it happen again."

"*Óðinn's skegg* (Odin's beard), Hervor! *Allt er gott* (all is good). Neinn thought badly of *þú*."

She looked at him uncertainly, he seemed to mean it.

"I'm considered young for an elf," she admitted, blushing furiously. "I can't always hide how I feel."

"With all you have been through no one expects any more."

She was shocked by the total idiocy of it. With all she had been through ...*with all that he had done to her,* he meant! She clamped her mouth shut and walked on in silence.

They had been travelling slowly because of the cart so by the time that the farm house appeared half way up the final hill the afternoon sun was already casting long shadows and shining golden on the grass on the roof and nearby meadows; both dotted with spring flowers. In a small dip behind the house a gentle stream burbled happily, that would be the house's water Hervor guessed. In the distance she could hear a rooster crow. Soon the sun would be setting: a fiery orb dipping below the mountains, turning the sky to blood.

Hervor couldn't but think that it was a beautiful place.

This early in the season the animals were on the low pasture near the house and Hervor was amazed at the number of them. This was a rich farm, big with lots of buildings.

"It's beautiful, isn't it Hervor?" Bjørn asked as Hervor paused to admire it.

"I don't like it." She said.

She would be dammed if she would admit it was beautiful to someone like him!

"You're lying," he laughed.

"She *is* lying," Inka said in surprise, looking over Bjørn's shoulder to study Hervor closely. "Isn't it a bad thing, Bjørn?"

"You're supposed to be asleep, missy." Hervor told her, "And wait till you're older, then you'll understand why adults sometimes lie."

They *both* started laughing at her then.

With a sigh Hervor let it pass and trudged on.

They had to ford a river that the house creek joined near the bottom of the hill and then they would follow a path up the slope. Someone had set stones in the stream and Hervor hitched her dress, grabbed Inka and ran lightly over them.

Harald climbed down and slipped off his moccasins, cursing the freezing water as he stepped into it to lead the horses. Bjørn waded into the water and waited, ready to heave on the spokes of the wheel. They yelled at their ponies and heaved mightily trying to take it in a rush but half way across one of the wheels dropped into a hole with a jolt. Despite Harald and Bjørn straining and cursing and rocking, their cart was firmly stuck.

Hervor collected the boys to lighten the wagon, leaving them with Inka. Then she ran back and grabbed the reins off Harald and pulled as hard as she could, calling out encouragement to the horses in Elvish. Their heads jerked up in acknowledgement and they began to strain harder.

After a hard struggle they finally emerged. Hervor wasn't so badly off but the men were wet and muddy.

"Serves you men right!" Hervor sniffed at them in disgust. "If you didn't steal so much, the cart wouldn't be so heavy."

For some unaccountable reason they found this funny.

From the stream the cart crept slowly along the deeply rutted path up the slope to the farm house. The dogs appeared and began to bark furiously and geese bugled out an alarm, then humans began to spill out of the house.

There was Harald's wife Sigríd, with their young daughter Freya, who was about the same age as Inka. Next to them were Harald's parents Valdís and Olaf, and Harald's foster-son Edmund.

Þórsteinn, Sigríd's older brother, waited just behind the others. He matched Bjørn in height and was almost as broad across the shoulders but the rest were half a head or so shorter than Hervor, but stocky and strong looking, even the women.

Hervor's heart began to beat faster, this would be where she and the children would be slaves to human farmers, how would they be treated? She felt like a condemned prisoner being taken to the gallows. She kept her head down and concentrated on encouraging the horses in Norse and Elvish as they struggled up the slope.

"By the Alfodr, it *is* alfir!" Valdís exclaimed loudly. "I scarcely would have believed it."

Hervor winced in anticipation, she must have heard about their arrival while they were still in Farsund.

"Und *fjorir* (four) liten *bairnr* (children)." Olaf added with a broad smile. "Freya the hunder! They be *villr (wild)* wit *gestr (strangers)."*

The dialect was even worse than in Farsund, and Hervor could barely understand it. Just then the three dogs broke free, much to the dismay of the adults. They shot forward, straight at Inka, who dropped to her knees and threw her arms wide, but instead of savaging her they wagged their tails furiously, jostling each other to lick her face and neck while she laughed and laughed and tried to pat and hug them all at once.

"Alfir," Valdís said by way of explanation, shaking her head. "Vel, ver need to get þeim allr inside."

* * *

Olaf's farm.

The inside of the langhús was divided by two rows of sturdy roof posts running length wise. This resulted in three aisles. The main central aisle had a hard packed dirt floor and was the main corridor, with space for three hearths. The other two smaller aisles were mainly given over to benches for sitting, storage and sleeping. One area near the central fire seemed to be given over to food and crockery storage and it looked like there was a box bed of sorts nearby for Olaf and Valdís.

The ceiling and walls were lined by wooden planks, darkened by decades of smoke.

Hervor could see well enough in the murky light but she wondered how the humans managed. The main light came from the smoke hole in the roof, the dying sun giving it a ruby glow through which she could still make out the blue-grey haze from the fire. There were no windows and only the cooking fire was lit. There were some shallow stone dishes with fish oil and cottongrass wicks on small stands; they would be for the evening.

The two women had insisted on hugging Hervor and the children, the men also greeted them warmly and then they were ushered into the house as if they were guests.

She

was not as bewildered by the warmth of the welcome she received this time, though she still didn't understand it. When she thought of slaves she thought of pens and cages, straps and collars. Still, it felt like a great weight had been taken from her shoulders. She was trapped here and desperately needed their help to care for the children. At least it seemed like they would be treated kindly.

Hervor was impressed with all the food that they had in storage. This was a rich household. Valdís didn't want to cook that evening but who can complain about smoked salmon, sausage, salt cured ham and smoked goat?

Something about the household was terribly wrong. Such a large langhús, such a large and wealthy farm, but so few people lived here. Olaf and Valdís should be surrounded by a huge family and yet they only had one son living with them and one grandchild.

And Þorsteinn, though he wasn't direct kin, seemed to have never married, why was that? Some wealthy chieftains took more than one wife, or a female slave or two, Hervor knew. So some poorer Norse men couldn't marry, but Þorsteinn seemed well dressed and prosperous. He could afford a wife and yet he had no female partner.

She didn't ask, but she felt some tragedy or series of tragedies had visited this family. There was no sign of this now though, everyone seemed loud and happy.

They seemed to be surprised and pleased that the elves immediately came forward and proved so tame and willing to help.

Hervor and Inka busied themselves helping Sigríd, Valdís and Freya prepare a meal. Brenda had invited herself into Olaf's lap and he looked thoroughly enchanted by the small elf. Niall and Nori had asked Bjørn what they could do to help and he set them to helping Þórsteinn repair some tack for the horses. Mostly it was Þórsteinn showing them what he was doing but they watched in open mouthed admiration and enthusiastically attacked every small job he allowed them as if it was a gift he had given them.

Hervor began to get the knack of their accent. When Valdís mentioned holding a feast the next evening with a lamb she had in a nearby enclosure, she seemed surprised when Hervor offered to do it all for her.

"Don't you alfir, er ..."

"No *fruvor* (mam) we eat meat too. We just have to thank the animal. The animal must not suffer and we must not waste. And of course we give a prayer of thanks to the Great Goddess for her bounty." She risked a shy smile. "I will kill it and skin it for you. Do you want me to cut it up or do you want me to build a fire pit and roast it whole?"

Valdís beamed at her, "Don't call me *fruvor* (mam, noble lady). I'm just Valdís. We'll cook it whole. Do you have a special alfir recipe?"

"No ... er free wife Valdís. I think our roast lamb will taste very much like human roast lamb. Just some salt, oil and herbs like rosemary. The smoke will give it the flavour for you."

"Enn for yor; yor enn the kynder are joining oss for the feast!"

Hervor looked at her, astounded. "Mam?"

"Valdís," the older lady insisted. "You enn the kynder villa *always* eat with oss enn yor villa eat whatever ver are eating."

Hervor bowed her head, a bit overcome. "You are very kind. We are happy with whatever you give us and we can sleep in the barn."

"The Barn?" Olaf shot an indignant look at Bjørn. "Wei kynder in the barn, without even a fyr to warm them, and this being so early in the season?"

Hervor paled, thinking she had said the wrong thing and caused trouble between her new master and these people who owned the house.

"If þeir are góðr enough to *verk* (work) on minn stadhr, þeir are góðr enough to sleep in minn hús!" Olaf insisted, his face colouring and his accent thickening. He bunched his fists up at his sides as if ready for a fight. Valdís joined her husband in giving Bjørn a hard stare.

He held up his hands in surrender.

"I am not the master of minn *faðir's* hús and she was safer in the barn. Minn broðiren asked if they could rape her."

"Your broðiren!!" Sigríd and Valdís shouted together, looking thunderous.

For a moment they were lost for words. Hervor quickly interrupted before things got even worse. After all Bjørn had rescued her from his brothers and they, against all expectations, were prepared to honour his pledge to her.

"Do you want pancakes or sausages made from the blood? We often give the head to the dogs. I think I can do something special with it but it takes a lot of time."

Valdís took a deep breath to calm herself.

"Yes Hervor, ver use blood too, enn the dogs are fine with the head but it will have to be chopped for them. You alfir aren't too squeamish are yor?"

"No mam, we elves are not and as I said, we never waste. I'll just go outside now and choose a green branch for a skewer so I can soak it in water overnight."

"Do you want a light?"

"No mam," Hervor turned her shining eyes back on the lady, "we elves can see in the dark well enough."

After they finished dinner and cleaned the wooden plates in soapy water and rinsed them, Valdís looked at Hervor a bit shyly. "I heard alfir can make coloured lights." It was a half-question. "It was something I always wanted to see, since I was a wei bairn."

She brought a pyramid of milky quartz out of a pocket on her apron and placed it uncertainly on the table.

"Of course mam." Hervor said. "A clearer crystal would be better. Not far from where we lived we could get lots of clear rock crystals. I will have to sing to this one, but let me take it to a darker spot."

She placed it on the bench away from the central fire and shaded it with her body while the others gathered around. She began to hum, softly at first, and then opened her mouth and clear silvery notes hung in the air. The crystal began to grow soft pink and then changed to blue. Inka moved closer and joined her voice to Hervor's pure tones; the two elf voices matching perfectly. The crystal began to chime, pure and clean, singing back to them and it started to blink green, red, and orange. The light reflected on their elvish faces.

After a while they stopped.

"We can't hold it, I'm sorry." Hervor apologised, a little breathless. "It's too cloudy."

But the humans were for a moment speechless. Tears were running down Valdís's cheeks and she used her apron to wipe them. "I always wanted to see." She whispered.

"Your singing ..." Olaf murmured, his own eyes moist. "It was the most beautiful thing I have ever heard."

Hervor yawned, "if you like ..."

"No child," Olaf said, "you have been travelling. I would love to hear more, but tomorrow or the next day is soon enough. We sleep on the benches by the fire." He lifted one of the benches, there was a storage place underneath and Olaf himself started passing out rough woollen blankets and sheep skins.

* * *

Olaf's farm, a feast

It was hardly first light when the humans of the house were woken by the dogs barking. They heard Hervor say something in Elvish and the dogs fell silent. Hervor and the elf children were already outside. They had found the outdoor fire-pit and had already started a shallow fire of dry hard wood.

Hervor had slaughtered the young sheep and it was hanging so the blood would drain into a large pot. She had found some of their obsidian and had napped some small flakes ready to skin it.

The naturally occurring volcanic glass was sharper than any metal, but was tricky to work with.

"Hervor, you don't have to work so hard!" Valdís said as she hurried outside. "You could have waited till we got up."

Hervor stood up from what she was doing. The elf children gathered around to look at Valdís with those penetrating eyes of theirs.

"Mam, I know four children are a burden that you have scarce looked for." Tears came to her eyes. "I want to prove that we are useful, so you won't send the children away."

"What!!!" Valdís's hands flew to her face in horror.

"Oh my dear child!"

She rushed forward to embrace the elf and stroke her silky red hair. Hervor had to keep her hands clenched by her sides so as not to dirty the older woman's clothes, so it felt like she was being hugged like a helpless child.

"Who said these children would be a burden?" Valdís demanded.

"Torgny," said Bjørn, he was stiff in the morning and his limp had returned. "Minn dyrr broðir."

"Let me show him the graves where I buried three of minn," Sigríd spat, in a full fury now. "And then let him say to my face that children are a burden!"

Sigríd exchanged a glance with Valdís and Hervor knew, without being told, that Valdís had lost children too. Then Sigríd too hurried over to hug Hervor.

"Bjørn was fostered *her* (here). I was raised nearby so Harold and Bjørn were my childhood friends and we are his family. Yor are willing workers, even the smallest. Never fear that yor are unwelcome."

"Takka Sigríd but we don't mind work, we really don't."

"Come then, Hervor we have copper tools, but it looks like yor prefer stone. Show oss how yor can dress a sheep. I bet yor can never match minn faðir-in-law."

A short time later they watched amazed at how deftly the elf worked and how strong she was, no matter how slender she looked. She hummed as she worked and kept giving them shy glances.

The hide was quickly stripped and hung, the hoofs removed and the long tendons were cut out and hung to dry. Then the guts were opened and the liver, kidneys, and sweetbreads were cleaned and left soaking in one lot of water. The intestine, for sausage skins, and the stomach, for blood pudding, were left in another, with salt added. Freya had joined in and now all the children were cheerfully helping.

"You don't waste anything, do you Hervor."

"No mam."

"You're not going to stop calling me mam, are you?"

"Er ..." She gave a shy smile. "No, mam."

In no time at all the fire had formed enough coals to be ready, the sheep was smeared with oil, herbs and salt and was ready to be skewered and suspended across two forked sticks.

"I'll never bet against you again," Sigríd laughed. "Yor alfir can work fast when yor have a mind to."

"Bjørn," Valdís said with elaborate innocence. "I am going to check on some onions, could yor koma enn help?"

Bjørn smothered a grin at the old joke. Valdís wanted to have one of *those* talks with him.

As they walked into the pit house, Valdís turned angrily to face him. "Tell me Bjørn, what madness possessed you to call that sweet girl and those wei bairnr your þrællr?"

Bjørn sighed, "I had to do it. As soon as I saw them, I wanted to protect them. Especially Hervor, she wounded me so I was able to make first claim on her. She refused to join us as a warrior. She wanted me to kill her, but I told her she had to look after the kynder.

"You well know what would have happened to her then. The menn of our army would not have treated her well. It was the only way I could protect them and bring them here." He pretended to study a string of onions. "I can't say I'm sorry. The kynder are a joy, and Hervor, well she is ..." for a moment he was completely at a loss as to what to say.

"She is a certain *fagr* (fair) thing." Valdís said for him, echoing his brother. "Olaf hasn't said anything yet but you know he neinn bruka the idea of slaves. What do you plan to do with her?"

"Já, she is beautiful," Bjørn sighed, he stared deeply at an onion and a small smile came to his lips. "And she has a *ballr* (bold) heart. Her world was destroyed, kyn and *frænder* (friends) *dauðr* (dead). She surrendered herself and has gan into the hús of her foe to *vørðr* (ward) *þar* (those) kynder. And what do I want to do to her?

Tears came to his eyes, "I would lika to make hir smile. I want hir to look at me with eyes shining with love. I want to make hir *bliðr (happy)*."

"She has good reason to hate human kyn. She may never wish you, Bjørn. She is your þræll, þú can take her *hvarr* (whether) or neinn she vilja."

"Neinn, that thing I can never do. I could never hurt hir."

"I remember when you came to us, all sullen and full of temper. You were how old? Eight, almost nine, and look at you now! I always wondered when some maid would get your attention."

"She speared minn leggr."

"I suppose that's one way." Valdís snorted with amusement. "But these are alfir, Bjørn, not humans. They do not abide captivity. You know in our tongue we use the same word for love and for freedom (friend). If you want her to truly love yor, yor must set hir free."

"I fear she would leave." He admitted.

A shadow of old pain passed across his face and Valdís's heart went out to him.

Bjørn's mother died when he was only two, then he was raised for a time by Valdís's cousin, Yvla ... until she was driven away.

"She is a bit like her isn't she? Yvla I mean. I remember her well. She always was an uncommon beauty."

"I don't know," Bjørn said, a bit wistfully. "All I can remember is a smile and long silky red hair."

"She loved you as her own."

Bjørn's face darkened with hurt and anger. "If she did, why did she leave me?"

Valdis merely shook her head, she wasn't going to discuss why Yvla ran away again. Bjørn was barely six and he had lost the first two women he had ever loved. He had always held back with females. It seemed he wasn't interested, but Valdís wondered if it was because of that. Did he fear that if he fell in love with another woman that he would lose her too?

Of course, elf captives were unlikely to stay, normally, but this was different.

"It's neinn the same, Bjørn. You heard Hervor, she needs our help with those dyrr wei bairnr, and she is welcome to it and more. But naming alfir your slaves is not the answer to winning their hearts, and naming someone a slave is not the way to keep them."

"I just need time to woo hir."

"Yor know alfir live for a long time. Yor will grow old and die while she is still young. Mayhap she will tire of þú."

"I don't care. I just want whatever time she would give *mik* (me)."

"You might gain her and later lose her anyway."

"I don't care." He insisted. "If I have to survive that, I will. I'm no longer a child."

"What you are is a fool Bjørn Alriksson." She moved forward to hug him and kiss his cheek, just like she used to when he was a small boy.

"Good luck though."

* * *

Olaf's farm, roast lamb and plum wine.

Hervor didn't want to admit it, but she had only *helped* roast a lamb before and not all that often. She sat, wondering what to do next, when much to her relief Valdís saw her hesitation and smoothly stepped in to supervise.

She got her to wait a short time and help prepare other food first so everything would be ready in the afternoon. Then she packed rosemary, lemon rinds, herbs, garlic and yesterday's bread into the cavity of the lamb, followed by a generous amount of berry wine and stitched it up tightly with twine. Then she placed a stick in the ground in the full sun and with a short stick marked five hours of cooking time. She supervised Sigríd and Hervor to skewer the lamb and suspending it over the fire with another short stick, tied onto the skewer so the roast could be turned.

Finally she strategically added wood chips to the fire so that the hotter parts would be under the thicker parts of the carcass. Olaf had dragged a stump up for Hervor so she could sit comfortably out of the smoke to cook while the rest busied themselves with other tasks.

By midday Hervor was forced to build a wind break and tie the neck back onto the carcass. Olaf disappeared into one of the pit houses and brought out apples, plums, cherries, and a wide range of berries for snacks.

"We can't eat all this," Hervor protested, giggling a little.

"He's just showing off," Valdís laughed nibbling at some berries with obvious appreciation.

By the afternoon the 'skin' was crisping: a beautiful golden brown, fat dripped off it sending up small puffs of smoke and a delicious smell. Everyone's stomachs had started to rumble. Despite herself Hervor felt comfortable and relaxed around these humans, even though it was only her second day.

Most who weren't preparing for the feast had given up any pretence of doing anything else other than watching the preparations. Brenda had fallen asleep in an untidy tangle on the ground; one arm wrapped around her rag doll and the other over one of the dogs, which sat, motionless, guarding the small girl.

Bjørn was showing Niall and Nori how to make a range of different snares to catch rabbits. The two small blond heads were bent in fierce concentration over a pile of twigs and twine. As Hervor looked across, she smiled to see the three of them so happy together. Just then Bjørn looked up and caught her smiling.

She quickly looked away; she didn't want him to think she was smiling at him!

Olaf appeared at her elbow and offered her a cup. "For the cook." He said.

"You be careful of that, Hervor." Sigríd warned, as she laid a flat stone at the edge of the fire. Once it was heated enough, she would add a pat of clarified butter fat, onion and wild garlic. She had carrots, root crops and cabbage cut up, waiting to fry, with a cloth over the food to keep the flies away. Valdís was making a special bread-dough from wheat flour, hazelnut and honey.

Hervor took a sip from the cup. "Is this plum wine? It's delicious."

"Olaf, don't give Hervor plum wine! It's too strong and she's not used to it." Valdís called out, from where she was making the sweet bread. "You be careful Hervor, it will go straight to your head."

It wasn't going to her head but it was giving her a warm feeling in the pit of her stomach. It made her feel relaxed and, being an elf, she loved anything sweet.

"I know how to make beehives so you can harvest honey and not destroy the colony." She offered, thinking of sweet things. Maybe she might be able to make sugar too from sweet beets like some elves could, but she wasn't sure how it was done so she didn't mention it yet. Elves were great experts in anything sweet.

Olaf's eyes grew large as he thought about extra honey. Humans could only harvest honey by destroying the hive. He took a cup for himself and drew up another stump so he could talk to her.

"I heard alfir can do that. A lot of the fruit isn't sweet enough for wine, but if I could add something sweet I could make honey-and-fruit wine and *mjøðr (mead)*. Does it work for *skeppa* (wicker hives) or do you need stump hives?"

Hervor had meant to tell him she wanted no more wine but she found her cup full again.

"I can show you. *Skeppa* (wicker hives) are easier. You weave a wicker cap on top with a hole leading up into it from the main hive. The bees use it for honey storage rather than breeding, so to rob the hive all you have to do is lift the lid. You don't get much honey each time, nothing like killing the hive, but you still have a healthy hive at the end of it and the bees can still swarm, so soon you can have several hives if you are careful.

"A hollowed out tree stump is harder but you get more honey than a wicker hive because you can choose what to take and not leave it to the bees. You need a large entrance hole, partly covered with bark, which you tie on. When you want to rob the hive you must be careful and use smoke and a sharp knife. You remove the bark and take the honey comb mainly from the top. You have to protect the hives from bears though."

She was surprised to see Olaf had filled her cup again. She didn't remember drinking the other one. How many was that? Three, she decided. She felt a bit light headed already. She tried to sip it slowly but it was so sweet and smooth it seemed to just slip down her throat without her willing it to.

"No more, thanks." She smiled covering the cup with her hand. "I shouldn't boast but I was the best elf at any form of foraging, including finding wild bees. All the other elves used to say I was."

"Well, my girl, it is very pleased I am to have you here at my farm then."

Hervor laughed, and then smiled at him, a little shyly. She thought her laugh sounded louder than usual. The world started to spin and rock in a strange way. She feared she might be sick but she couldn't stand to reach a nearby patch of grass.

"Olaf!" Valdís shouted. "What have you done with my cook?"

Hervor bolted up, hand pressed to her mouth and did a wobbly run for the grass to vomit. She was mortified.

"Oh, I'm so sorry; I am spoiling your dinner. Please forgive me."

Tears came to her eyes.

Sigríd appeared at her shoulder laughing. "Don't worry, sweetling. It's not a real party unless someone throws up; though it's usually not till much later."

She and Valdís dragged Hervor to her feet and Valdís used her apron to dab at her mouth.

"I swear I'll kill that man some day." Valdís chuckled as they helped the unsteady elf back to the langhús. With a laugh and a reassuring pat or two, they left her on a bench near the fire with a blanket, water, a cloth and a wooden bucket to vomit into.

It was the last thing Hervor remembered of that day.

* * *

Gokstad, Ragnarr's stronghold in Vest-fold, South East Norge
(Norway)

Brice tried not to pace as he waited with Aranwen at the harbour of Gokstad. The reaction of the inner council of the Illvættir to the events at Ālfheimr had been catastrophic. He was glad he wasn't physically present or he might have been assaulted.

Four of the council were particularly ferocious, led by Máedóc. Máedóc demanded he be put in charge of eliminating the elves immediately. He said that the task should have been his from the start. He kept giving angry looks at three who sat in the corner, saying very little.

Brice felt icy fingers clutching at his heart.

He had been used.

There must be some in the council wary of Máedóc's growing power. So Brice had been given the job of eliminating the elves to prevent Máedóc from taking it.

Without even knowing it, he had made an enemy of the council's most powerful member. And now he would have to face him. Máedóc was on his way with his partner Fáelán to assume command. The horns announced the approaching ship and Brice felt his stomach tighten.

"That's them," Aranwen said unnecessarily.

A large broad ship emerged in the distance, moving fast. It had a square hemp sail, bleached white and bearing a picture of a fire-breathing dragon. Tall, red haired men in blue and green tartan pulled strongly on oars but the ship glided faster than it possibly could. Large shields with iron bosses lined its sides. It

didn't stop, boxes appeared on the shore with a loud 'crack!'
Máedóc seemed to leap from the prow then walk across the last
few feet of water to the shore.

"Very impressive," Aranwen said quietly.

Fáelán followed, but had to wade to the shore carrying his
boots as the ship turned to leave. Máedóc spied Brice and
immediately stalked up to him, ignoring Aranwen.

"If it were up to me, I would send you home right now."
Máedóc shouted. "You had one small village to destroy and you
had THREE daimôns to do it with and what did you do? You got
Eiríkr killed and you let an unknown number of elves escape.
Worse than that, you lost half of our allies with some silly
argument and now you haven't been able to maintain a simple
secrecy shield for an attack on the north. I suggest you pray that
attack goes well. Now, keep out of my way and do exactly what
you are told, or I will crush you. Do you understand me?"

Máedóc glared at him and Brice forced himself to break eye
contact and bow his head. He tried not to show his own anger.
This degree of hostility was a shock. Part of it was calculated to
cow him, he knew, but he had no doubt that when the killing
started, Máedóc would be coming for him.

Chapter 8: Hervor and Bjørn

Olaf's farm, the morning after the feast.

"Uugh," Hervor said as she woke.

She ached all over. Her head was pounding. Her mouth was dry and tasted foul; she tried moving her tongue around but it only seemed to stick to her teeth. She wondered if she was going to be sick again.

Elves, especially slender female elves, couldn't drink like humans she decided.

Why on the Goddess's earth did she drink so much?

The central fire had burnt down in the night and it was dark and chill, though her befuddled senses told her it was first light outside. She still wasn't used to the lack of windows in human houses and how dark it made them. What if enemies came? What if they simply wanted to look outside?

She drank some water, washed her face and then stumbled outside to the hut that contained the pit latrine. Fortunately it didn't stink as much as it would in the heat of summer, but she still choked back a wave of nausea.

She moved gingerly back inside, pale and shaky, and busied herself blowing the fire into life and laying down some fresh kindling. The hearth was 'U' shaped, lying in the line of the central isle. It was open at one end and had a large vertical stone at the other so it would draw well and minimise smoking.

The men were all snoring loudly, even Sigríd, but Hervor had a feeling she was being watched and turned around to see. Inka looked asleep, lying on her side snuggled up to Freya with an arm possessively over the human girl's blanket-covered body, but there was a glint of eyes just beneath her closed lids.

Valdís in her bed with Olaf sat up and wished Hervor good morning.

"You are awake, mam."

Valdís laughed. "How can I sleep? With *that* bear growling in my ear?" She jerked her thumb and smiled wryly and a little fondly at her husband. Even Hervor thought he sounded like a pig snuffling food. It was the sort of thought she would keep to herself.

"Mam, I'm sorry about yesterday."

Valdís chuckled again. "Hervor dyrr, there is no need to apologise. I should have warned yor."

"I don't think I'll ever drink again."

"We all say that."

"If you allow me, I will milk the cows before we all wake and break our fast."

"I will allow yor," Valdís fought to keep a straight face, "as long as you are up to it."

"If I'm going to feel miserable, I may as well be doing something to distract me."

"Do you want something to eat first?" Valdís asked. "We have plenty of left overs."

Hervor gave the human woman a pallid look, "maybe later, mam."

"Most of the others will be sleeping in, even the bairnr. They were up late. Little Brenda was the worst of them, she really loves a party that girl."

Hervor groaned. *Oh, no!*

She should have sent the young ones to bed herself, not that she was in any condition to. These humans were going to spoil them and the children were sure to take every advantage!

And yet ... it warmed her heart and brought tears to her eyes to think these people would care enough to spoil the children.

"Mam, thank you for the wonderful welcome you have given me and thank you for caring for the children."

Valdís gave her a warm smile. "They are good bairnr, and all bairnr are precious."

She read something in Hervor's expression.

"Yes Hervor, I lost a daughter and a boy when they were very young and I had two fine sons before Harald. They were in a canoe during a great storm. No one ever knew for sure what happened to them. As you know, Sigrid has had her own sorrow ... and so I have only one grandchild, precious though she is."

"I'm sorry," Hervor said.

Another elf would have known how sorry Hervor was, but Hervor wanted to say it. Olaf and Valdís were good with children and while Freya was a delightful young girl, they deserved more than just one.

"When I heard Bjørn was bringing a young alfr wif and wei bairnr her I hoped that maybe ... I mean, this house has been too empty for too long, but I didn't know if yor ... vel, yor being alfir and all." Valdís's eyes misted over and she coughed awkwardly. "Vel, I just want to say we are happy to have yor her."

"Takka, mam. It means a lot to us, really it does."

Hervor felt her heart much lighter. She smiled at the older woman but she didn't know what else to say, so she put on her coat (and moccasins this time to keep her feet clean) and walked a little unsteadily to the barn.

While she was cooking the day before Hervor made the mistake of asking Olaf how he got so many of his cows to calve in the early spring. Calving or milking too many over winter would require a lot of supplementary feed on top of the normal hay.

Firstly, Olaf explained to her what she already knew. A bovine pregnancy took nine months and the first three to four months after delivery were spent feeding the calf. The milk was richest then and the cows lost condition while feeding in the first few months. Only after this period were they milked for human (and elf) consumption.

They could be milked for up to nine months but it almost never came to that, they usually stopped themselves if it was winter, with its poorer feed, or they could be made to stop by slowing down the milking. Then they needed a minimum of three months to regain condition, often more, before they were allowed access to the bulls.

So how could he organise so many of his cows to calve in spring? Olaf was more than happy to explain it to her ... at great length, and on a cow by cow basis, till her eyes began to glaze over and the women had to rescue her and insist Olaf stop his boring talk and talk of something else.

Olaf only had two milking cows at the moment so Hervor fed them some oats and told them what clever cows they were. Then she cleaned their udders and undersides, carefully trimmed the hair on the tail of one of them and then set to work milking the first one.

"Meow!"

Unlike the Norse cows and horses their cats were HUGE, near as big as their dogs!

There were five of them. They had the important task of keeping the rats and mice in hand and their reward was a saucer of milk each.

She carefully laid out five saucers like she had been told and made sure the big ginger and white cat didn't steal milk from the others. If he got any fatter, Sigríd had warned her, he would leave the mousing to the others as well!

She was absently stroking and massaging the second cow, thinking how much of the milk would be drank fresh and how much she should add *skyr* (runny yoghurt) to. Fermented milk gives *skyr* or curds and *mysa* (whey) and of course adding skyr to milk speeds up the process.

The Norse loved their skyr. They drank it or added it to porridge, cereal, jam, fruit, bread and even fish. The elf children were picking up the habit ever since they first landed in Farsund.

Her mind drifted to recipes for butter and soft cheese.

"Góðr Morgen, Hervor!" Bjørn appeared at the entrance looking rested and cheerful.

He must have come in search of her as soon as he had woken.

"Coming to check on your slave are you?" she scowled at him. "Well, you didn't have to worry. I've already started work as you can see. I will make you breakfast as soon as I can."

"There were plenty of left overs," Bjørn gave her a broad smile. "That lamb roast was delicious, it was a shame you missed it."

Hervor could feel the blood rush to her face, even the tips of her ears. She bowed her head in embarrassment. "Master, I apologise for my behaviour yesterday. I shamed you in front of the people of the house and I'm sorry."

Bjørn surprised her by throwing his head back and laughing long and hard.

"Hervor, Hervor no one thought badly of yor. We all have done that at einn time or another and yor have not drunk alcohol before, I would guess. I'm just sorry yor missed your welcome feast."

"That feast was for us?" Hervor was almost speechless; tears came to her eyes unbidden. "I thought it was your victory feast. We are only slaves."

"Hervor," Bjørn looked at her intently with those light blue eyes of his. He was so tall and muscular and handsome, it took her breath away. "We each of oss want yor to be happy *her* (here), me most of all. I brought yor her because I knew yor would be safe and cared for. I grew up her and love this place. Now I'll give yor some time to finish milking or Valdís will never let me hear the end of it."

Hervor sat there, her head spinning with confusion.

She had suspected Bjørn was waiting to get her to his home where he had some sort of dark plans for her. Now they were here but all that happened was that he seemed more relaxed away from his father and brothers, and all he had showed her and the children was continued kindness.

And last night's feast was for them! It was hard to believe but the people on this farm weren't treating them as slaves at all.

And yet, they *were* slaves a voice inside her said.

Bjørn said he had brought her and the children here to look after them. It was looking like it might be true. She had no idea why he would want to do such a thing after capturing them. But none the less he had brought them here as slaves!

Eventually she gave up, it was impossible to understand these crazy humans, especially Bjørn who seemed to be crazier than most.

As she got back with the milk, the people of the house were waking up. The first thing she noticed was all the talking and laughing the humans did, and they were so loud! Sometimes they even had several conversations all going on at the same time, talking over the top and interrupting each other.

It made Hervor feel breathless just to listen. A lot of it was teasing, especially between the men and women, but she had to admit she found the banter pleasant and she felt the genuine affection underneath it, barely hidden. It was impossible for her to join in of course, even if she felt confident enough. Elves simply weren't used to doing all that talking! She didn't know if they even could.

All she could manage was a few shy comments when Sigríd, Valdís or Olaf tried to bring her into the conversation.

The young boys eagerly left with the men. Freya took Inka's hand to show her the care of the different types of poultry: chickens, ducks and geese. Valdís was going to bake in her clay oven and asked little Brenda if she wanted to help, not that Brenda would be much more than good company.

After she and Sigríd had cleaned the platters, put the bedding back away and spread some fresh herbs on the floor, Sigríd took her to show her around the farm and explain more of the women's tasks.

She spent more time telling Hervor funny stories about growing up with Harald and Bjørn. As a youngster on a farm there was always plenty of work and they had to visit and help their neighbours, just like elves did. But there was still time for fun, the three of them exploring, competing, stealing fruit, stealing cream from the top of the milk and stealing Valdís's cakes. Harald was slightly older and often in charge of their small 'gang'.

Sigríd admitted that from when she was small she had decided to marry Harald when she was old enough. She had a fine way of telling a tale with a lot of amusing details and she soon had Hervor laughing. Some of her comments about family members (such as describing Olaf as a 'fussy pants' farmer) was mildly scandalous to Hervor, something an elf might think but would never say, but Sigríd had such a bluff easy manner with genuine affection for her family that it didn't seem so bad coming from her.

She told Hervor about a lot of childhood adventures, some of which had gone wrong in amusing ways, and about something called practical jokes. Hervor never found out why they were called 'practical' but they involved things like Harald hiding a frog in Valdís's handiwork box. Apparently frogs often figured in practical jokes played on older women.

When they broke into Olaf's large stock of berry wine, Sigríd had fallen asleep in the sun. Bjørn and Harald had carried her on a blanket into a pit house and jammed the door closed. She woke to total darkness, hung over and with no idea where she was or how she got there and it took a lot of shoving before she could get out.

Her revenge was to sew the legs of their good pants shut. She was only sorry that she wasn't there to see them hopping around, trying to put them on in a hurry due to visitors; Bjørn told her it was hilarious.

An outsider would have seen Sigríd and Hervor as a strangely mismatched pair, the short stocky human farmer's wife and the slender elf giggling together, though Sigríd was doing most of the talking. Hervor realised she liked Sigríd; she really liked her a lot.

* * *

Olaf's farm, the morning of the fourth day.

Hervor couldn't help it, she found herself beaming at Bjørn as he strode energetically into the cow barn the next morning. He looked surprised and then his face broke into a boyish grin.

"You get up too early," she said. "I haven't made you breakfast yet."

"There are still plenty of left overs. I have eaten."

"I would have served you, if you had waited."

"I have brought you something." He said instead, producing an enormous bunch of flowers from behind his back. "I picked them myself." He said proudly.

"Oh." She took the flowers off him and looked at them.

Of course he picked them himself, how else would he get them this early in the morning?

But she was completely at a loss as to what she was supposed to do with them. Why would anyone pick flowers?

Let's see. She looked at the bottoms. It was just stems so she couldn't plant them ... maybe she could put them in water inside the house.

"I'll give them to Valdís ..." she said uncertainly.

He seemed to be watching her intently.

"I collected them for you." He said again.

Yes, you said that, and what am I to do with them?

He seemed disappointed. She realised he had gone to a lot of trouble.

"These are very pretty, Bjørn. They will brighten up the house, takka."

He seemed to relax a bit and flashed her that smile that somehow made her heart beat faster.

"Hervor are you happy now that you are here? I would like you to be."

The question took her by surprise. She thought of the wonderful and surprising welcome she and the children had received from these humans and how kind Bjørn had been them.

"Master Bjørn." She took a deep breath. "At first I was very angry with you. You made me and the children slaves. You may see nothing wrong with it, but we elves see it a great crime to come to someone's home and say that they are your slave. Now unless we can buy our freedom even our children will be born slaves. For an elf that is a terrible thing.

"I didn't know what it would be like to be your þræll. I understand some of your people are harsh with their slaves, but you have been kind beyond all expectation. You and your family saved me and the other injured elves from the Illvættir. You protected me from your brothers and you brought me to this farm with its wonderful people."

"Þú are grateful, já, but is that all þú feel towards me?"

She sensed his disappointment but didn't understand it.

"No, much more!" She protested. "I am *very* grateful and I'm relieved, the children also."

"Hervor, don't þú think of me as a man?"

"Yes of course I do." She said, flustered. "You are a *good* man, Bjørn."

"HERVOR, WILL YOU LISTEN TO ME!"

She looked at him in shock, tears came to her eyes.

Her happiness of only moments ago had fled. What had she done wrong?

"Yes master! I'm sorry master; please don't be angry with me, master. I don't know what I have done wrong."

"Don't call me that!" He stood up. She had never seen him angry like this before.

"Arggh! It's not your fault!"

He turned and stormed out.

"Wait Bjørn, no!"

Hervor put cloth over the jars of milk and ran, flowers in her hand, to the door. Bjørn was ahead of her, stalking up the hill. Distressed and not knowing what to do, she ran to the house urgently searching for Valdís.

"I've upset Bjørn badly and I don't know what I did wrong."

"Well child, you can't have upset him too much if he gave you flowers." Valdís said with a small smile.

Hervor lifted up the bunch and waved it around.

"What am I supposed to do with them?" She asked.

"My young elf," Valdís explained slowly. "A man gives a woman flowers when he is courting her. Of course you both live in our house and you are his þræll so it is all a bit silly, but Bjørn has never courted a woman before."

Hervor looked at her owlishly, her mouth in an "O".

So that was what was going on!

"You think Bjørn wants to court me?" She said, in shock. She felt a little dizzy. "You think he might be falling in love with me?"

"And I thought alfir were supposed to be uncommonly clever," Valdís laughed. "Haven't you noticed how he looks at you?"

So that's it! She remembered Bjørn watching her like he did. It made her so nervous because she didn't know what it meant.

It was because he was falling in love with her!

"But what am I to do? I am his slave."

"Bjørn has no need for þrællr." She paused. "He did it to protect yor enn the bairnr."

Hervor nodded her head in slow understanding.

Bjørn was a single man, he didn't own the farm, and he had no real need for þrællr. Except for a sex slave maybe; no ... she couldn't see Bjørn forcing a woman. She giggled, he was too sure of himself for a start ...no, he was too honourable for that, she admitted.

From the very first, he protected her and the children. But it was all so strange. It was he who had come to her home to kill and steal and enslave her people, wasn't it?

But protecting them by making them his property? Couldn't he just have ... she admitted she wasn't sure what else he could have done, surrounded by his father's army ready to rape her!

She began to count the problems to herself, ticking them off on mental fingers.

"But we are *still* his slaves. It would be a very shameful thing for an elf to allow themselves to love someone who had made them a captive. AND he is the enemy of my people. AND I am an elf and he is a human. AND I already pledged to let an elf man court me. It wouldn't be right to have two men courting me."

"I wouldn't have minded having two gorgeous men wanting to court me when I was your age." Valdís gave her a cheeky grin. "And as for all the rest Hervor, you and Bjørn will just have to sort it out."

* * *

Lofoten Archipelago, Land of the Midnight Sun
The raid on Vágar

The storm had gone as quickly as it came and for the last two days the small fleet was now making its way steadily through Lofoten Archipelago. Waves gently lapped. Paddles made a soft fluid tinkling noise, knocking gently on the wood of the canoes. There was no talking, no drums, just the canoes knifing quietly through the calm water, slender, confident and predatory.

A blue throat called: a thin whistle followed by two sharp claps. A wood pigeon answered 'whoh-hew-hew-hewyew'. Somewhere in the distance a willow warbler sang its high pitched medley: hoping for a feathered lady.

They passed a small number of harbour seals, resting on a muddy beach. A low curtain of cool mist swirled off the water.

The Lofoten Archipelago, where they had sought refuge from the storm, was dramatic in its beauty: towering mountain peaks, open sea, sheltered bays and virgin islands. Every night the sky was lit up with the glorious feathery reds, yellows, blues and greens of the northern lights.

The island of Vágøy (sometimes called Austvågøya) was really a mountain rising from the sea. Time, the sea and rivers had worn a thin rim of coastal lowlands which clung to its base. The village of Vágar lay on the eastern side and slid into view as they rounded the headland.

There was no smoke from the houses, no horn warned of their arrival. There were no grim warriors waiting to fight them or others fleeing in panic.

"It looks deserted," Rúgálfr said as they beached their canoes, "but I bet we are being watched."

Garðr wasn't about to argue with a statement like that when he was hunting elves.

The village lay along a slender green finger of coastal land poking out into the bay, backed by the dark granite mountain. The beach was narrow and made from pebbles and black sand.

The village itself consisted of neat log cabins, three deep, with wharves, boat sheds and smoke houses. The bark had been left on much of the logs but any naked wood was painted with some sort of oil to bring out the rich colours of the pine wood. Door posts and corner posts were painstakingly carved in swirling patterns. A closer look showed birds, animals and fish peeping out behind what looked like thin curling ribbons of wood.

The window boxes were filled with flowers and herbs. Strings of clear crystals and bells dangled between houses and trees. Trees, shrubs and plants grew out of every available space making it seem more like a forest than a village. All the houses had windows but the wooden shutters were all wide open as if in friendly greeting.

"It is a place of uncommon beauty." Garðr murmured, half to himself as they drew their canoes up. "Something both eldritch and wondrous will be lost forever when we kill the last elf."

Speaking of which...

"Take a couple of dozen menn and search the town. *Sja* (see) if yor can find what has happened and where Þeir have gone. Ver aren't her for plunder but *þessi es* (this is) a rich place, so keep yðvarr eyes open."

There were over fifty houses with a scattering of smoke houses, pit houses and boat houses. As the men assembled, Rúgálfr chose ten teams of four men each, while the remaining men attended to the canoes and set up camp.

"Look at all that dried cod! It's enough to foeða an army in *þessi* (this) hut alone." Harékr called out to him from the entrance to one of the pit houses.

"You can have as much as yor can eat, till yor are sick of it." Rúgálfr laughed at him. "But ver are here to kill elves, not to capture their dried cod! See if you can find something better."

Harékr was looking back at Rúgálfr as he stepped down into the dark of the pit house. He didn't even see the trip cord or the heavy log tied to the ceiling. It had fire-hardened wooden spikes. It hit him like Thor's hammer, throwing him back through the doorway to lie, moving feebly, with blood spreading over his *kyrtill* (shirt).

"Traps!" Rúgálfr screamed out. "Everyone be careful!"

"Harékr!" His cousin cried out as he ran towards him, then screamed as his foot pushed through a layer of dirt and leaves into a pit of spikes.

"I segja be careful!" Rúgálfr yelled in disgust at the stricken man.

He nodded for two of the men to help him and got the rest of his teams to cut branches and sweep for more traps. There weren't all that many, the elves couldn't have had much time, but they found bare-foot tracks heading around the bay.

"Alfir fleeing and neinn covering þierra tracks?" Garðr snorted in disbelief. "It is a trap and Þeir won't be alone."

"Alfir neinn set spiked traps." Rúgálfr said in realisation. It meant that there had to be others.

"But Fenni do." Garðr agreed. "Our enemies are already banding together against oss. In the morning we will have to hunt them both."

"They say that hunting alfir is an unlucky thing, no matter what the numbers say." Rúgálfr warned him; crossing himself with the sign of *Mjøllnir* (Thor's hammer).

"Ver vilja see. These enemies are few and we are many, what can they do to us?"

They erected their tents around a single log cabin separated from the rest of the village. It had a short section of beach to store their canoes and plenty of brush they could cut for rough fortifications. Early the next day Garðr left Birger with a hundred men to guard their improvised camp while he took their main force elf hunting.

"The alfir build their houses too close." Rúgálfr said trying to watch in all directions at once as they crept through the village.

"It gives them more room for trees." Garðr suggested.

"Trees!" Rúgálfr snorted in disgust. "They should clear them so no one can sneak up on them. Then again, I hear it is impossible to sneak up on alfir in the woods."

"These are fisher folk, not woodland alfir." Garðr said.

Let us hope they aren't as dangerous.

They followed the foot prints to the right, along a thin beach overshadowed by tall cliffs. The men eyed the heights warily as they passed. There were plenty of sea birds: gulls cried sadly, a white tailed sea eagle swooped for a fish and swarms of small birds soared and dove backwards and forwards between clefts high up on the cliffs ... but no elves, at least that they could see.

There was one group of elves watching them from high above, where they couldn't be seen. The action of waves had caused an overhang, so trying to drop rocks on the Norse would be no good; besides Hagbarðr had told them to let them pass. He wanted them as far away from the village as they could possibly get before they attacked.

The Norse came to the other end of the beach and picked their way around the headland, where they found the tracks again leading into a small river valley with peat bogs and enough land for a solitary farm house. One of the scouts trotted back to tell them that the farm was abandoned and the tracks disappeared into the peat bog.

"We are wasting our time." Rúgálfr spat. "I think we should just torch the village and be on our way."

Just as Garðr was about to reply they heard a signal horn, faint in the distance.

"*Tord* (shit)!" Garðr swore. "They are attacking our camp! Time to see how fast we can run, our scouts will have to follow later."

At a normal pace they were an hour away. If the attack was well planned, a lot could happen in an hour. They would have to run, but still arrive capable of fighting.

"Here they come!" Jossur whispered to the waiting elves as the main Norse force approached at a fast trot.

The Norse were only a few yards short of the headland when a dozen elves appeared above, firing down on them. Most of the men had their shields slung over their backs so they could run and Garðr had ten dead and five injured before he could react.

He barked a series of commands. His rear guard rushed to help the wounded and gather the dead. Rúgálfr and Egill led a hundred men charging up the slope to deal with the elves while he led the rest on to the village.

Rúgálfr knew it was a trap as he forced himself up the slope. He didn't much care. This was his first chance to fight against Northern Elves. Elves specialised in bowmanship while his men used spears, stone axes and shields. It would be interesting to see how the two matched up. Their Southern brethren did poorly at Ālfheimr, maybe these would be easy to fight too.

Another dozen elf archers appeared on his right, searching for targets. By the time he reached the top he had lost more men. Ringed by thirty elves with heavy war bows, he formed his men into a shield wall. They weren't proving easy to fight so far.

"Human!" One of the elves called out. "My name is Dómarr and my father is *Yfirmathur* of the northern elves. Those you left at your camp are already dead. We will let you leave if you promise to never fight elves or Sami again."

"Bullshit!" Rúgálfr roared and charged, his men pounding after him. "We will leave when all you elves are dead."

The elves in front of him ran for the rocks.

"They can run like mountain goats," Egill laughed, "but they don't stand and fight like real menn."

Rúgálfr scowled at him, it was far from a laughing matter. The charge had broken their shield wall and left them open a third time to the elvish archers, and just a few of them were proving wickedly effective.

Still, it didn't go all the elves way. One of the elves moved too slowly and lost his footing. His scream was cut off as his body bounced off the rock face, ending on the rocks at the bottom with a meaty thud. Víðarr caught two elves with throwing spears and *Ásgeirr* (heaven's spear) grabbed the thrusting spear of one of his dead friends and with a short run up and a grunt hurled it at one of the elves. The elf took it in the chest and with a muffled cry followed his friend over the cliff.

As the elves ran and scattered the humans let out a ragged cheer. Yet it was only four elves dead compared to thirty Norse either dead or injured so far.

"I feel like a bear being baited by dogs." Egill spat.

"The signal horn has stopped." Rúgálfr said. "Let's collect our wounded and get back to Vágar. I don't feel like losing any more men chasing a handful of elves over the rocks."

* * *

By the time the advance guard with Garðr had reached the village it was mid morning. Columns of smoke marked the cabin they had used as a base and where they had stored their canoes. They were half way through the village when they came across the first of the dead, shot in the back fleeing back to their camp.

They found Birger badly wounded but still alive.

"We decided to look for plunder but we were cautious, or at least we thought we were." Birger winced. "They must have been watching us the whole time. Next minute there were Fenni and elves everywhere. I didn't even make it back to the camp. How did we do?"

"I don't know, they must have taken their dead with them and some of our canoes but not good I think."

They had set out with six hundred men. They were supposed to catch the elves by surprise, levelling this village and then wiping out any small settlements as they worked their way back south. Now they were marooned without canoes, some taken, some burnt. He didn't know how many were left until Rúgálfr and the scouts got back, maybe he had three hundred and sixty men left. Night would come, and elves could see in the dark.

* * *

Calving at Olaf's farm

Hervor got up early as she usually did and went to the barn first to check on the cow Olaf had brought in, because her time was near. She was only in her third year so it was her first time and she was even smaller than most, so Olaf was especially worried about her.

As soon as Hervor walked in she could sense something was far wrong. All three cows, including the two milking cows, looked anxious. The young cow was standing bunched up with her tail sticking well out. Hervor ran to her and put her hand on the cow's side, it was slicked with sweat.

"Hervor!"

Thank the Goddess! It was Bjørn up early, wondering where she was as he always seemed to do, but this time she was overjoyed to hear his voice.

"Bjørn!" She screamed, tears in her eyes. "Please help me! Bring Olaf, the calf is stuck."

It seemed like no time at all before people came running and crowded into the barn behind her. Olaf appeared at her elbow.

"How long has she been in labour, Hervor?"

"She has no way to tell me," Hervor replied, she had got the heifer to lie down and was stroking her side. "I think half the night. The calf is alive but they are both getting tired."

Olaf reached up to lift down the leather straps he used to assist difficult births.

"Shouldn't we wait and see how she progresses?" Bjørn asked.

It was what Olaf would normally do.

"Bjørn, I have an elf here telling me it's urgent and I'm not about to ignore what she says."

He reached inside the cow. "Hervor's right. The sack has ruptured and I can feel the calf."

He pinched a soft part of its foot and it pulled feebly away. "It's alive, but tired."

He attached one of the straps to the leg of the calf and passed it to Bjørn and then attached the second one to the other leg and passed that one to Harald. "Now we wait for a push from the mother, Bjørn pulls first."

"Now!" Hervor called, her face was a mask of anxiety.

Bjørn pulled and the waiting people held their breath. Hervor was murmuring to the heifer, its head kept coming up, its eyes wild with fear, but it hadn't made a sound yet.

"Good, one shoulder is through" Olaf said in a taut voice, "now for the second one."

This was the vital one, once both were past the narrowest part of the cow's pelvis they could pull harder.

Harald took hold of both straps. He would pull mainly on the one where the shoulder hadn't passed the pelvis. No one could help him now, it would be too much force and he needed to get the balance right.

No one spoke, not even Brenda, no one wanted to spoil Harald's concentration. After a few moments Olaf signalled and his mouth split into a grin, the other shoulder was clear!

Harald put a foot on either side of the opening and now he pulled with all his strength, grunting with the effort, enough to lift his bottom off the ground.

The heifer 'mooed' and the calf's head appeared, sliding out slowly and then it all came in a rush, sliding into Harald's lap, covered with blood and ichor. At least it was moving; its mother staggered up and went closer to lick its new calf.

Tears of joy came to Hervor's eyes. The humans were laughing with joy and relief. The danger was over and before them was the wonder of a new life.

Olaf grabbed Hervor and spun her around and kissed her fiercely on the cheek, while Valdís was shouting that he was too dirty.

"I don't care," Olaf laughed with joy. "This girl is a hero. It's a heifer and I'm going to call it Hervor."

"Þar yor are, Hervor." Valdís chuckled, "that's a mighty honour indeed, coming from my maðr Olaf."

Bjørn and Harald came (in jest) to hug her. They were still covered in goo from the delivery. Hervor squeaked a bit like a mouse and ran from the barn while everyone laughed.

"See Hervor," Sigríd screamed after her and then broke down laughing. "If you want any attention from the menn around her all you have to do is help to deliver one of their calves."

* * *

Olaf's farm and chickens

Inka and Freya were busy helping Valdís so Hervor hurried to attend to the chickens, letting them out to scratch and then gathering the eggs. Barley wasn't good for chickens so she gave them a small handful of wheat and collected some of the weeds they liked.

As she worked, she thought about the farm and admitted to herself just how much she had fallen in love with it after only a short time. The children were happy here, after all they had been through and all they had lost.

Hervor might have been a jarl's daughter but she was more an elf of the hills and woodland than a fine lady. She loved the outdoors and exercise and she had grown up in a harsher land than this.

She didn't know if she would ever love the farm as much as she had loved Álfheimr (Elf-Home), but her home was gone. There was something about a farm, all the animals and the growing crops that made it feel alive and happy and it had its own smell too, rich and wholesome.

She had expected she would be very wary of humans but even from the first she couldn't think of them as her enemies. She found she liked them, especially Olaf, Valdís and Sigríd. And they treated her and the children as part of their family, not at all like slaves.

She had to admit that maybe in one way, humans were better than elves. Elves were reserved, especially around strangers. Humans, or at least those who lived in small villages like Líðandi and farms like Olaf's, had an instant welcoming warmth to any visitors that was enchanting.

The children were quicker to trust of course, especially Brenda. Brenda seemed to automatically love everyone and everyone simply adored the little elf. She seemed to carry sunshine wherever she went.

The girls Freya and Inka had become instant friends for life, and the twin boys had become inseparable from the human men; Hervor rarely saw them now except at dinner time or at a distance.

Elf men are quieter than their women but some said it was because as boys they never stopped talking and asking questions. The human men didn't seem to mind, they always seemed to wear smiles as the young boys followed them around chatting in high pitched piping voices. They would just ruffle the boys' hair, or give them mock punches or a light box around the ears, when they were tired of the endless questions and comments.

The two human women told Hervor that they were glad she and the children had come. The house felt happier now, filled again, after being a little sad for so long. They were delighted to meet real elves and loved their 'little magic' and elf singing. In the end, the only person Hervor continued to feel nervous and flustered around was Bjørn.

She tried to think why.

He kept turning up wherever she was working. At first that made her very nervous. She was a female þræll of a young and handsome master. Hervor could look after herself *normally* but the presence of the children made her helpless. That made her short and irritable but instead of punishing her rudeness he seemed sympathetic, even amused.

Sometimes he seemed hurt and that was the worst for her. It made her feel guilty.

Over time she found herself beginning to trust him more and more and often found herself looking forward to his visits. He was always strong and patient, gentle and kind, not to mention pleasant company and, yes, he was pleasing to look at: blond and tall with broad shoulders and a wonderful smile and deep masculine voice.

It was all so confusing.

One minute she was angry with him, the next minute guilty, the next minute nervous, the next minute full of gratitude and the next minute her treacherous heart felt like taking flight with joy whenever she saw him coming.

Hervor stopped.

She felt a jolt through her body as if she had been hit by one of the thunderbolts from the Norse God, Þórr.

So *that's* why she still felt so nervous around Bjørn!

She should hate him. Instead, she was beginning to have romantic feelings towards him!

It couldn't be! It was forbidden! He was her slave master!

Maybe she could like him, but she could never love him. She had to keep that firmly in mind, she decided, and then she wouldn't feel so flustered.

Valdís said he was in love with her and that only made it worse. But it didn't matter. She set her jaw firmly, all she had to do was to resist the attraction she felt for him.

After all, how hard could that be?

* * *

Planting Onions at Olaf's Farm

Hervor especially loved working with Sigríd and Valdís. It gave them a chance to chat and it made the day fly. Today they were going to plant onions together and Hervor was digging the holes with a digging stick. Onions could be used in almost any main dish so they needed an awful lot of them on the farm. Most of what they grew was for their own use but Olaf and Valdís also traded locally and at the fortnightly markets.

Elves and humans did the same thing with onions: planted the seeds in spring and pulled the bulbs up in autumn. The yearling bulbs were replanted the next spring, only more carefully: further apart, with better soil and more manure. It is at the end of their second year that onions are best to eat, or will seed well if they are left undisturbed.

Onions didn't need to be planted deep. Hervor was using a long fire-hardened digging stick with a branch she could put her foot on if she needed to, but had already decided she would choose a shorter one for working on all fours next time.

Valdís was putting yearling bulbs in the holes and Sigríd, Freya and Inka were bringing up the rear, arranging the mulch and manure and minding Brenda, who was dividing her time between talking to the older girls and the rag-doll Bjørn had given her.

As Hervor's mind drifted, she thought of how everything needed to be stored in its own way, for instance cabbages needed to be stored with their roots on and kept damp and cool.

Turnips could be left in the ground under the snow over winter and dug up when needed.

Food could be preserved for long periods by drying, salting, smoking or pickling. In winter meat and butter could be frozen in ice-houses or stored in the water beneath frozen ponds. Surprisingly, fat or butter could be buried for years in peat bogs in little wooden pots. The contents would emerge still fresh, though with a strong peaty flavour that Hervor didn't like very much, but which the humans loved.

Pit houses were so named because they were built over a pit that became the sunken floor. It kept them warmer in winter and cooler in summer. Valdís and Olaf seemed to have the right pit house, or the right corner of the right pit house, to store everything. As Hervor worked she wondered if there was anything that they didn't know about farming, cooking or preserving.

"Bjørn never married, neinn?"

Hervor had told herself to try to stop thinking of Bjørn. She hadn't even realised she was going to ask about him until she did.

"Neinn," Valdís said. "I've never known him to be interested in any maiden before you came. I think he was avoiding falling in love. His mother died of the fever when he was only two. King Alrik took my young cousin Yvla as his second wife. She was an uncommon beauty but barely more than a child herself. Nonetheless, she was a good mother to his three sons. Three years passed and there was no sign of another child. Many men and no few women demanded the King put her aside or take another wife, but he refused. Some used to call out and pass comments when she passed. Then one day she just disappeared. They tracked her into the wild back country but after that they lost the trail. Most think she could no longer face her shame."

"Oh." Tears came to Hervor's eyes at the thought. "That poor woman."

"That bloody fool, you mean." Valdís said bitterly. "Alrik and the three boys loved her dearly. It didn't matter that she couldn't have children of her own. She should never have listened to all that malicious gossip."

"It's hard when it is about you." Hervor said.

"I suppose so, but after that Alrik almost went mad with grief. He long searched and he sent ships out to neighbours in case they had some news, but she was never found. There are still many dangers in the back country.

"The three boys went wild for a long time. They had lost two mothers and their father was distracted by loss and the usual wars and raiding. The older boys recovered, but Bjørn remained sullen and sickly, that is why he was sent *her* (here) to the farm."

Hervor couldn't imagine Bjørn ever being sickly.

"What did she look like, Yvla I mean?"

"Why she looked a lot like you, Hervor, except her eyes were blue. She was slender for a human and had lovely shiny red hair. It was her best feature. When I first saw you it felt as if my cousin had returned. Maybe that's part of the reason that Bjørn fell in love with you when he first saw you."

"Well I didn't fall in love with him," Hervor replied hotly. "I wanted to kill him, and his family."

"That's nothing," Sigríd giggled. "I've often wanted to kill Harold."

"Anyway," Valdís continued. "I think because Bjørn lost the first two women he ever loved he didn't want to fall in love again, until he met you.

"Hervor, you don't have to work so fast."

"So some of his confidence with women is a bluff," Hervor said.

It seemed unfair to talk about Bjørn behind his back but even elf women talked together about their men, Hervor knew.

"Norse menn *are* tough, but not nearly as tough as they pretend to be. All menn pretend to be tougher than they are, to impress their women. And we women have our own games that we play, but we are not so easily fooled by it all. Underneath Bjørn can be soft. He's always been good with kynder."

"Such a good and handsome man," Sigríd had a small smirk. "Don't yor find him tempting, Hervor? If I weren't married I would."

"I'm his þræll!" Hervor sat up straight. "What does it matter what I think or not think?"

She found she was pounding the soil too hard.

Sigríd moved closer to put her arm around her.

"Hervor dyrr, I didn't mean to mock yor."

Hervor coloured, she felt ashamed of herself.

"I'm sorry I don't mean to be such poor company." She laughed a little. "Yes, I have noticed Bjørn to be comely enough."

How could I not?

"You are still very young for an elf, aren't you?" Valdís asked.

"Já," She said. "But if I ever fell in love it would have to be more even, not me and my slave master."

"It is never even," Sigríd laughed, "women are always more important. Alfir can carry human babies can't they, Hervor?"

"Já, there is no problem with that, elves and humans are close cousin-species but," Hervor blushed again, "it would be hard, me and a human, I mean. Many humans barely live past 50 years. It would be hard to fall in love with someone and lose them so quickly."

"I'm forty nine. Do you think I should get ready to die or do I have time to finish planting these onions first?" Valdís asked her with a teasing smile. "And what about Olaf? He is in his late fifties, is it worth making him dinner or will it be wasted?

"I suppose you would get tired of a human if he got old." Sigríd said.

"An elf tire of their love, just because he or she got old?" Hervor was appalled, "elves are slow to find their true love but once we do, we are never fickle."

"And so my young alfr," Sigríd nudged her playfully. "It sounds like you have already thought about you and Bjørn becoming lovers."

"Neinn!" Hervor said, a little too quickly. She leapt up, blushing deeply.

"I have never had such thoughts, ever!"

She was so agitated that she thrust her stick through one waiting onion and then trod on another and finally stumbled over a third. "Oh, I'm sorry."

She looked back to see the human women smirking at her and the two seven year old girls, one human and one elf, grinning in amusement. Even Brenda was looking at her and smiling.

Maybe they saw her more clearly than she saw herself. Just then, though, she would have preferred to be left alone while, she continued to try to fool herself.

Chapter 9: Hjørvard and the Tainted Gift

Village of Kholm, Repairing the Dwarf Ship

Small splits in the hull of the dwarf boat could be sealed by hemp soaked in pine tar and forced in by a hammer and chisel, but several of the hull's planks had been too damaged for that.

Báfurr was in a friendlier mood when he explained the problem to Sindri. A single line of hull planking from the stern to the bow was called a 'strake'. Large boats used one long piece of timber for each strake, tapered to join at the bow and stern. The bottom of each plank was laid over the top of the one below (something called 'clinker built') before they were tightly bound together with sinew. In the mountains where the dwarves came from old, giant trees were not hard to find.

The hull was built first and then the internal frame was inserted, layer by layer, using steam to bend the timber into place. The hull was then nailed to the frame but the greater strength came from the hull.

"The men of Kholm don't have any cedar. For planks they mainly use ash but they have some cured pine that's not too soft. It will do till we get home. The real problem is that their planks are short. Normally we would remove the frame entirely and loosen the strafes above and below and fit new strafes and then re-insert the frame. Now we will keep as much of the original planking as is solid, cut out the rest and insert shorter planks into the gaps.

"We have copper to nail them onto the frame but we will need a much stronger frame than was intended. It's a terrible hodgepodge and it will be heavier for portage. I just hate to do something like this to one of my boats."

They removed the decks, cabin, benches and mast to expose the underlying frame. Then they replaced the weakened hull planks, which showed them where the frame needed reinforcing.

"This is one reason that no one does it this way," Andvari said as they watched the others struggling to fix it. Andvari was better, but still too sick to help and Sindri knew too little about boats.

"I have often wondered if you could build a boat around a strong frame." Andvari told him. "Build the frame first and then you could use shorter planks to build a boat of any size you liked, you could join two planks to a short thicker one at either end so you wouldn't need to taper the strakes and it would be stronger and easier to repair. Trying to strengthen the frame after the boat is built is the worst of both possible worlds."

The next step was to float the boat and check for leaks before putting the benches and decking back. Checking for leaks was something Andvari was an expert at and Sindri went with him.

"All the new joints are leaking!" Sindri cried out.

That set Andvari laughing so much that it ended in a bout of prolonged coughing.

"That's because of the way we have had to fix it with smaller pieces of wood. Cured wood is dried in the air. That makes it shrink. Once we get it back in the water it swells again, not too much with this sort of hard pine, but the seals will tighten soon enough."

Sindri looked at the moisture leaking into the ship dubiously.

"Don't worry, my friend" Andvari reassured him. "With Báfurr in charge the repairs have been done properly."

When they replaced the mast, decks, seating and the small storage cabin, none of the original joints fitted, but this didn't seem to upset Báfurr, who seemed to be in a better mood now that he had one of his ships restored to him.

Just before they left Sindri made the mistake of asking Báfurr whether they were going to leave Andvari behind and pick him up on the way back. He was trying to be considerate, but it was taken the wrong way.

Báfurr looked at him as if he was something brown and smelly that he had just stepped in.

"You have lost me one boat and most of my crew. They were not just crew to me, they were friends. I'm not leaving any more of them behind for you, *my Lord* Sindri."

If he didn't have Báfurr's personal oath, the journey would have finished there and then.

* * *

Olaf's farm, memories

Hervor felt like she was in a bottomless pit, falling endlessly, drowning in an ocean of sorrow and loneliness. Elves do not easily forget and sometimes the memories flooded over her. She clutched at the cow she was trying to milk, unable to go on.

"Góðr Morgen, Hervor!" Came the strong voice outside.

"Bjørn, please don't come here!"

"Why?" He barged in. "What's wrong?"

Maybe a slave has no right to privacy. No, that's not fair; it's just the way he is.

She turned her back on him and leaned her forehead on the cow, trying to wave him away.

"Nothing's wrong, just let me be."

He pulled at her shoulder.

"Hervor, you've been crying." Tears touched his own eyes at the thought.

"It's nothing please, I'm sorry Bjørn."

He pulled her up, taking her into his arms, wiping the tears from her cheeks with his hand.

"It matters to me Hervor, *you* matter to me."

"Já, it matters." She said bitterly. "I am a slave and you are my slave master."

She felt him stiffen. He had that wounded look in his eyes. He is a good man, a voice inside seemed to say, making her feel guilty again.

"I'm sorry Bjørn. I am just being silly is all."

"Then tell me what's wrong."

She opened her mouth to say it, but all that came out were hot tears.

All she could do for the moment was sob helplessly, clutching to him.

"All their faces, I can see their faces." She finally managed, "My father, my mother, my little sister; all my friends, the old ones and the little ones."

She took a shuddering breath. "They had no chance, Bjørn!"

"It wouldn't help if I told you how sorry I am."

"Sorry?" Hervor laughed bitterly. "You want to say you're sorry, *now*? You came to rob and kill and you brought those murderous devils ..."

She took a shuddering breath and sighed deeply. All the fight drained out of her and she rested her chin and her hands on his chest.

"You are right. You didn't know ... though if you had studied the history of the Illvættir you would have! It doesn't help with what happened, nothing will."

She spoke more gently, and looked into his face. "It helps me with you though."

One minute she was looking into his eyes and then the next minute her arms were sliding around his neck. Their lips met and she was kissing him, clinging to him, urgent in her need. She didn't even know how it happened. It was as if her lips and arms had a will of their own.

For a big man, Bjørn was gentle and strong. It was everything she had dreamed of, yearned for. She stood there with her arms gripping him as hard as she could. The voice in her mind was screaming for her to stop it, stop it now, it was all so wrong!

She couldn't be falling in love with her slave master!

No! No!

But for a moment she had no power over herself.

Then it was as if she had awoken in a fright. With a cry she broke away from him and fled, running as fast as she could. Not sure where she was going, she just had to get away. She heard Bjørn calling out to her but there was no way he could catch her.

He gathered the milk and went to ask Valdís what he should do.

* * *

Úlfr, Jarl of the elves

Úlfr (wolf), the new Elf Jarl had dismissed the remnant of the *hirð* (men's court). He was sitting with Hákon, the blind *seiðmaðr* (*sorcerer*) and his brother Brynjar.

This was a poor place. It had been a Sami mountain village, abandoned long ago. Spring came late to this place and the sun had little power. The wind outside was howling, searching for any cracks they had not sealed with mud. They only had a thin brush wood fire so the three men wore their coats.

"It just came to me that Hervor lives," Hákon said. "She is a captive of the Vest–Agdir. She has Brenda, Inka, Niall and Nori with her."

Brynjar felt like his heart stopped, he had assumed Hervor was dead in the fire with all the others. Now he felt joy to hear that she was alive, but anguish to hear she was captive to their enemies!

"Is there any way to rescue her and the children?" He asked.

"Not for us. They are treated well and the Vest-Agdir have turned against the Illvættir. Hervor and the children were meant to go there. They each have their own tasks, even the children have their tasks, though theirs are not the same as Hervor's."

"What do you mean, tasks? What is it they are there to do?" Úlfr asked.

"I don't know yet." Hákon said.

"Old man," Úlfr said, but he was smiling. "Must you always speak in these riddles of yours?"

Hákon laughed. "It comes to me in riddles. It doesn't come to me plainly and then I turn it into riddles. A large Vest-Fold force went against the Northern Elves but their *Samit* (Sami) allies gave help. None of the Norse will be returning south. As we speak forty Northern Elves and two hundred Sami are making their way to Álfheimr. Old Steinkell also lives and is hiding out in the hills with over two hundred elves, mostly elderly and children."

"Are there many others scattered throughout the hills?" Brynjar asked.

"Of refugees, there are too few," Hákon said.

In the fire Brynjar could see the elf stockade burning and he remembered the screams.

"With so few of us, what hope can we have?" He asked.

"There is always hope." Hákon said. "What do you know of the Prophecy of Gudmund?"

"What most elves know, nothing more," Brynjar admitted. "When we face daimôns again the spirit of Hjørvard was supposed to infuse the heart of a successor, the man who is Hjørvard returned. Well, we faced daimôns and no great hero appeared to save us."

He got up and put a little more brush wood on the fire. It flared briefly, sending most of its heat up the smoke hole.

"It hasn't happened yet but that doesn't mean it won't happen," Hákon said. "There is more and it is tied in with an even older prophecy. Let me tell you some words of Gudmund's prophecy:

'No man will ever replace our beloved prince who has died today and yet one day when the Illvættir hunt us again, one will be found infused with his love and courage; not a Jarl or King but nonetheless a true heir who will take the name of Hjørvard and who will wield a weapon against the daimôns. One who will guard us and keep us safe on the long journey to the new home for the elves.'"

"Could it be Dómarr?"

"Perhaps, but it was your father who was the Jarl and your brother is the new Jarl, so you are the closest elf we have to a prince and an heir to a prince. I thought before that it was time for the new Hjørvard to appear, now I know it is."

"It isn't me, old man." Brynjar laughed. "When I faced those daimôns I wasn't infused with the heart of any hero. I was so frightened I almost soiled my pants."

"You did well enough," Hákon smiled at Brynjar's description of himself, which he knew wasn't true. "I think it is you who is 'the man who is' and you will be offered a way to fight the daimôns."

"We did have a way to fight them ... we just didn't have a way to win against them."

Brynjar turned back to the fire, for a moment lost in his own memories.

Hákon didn't remind him that it was he and his brother who rallied their survivors to banish both the daimôns. Nor would he mention how against all odds they had helped the few they could to escape, or even that one of the Illvættir had been killed. It was all true, but they couldn't afford any excuses for the disaster that happened, not now.

"We will return to Ālfheimr." Úlfr decided, changing the topic. "We will gather all we can and then we will flee north. Now that the Illvættir know where we are none of us will find peace in the south."

They would find a new life in the north amongst the Sami and their northern kin. It would be hard, even for those of his people not yet touched by war. He would be asking them to leave almost everything and start over, but if they remained in the south they would be hunted down and killed, one by one.

"Won't going to Ālfheimr be dangerous?" Brynjar asked.

"No," Úlfr said. "The hinterland with its steadings, forester's cottages and tiny fishing villages is still intact. We can billet most of our people there and just have a small force at Ālfheimr which would melt into the hills if there is a raid. Anyway, our new enemies will have to get past Vest–Agdir before they can attack us again."

"Isn't that just a little bit ironic?" Brynjar asked. "One of the human kings who helped destroy us is now protecting us. I wish he had thought to do that just a little earlier."

"If Konungr Alrik had not gone to Ālfheimr he would not have seen what the Illvættir had intended to do to us, or maybe he wouldn't have cared what someone else did to the elves." Hákon said. "As it stands the Vest–Agdir men are angry because they feel they were tricked. Alrik won't help the Illvættir any more and he knows they will attack him now. He may be our only hope. If he is defeated then our enemies will be backed by the biggest army this country has ever seen and there will be no safety even in the north."

* * *

Olaf's farm, avoiding Bjørn

Hervor got up at first light; she milked the cows, stoked the morning fire and set out everything for breakfast. She wanted to avoid Bjørn so by the time he was up, she was gone.

Of course Bjørn was not an easy man to avoid.

She had just let the chickens out when he finally caught up with her, carrying armfuls of the chicken's favourite weeds (clover, dandelion and smart weed) back to where they were scratching about. She wondered if she could distract him with mundane matters.

"That speckled hen is broody again, she's sitting the nest now and fighting any of the other hens that get near." She told him as he approached. "I've sorted some eggs ready for a clutch and will move her to the brood pen tonight."

"You're avoiding me," Bjørn smirked, "because you love me."

Hervor couldn't stop herself from laughing. "Someone has a high opinion of himself."

"And why wouldn't I?" Bjørn demanded. "See, you can't stop smiling whenever I'm around."

"That's because you are ridiculous."

"Isn't the word 'irresistible'?"

A pile of dandelion plants slapped him in the face.

"Now Bjørn!" Hervor called as he circled around to catch her. "Bjørn! I have work to do, let me be!"

Next minute her shrieks rang out over the valley, causing Olaf to come charging out of his house. He saw Bjørn grab Hervor around the waist and dump her over his hip onto the ground, a load of weeds for the chickens went sailing into the air and ended up scattered all over and around them.

"Help!" She cried out. "He won't let me do my work!"

Olaf burst out laughing and walked back inside, shaking his head. Several of the children came out to see what was happening.

"If you want me to let you up, you'll have to give me a kiss first." Bjørn looked down at her with a smug expression of triumph on his face.

"What?" Hervor shouted in outrage, struggling against him, "that's not fair, I have work to do."

But he had her pinned. Being nimble and quick was no use against a human man's weight and strength. She struggled for a while, kicking her legs and twisting before she finally had to give up, laughing. He was such a boy!

She reached up to give him what she intended to be a quick kiss on the lips. The kiss was so much slower than she intended ... and, yes, she did close her eyes when she kissed him.

She tried to pretend it didn't feel like she was melting into the kiss and she didn't want to grab him and kiss him again ... and maybe again.

"Can I get up now, master?" She asked, grinning despite herself.

He stood and brushed himself off and offered her his hand.

"Takka Bjørn, but that wasn't a fair fight. I was trying to work."

"You're thanking me for the kiss." Bjørn suggested.

"No!" Hervor flushed and kicked him in the shins with her heel. She wished she had something heavier than bare feet.

"All I did was to thank you for helping me up. I never said I love you, and I never will."

If she said it often enough, she might believe it herself.

* * *

Ālfheimr

The rain was sheeting down, running down the faces of the men and the elves as they dug their paddles slowly and rhythmically into the grey water. Grey skies, grey water, it fitted the dark mood of the two hundred Sami and forty Northern Elves as they paddled into the harbour.

Dómarr remembered so many happy visits, but there was no longer any horn to announce them or crowd of excited well-wishers, only silence and the skeleton of the fortress. Álfheimr had become a ghost town, a place of endless sorrow and sad memories.

A great barrow had been raised to bury the dead and flowers had been planted in patterns over it: yellow ballblom for the dead children, purple primula for lost family and friends, bluebells for remembrance and finally white King Solomon's seal, a sign of enduring grief.

Once they had pulled up their canoes, Nilse, in the way of the Sami, led the others to circle the grave while he beat his drum and chanted. Then he lit a small fire and sprinkled it with green leaves, singing while the smoke drifted up into the air. They all bowed their heads in prayer. After that, they settled to wait.

This place would be watched by more than the dead.

* * *

Olaf's farm and staff-fighting

The next morning the sun came out and chased the clouds away. It was going to be a glorious day for spring, though still a bit wet under foot.

"I think it will be clear today." Valdís commented, as she came back from outside.

Hervor had slid a cooking stone into the fire and was offering skyr, bread, fried eggs and ham to Þórsteinn and Bjørn, who had come back after doing some work with the lambs. She was singing softly to herself as she worked. Edmund and the twins had already eaten and were somewhere outside.

"After my chores, can I go into the forest?"

She tried to sound casual.

Valdís was normally in charge of organising the women's work but, because she was Bjørn's 'slave' getting permission to wander on her own might be a problem.

"Olaf has asked me to get herbs for his wine and the bees will be swarming soon, so I want to spot their hives."

Bjørn stiffened; he cast a worried glance to Valdís. Þórsteinn didn't say anything but he stopped eating and sat watching Hervor and the others intently.

"I heyra other alfir have run away." Valdís said, watching Hervor closely. "Not that I blame them, mind."

"Forcing me to stay near the hús won't stop me running," Hervor replied hotly, "not if I want to!"

Then she saw the hurt in the older woman's eyes and shame and guilt washed over her.

"*Moðir* (mother) Valdís, dyrr, please forgive me for saying such things. I promise I won't."

You could not trap me with a cage, and yet here I am trapped by your love.

Valdís tried to pretend that tears didn't come to her eyes.

"Some bears have been sighted." She added.

"I'll take a walking stick, bears won't bother an elf."

"Do you know how to fight with a stick, girl?" Þórsteinn asked. "Would yor leave her neinn defence, Bjørn?"

"*Koma viðr* oss (come with us)," Bjørn said, standing and finishing his skyr in a single long draft. Þórsteinn quickly mopped up the yolk in the bottom of the wooden bowl with a large slab of bread and stood to follow.

The two men led her outside and took two tall stout ash walking sticks leaning against one of the sheds. They had been treated with linseed oil and had fire-hardened tips. The only strange thing about them was that they were about seven feet tall.

"Do you know how to use these?" Bjørn asked.

Hervor felt like laughing, "for walking, yes, but they would be better if they were cut a foot or so shorter."

"As a weapon." Bjørn wasn't smiling.

He gestured for Edmund and the twin boys to join them. Þórsteinn and Bjørn each took cloth and twine to bind the tips.

"I was considered the best elf for my age with a bow. Even amongst the older elves, few could match me."

"Þrællr are not usually allowed weapons." Bjørn said. "But these are better. They are cheap and easy to make and don't look like weapons."

He tossed her the one he had padded. She caught it easily and swiped it through the air a few times.

"Not like that, use thrusts. They are harder to block and more deadly."

He showed her the low guard position, the two handed thrust, a single right handed thrust and a right handed thrust guided by the left hand. Then he took the other quarter staff from Þórsteinn and they crossed tips.

"Thrust for my face," Bjørn invited. "Don't worry, you won't hurt me."

Hervor burst out laughing.

Are you really sure you want me to do this?

Every time she tried to look at him she broke into giggles.

Bjørn gave her a cold stare and waited.

Finally, she managed to get serious and tried for a thrust to his face. She felt the tip of her staff blocked and forced to the ground. She ducked back and to the side as Bjørn stepped forward for a soft jab to her face. Her staff was no longer trapped and she brought it spinning around to block him, in position to make another thrust to his face.

"Stop!" Bjørn called.

Edmund and Þórsteinn were doubled over laughing. Niall and Nori were both struggling to keep straight faces.

"Yes, very funny." Bjørn said to them.

He turned to Hervor. "Are you sure you have never done this before, alfr?"

Hervor shook her head. "No Lord, but I'd like you to show me more of it ... *please.*"

"Alright, but no improvising until you learn what I am showing you."

Hervor gave him her most solemn look. "Yes Bjørn."

It almost made him undone, she looked so gorgeous. All he wanted to do was grab her and hold her and kiss her, careless of any audience.

* * *

Ālfheimr and the search for Hervor

"It is true!" Dómarr punched the wall of the cottage. "Hervor is alive and being held as a slave. I have to go there and find her!"

"It would be dangerous to try to get a canoe past Vest-Agdir." Onela warned him. "Konungr Alrik's men have started patrolling the sea around their land."

"Yet I must find a way. One of those who escaped said she let herself become a captive so she could protect the children. She is brave and strong and her heart is full of love. I feel I am on fire when I think of her and those small children in the hands of those savages."

"Nilse would know the inland routes over the mountains. They will be safer. Perhaps he might agree to help."

They found Nilse sitting before his fire; he looked up calmly as they entered his *lavvu* (tepee). He seemed to be expecting them.

"You want to search, elf." He said before they had a chance to explain why they wanted him. "But do you really know what it is you are searching for?"

"That is easy," Dómarr laughed gently as he sat down opposite the noaidi seer. "I want to find Hervor, the woman I love."

Nilse smiled. "A man once offered to show me a river he said he knew. I told him that it was impossible."

Dómarr smiled at the old lesson. "The water of the river is constantly flowing past, like a person's thoughts and their experiences. Every time you return, it is a different river, a different person. Yet, the banks have changed little and the flows and currents are much the same."

Nilse threw his head back and laughed. "It serves me right for arguing philosophy with an elf. What you ask will take six weeks. I need to go south anyway and was only waiting for you. If you wish, meet me at the harbour at dawn. I will take you to the one you call Hervor. Hákon has shown me her and the children so I will know where they are and can watch them for you, until we get into the south that is, where the influence of the enemy is too strong."

"I hear the warning that she may not be the same woman that I remember." Dómarr said. "Though I wonder why you would feel you must say such things to an elf. Remember that Hervor is also an elf, and elves do not change as quickly as you humans do. Help me search for the Hervor who is, whilst I hope that she is still the Hervor I wish her to be. Why must you go there, holy one?"

"Many reasons." Nilse looked tired. "I need to give warning to enemies who will become friends, and a group of dwarves are coming here to Ālfheimr bearing weapons to fight daimôns. To use the weapons one has to wear the armour. It was built for the Jarl's brother but it has not been prepared in the way that was intended. I fear that the man who can wear it now does not exist. I want to search for that man, the one who does not exist, and ask him what he intends to do."

* * *

The Path over the Dovrefjell

Nilse appeared, paddling a four-man dugout with an outrigger for ocean travel. Jossur and Gyrd had insisted on coming as well. The elves wore Sami leather clothes including hats to disguise their hair and ears as well as packs, quivers and their bows over their shoulders.

Not much of a rescue party, Dómarr thought to himself: three warriors and a seer.

"More will not help." Nilse said as if reading his thoughts. "A larger group would only increase the chance of us being caught."

He swore them to secrecy about the path he was about to show them. They agreed, but it only fed their curiosity. What was the great secret the Sami were hiding? They were astounded when Nilse made for a deserted stretch of coast not far from Ālfheimr.

They camped that night in the wilderness by a deep wide river. The mosquitos were ferocious, gathering around them in a great cloud. Nilse had a large tub of mugwort lotion and pungent herbs for the fire, but neither seemed to be particularly effective. They were finally forced to take refuge under their blankets to sleep.

By mid-morning of the next day they were paddling well into the heart of what the Norse called the *Upplænd* (back country). Nilse got them to turn into a small tributary and not much further on lift the canoe onto the river bank, empty it of supplies and untie the outrigger. He pushed a heavy thicket of willow aside to reveal the entrance to a low cave. There was already one small canoe there and they carefully added theirs and then replaced the camouflage.

"We keep the ways of our land secret but each year the Norse only get stronger." Nilse said. "One day they will come with their kings and their farmers say the land that we have walked on for over a thousand years is really theirs."

Carrying their supplies in small sacks over their shoulders, Nilse led them only a short way to where a group of four Sami waited for them next to a *lavvu*. There were five dun horses grazing nearby, one to carry supplies.

"Sami walk with reindeer and that means we can travel fast on foot when we have a need to, almost as fast as an elf can, but we are in a great hurry now so we will ride." Nilse told them.

"I cannot ride." Gyrd admitted.

Nile laughed. "Then at the end of this trip you will not only be stiff and sore, you will be able to ride very well."

"You can get horses over the mountains?" Gyrd asked.

"We get reindeer herds over the mountains and these are fjord horses, strong, intelligent and sure footed. They came to this land when the Sami first came. You will see. The path I will take you will be more long than difficult. That is our great secret. Without a guide you would never make it but the mountains only look impassable to someone who doesn't know. Once enough of the Norse know this we will lose more of our land to them. No more questions, let me surprise you."

They followed a narrow path through a forest mainly of pine. The horses seemed to know the way and followed with hardly a stumble, stepping over rocks and tree roots. There were short downhill sections but mostly it climbed higher and higher until they seemed to be climbing forever. The trees began to get sparse, surviving mainly in shelter. The air was cold and dry.

The last of the trees were sad twisted things with thick ancient trunks and branches hugging the ground and hollows, growing away from the prevailing winds that would freeze their sap in the winter. Some looked like maidens frozen in torment, their hair flying in a wind only they could feel.

Eventually they left the last of them (and the mosquitoes) far behind and found themselves riding across a vast region of rocky alpine tundra, grassy meadows, flowers and marshes. The air was noticeably thin, making them feel a little breathless.

In the distance they saw Sami with large herds of reindeer trotting along, heads held high, topped by a forest of antlers. Nilse waved to them but made no effort to approach.

"These are the lazy reindeer and their lazy herders." He chuckled. "Reindeer migrate from their winter refuges to their summer feeding grounds. For most it is a long and arduous journey but these reindeers live in the forests below. All they do is climb up the mountains once the snows have gone."

The mountain tundra seemed endless, interspersed with valleys, lakes, rivers and bogs. In the distance they saw great mountain peaks. Dómarr had imagined climbing steep mountains, traversing glaciers and crossing rope bridges on foot. It felt like an anticlimax to be riding across alpine tundra.

"I thought you were taking us over the mountains." He said.

"What I am doing is taking you over a section of mountain plateau." Nilse smiled. "This is the path the reindeer take. If you would rather hike and climb mountains with the horses on your back I can take you another way, but I am in a hurry and I thought you were too."

It began to drizzle and this continued for most of the time they were on the high plateau. They were glad of the *lavvu* (tepee) the Sami had packed for them. Inside they could light a small fire of brush wood. In the winter, not having a shelter in a storm would have been fatal.

"How is Hervor?" Dómarr asked Nilse one evening as they sat by the fire.

"She and the children are being treated well." Nilse told him.

"I am grateful for that at least." Dómarr said.

"The children will not want to leave."

"What, elves wanting to live amongst humans?" Dómarr spoke for his friends too, they were incredulous. "How is such a thing even possible?"

"They have a new family, Dómarr, it is a Norse family and they love them."

"And Hervor?"

"Ah, you ask me the key to a woman's heart? Even a noaidi cannot give you that. She too loves her human family, for Hervor has a loving heart. There is a man there who wishes to win her to him."

"A human man?" Dómarr scowled. "It is Norse that have killed her family and made her a slave! Hervor is not a child to forget such things!"

"That is something that we will have to see."

It was all Nilse was prepared to answer.

* * *

Olaf's farm and another talk in the pit house

Every day now Hervor hurried through her tasks so she could practice with the fighting staff. Norse quarter-stave fighting was based on the use of the spear and concentrated on the thrusts and blocking. Hervor mastered these easily enough but she was more at home with dodging, sweeps and jumps.

She quickly outpaced Edmund and could hold her own with Harald, sometimes Bjørn and sometimes even Þórsteinn who was the best of them all. Olaf often paused to watch, though he expected his fighting days were well and truly over.

Today Hervor was facing off against Þórsteinn. They were both wearing padded armour.

Hervor couldn't match the strength of these Norse men but she definitely made up for it in speed and agility. "Whack! whack!" they were both moving fast; Þórsteinn began attacking savagely and Hervor's defensive movements had become a desperate blur. Þórsteinn charged in, crowding her, and suddenly ... Hervor wasn't there.

"What was that?" Þórsteinn bent over, laughing. Sweat was running down his face.

Hervor had dug her staff in for an improvised running vault away from him. She laughed back, bent over, panting and flushed with exercise. "You had me Þórr; I had to get out of there."

"Well, I think we both should rest and let the others have a turn."

"Bjørn," Olaf's voice was hard as flint. "I'm wondering if we could have a talk first."

He jerked his head towards the pit house for onions.

If Olaf was going to talk to him now, Bjørn thought, things were getting serious.

As Bjørn followed him in Olaf turned to him, unsmilingly.

"What are you doing with her, Bjørn?"

"It makes her happy, Olaf. It is a joy to see her happy. It is a joy to spend time with her."

"I don't mean the stick fighting. If you will not set Hervor and the bairnr free, name your price." Olaf met his gaze levelly.

Bjørn felt shocked. It was as if Olaf had hit him.

"I don't think you can afford it, old man."

"Don't play the fool with me, boy! I haven't said it yet but you know I don't like the idea of slavery. That girl is a *skjoldmøy* (shield maid), a Jarl's daughter and an alfr. She is not a drudge. You have no right to call her and the kynder þrællr. After that disgrace at Álfheimr, it is a stain on your honour and if you won't set her free, I will."

Bjørn held his hands up in surrender. His brothers and father would not agree, but Olaf was more his family than his real family was.

"Just give me a little time, please Olaf."

"Alright, *boy*." Olaf growled. "But I don't like it and I won't wait forever."

* * *

Gokstad, Vest-fold, Ragnarr's Stronghold

Máedóc exchanged a look with Fáelán as they waited for Ragnarr to assemble his war council. Fáelán was almost feminine in his beauty and he still had the ability to make Máedóc yearn to run his hands all over his body and his hard cock. Fáelán's head jerked up, he shot him a sly smile; some of Máedóc's thoughts must have leaked out to him.

They would have to be careful. The Norse did not like sorcerers, they already saw them as womanly. The most deadly insult a Norse could ever give a man was to accuse him of acting like a woman in a sexual relationship with another man.

No, there was definitely no need for them to know that the two new sorcerers had been male lovers for three thousand years!

Brice and Aranwen walked in, avoiding eye contact with him.

Ragnarr in his corner smiled as he studied the body language between Brice and Máedóc. It didn't escape him that Máedóc was now the leader of the four sorcerers, not Brice, and Máedóc had not hidden his distain for Brice since he had arrived.

On the other side of him Anathon, the king of the Grener, sat surrounded by some of his advisers. He was seemingly engrossed in a game of knucklebones but Ragnarr knew he was really waiting to see what else he might be offered for his co-operation. His Kingdom was very large but lay in the thinly settled upplænd immediately north of Vest-fold. He had tried to conceal his delight to be given Vissedal on the edge of Vest-fold, a narrow strip of land but rich in farmland and with good river access to the sea. He and his people had been building canoes almost as fast as they could ever since.

Well, everyone was here...

"I think what we have to discuss today is rather simple," Ragnar nodded to Máedóc, "you want our help getting rid of the alfir. I want Farsund, and Anathon wants Líðandi."

"You did poorly in Vágar," Máedóc reminded him.

If he was any closer, Ragnarr might have been tempted to strike him. He forced himself to smile and shrug instead.

"Vágar was always a risk. It was deep in the Finmark and too far north for your daimôns. Also, the spell that was supposed to maintain secrecy failed." He schooled his face to show no expression. That wasn't Máedóc's fault but it still reflected on him and he knew mentioning it would annoy him. "If I take Farsund I will have the biggest army this region has ever known, with no Vest Agdir to get in my way. Nothing would stop me then from using my main force; a few Sami or a few elves would hardly give me trouble."

Personally Ragnarr didn't like the Illvættir witch-men, their arrogance and their slimy ways. Their witch-woman was comely enough, but showed no interest in human men.

She was a stuck up bitch too!

Still, he didn't have to like them and he could afford to keep his temper. Máedóc was going to help him take Farsund. With the addition of Farsund and the Vest-Agdir men in his army no other Norse king could stand against him.

He felt a thrill of hunger. He would become the first king to unite all of Norge, the most powerful king this country had ever seen.

"You tell me Líðandi has the Jarl's sister, and four elf children." He smiled at his new friend Anathon. "I think we should start there."

"After Líðandi, we will take Farsund." Máedóc agreed and then he turned his attention to Anathon. "Fáelán will go with you to make sure nothing else goes wrong, like it did at Vágar."

The Grener king was stunned by the insult, there had been no Grener men at Vágar.

"I will take your man if he wants a sea journey, but I have no need or want of him. Killing four bairnr and the alfr wif will be easy. They live on an isolated farm and as a þræll the wif will be forbidden to hold a weapon."

Brice smothered a smile; they had not been watching Hervor like he had.

Chapter 10: The Way of the Norse

Olaf's farm

They had finished clearing up after dinner and the three younger children were asleep. Sigríd had put some larger logs on the cooking fire to make it last till the morning and lit some of the small lamps so the men and women could continue to work as they talked.

Sigríd's older brother, *Þórsteinn* (Thor's stone), had come back *changed* from the last of his Konungr's wars. He would never talk about it and it never affected his work but sometimes he didn't sleep well and sometimes he drank alone. Tonight he had withdrawn to his leather work in silence, as he sometimes did.

Bjørn and Olaf were teaching Edmund the meaning of the Norse sagas and legends.

Hervor had joined the women in their corner of the langhús with some unspun wool, a distaff and a spindle. Inka and Freya sat on either side of her to learn how to make wool yarn.

The distaff (meaning 'flax staff') is a simple wand to wrap unspun fibres around, to keep them out of the way. The 'drop' spindle is also simple. It is the size and shape of a child's wooden spinning top: a round dowel through a small wooden wheel. Hervor's had its wheel near the bottom and had a copper hook drilled and glued into a small hole at the top of the dowel.

Unspun wool comes out half-way between a roll and a loose ball. She needed to draw some of it out and then twist and spin the fibres together, to tangle them into wool yarn.

Hervor didn't like handicraft as much as some elf maidens did, but this was simple and easy for her nimble fingers. She hooked some wool fibre from the unspun wool ball on the distaff and then let the 'drop' spindle hang from it and then spun it, gently pulling and stretching the wool between her fingers, so the yarn was made above the spindle.

Once a length of it was finished, she wound it around the dowel of the spindle and then hooked the next segment of unspun wool. She held it up for Inka and Freya to see.

"I have yet to see you drop a spindle." Sigríd said in admiration.

A dropped spindle meant the yarn had broken and had to be re-joined by twisting it together. It made it uneven and weaker.

Hervor smiled, "I'm not as good with handicraft as most elf maids, but this sort of thing I can do. I was thinking of needling socks for all of you."

Olaf was the best at making moccasins but the moccasins the humans wore tended to get soaked through on wet days, so they stuffed them with grass. Socks would be better and there is nothing better than thick socks at night. Elves preferred bare feet for most things but even they couldn't resist warm socks in front of a fire at night.

Norse women didn't knit like elves did, and Hervor had just learnt the Norse technique of making socks and woollen gloves with a single needle. It was a bit slower than knitting but much better, each stitch was knotted and garments wouldn't unravel like knitted ones could.

"A new kyrtill for Bjørn wouldn't hurt." Sigríd muttered. "Look at that old thing he wears."

"You're right!" Hervor smiled in agreement. "Mother Valdís, would you teach me how to weave?"

The hand loom was the mainstay of Norse garments; wool for outer garments (and sails) and flax (linen) for softer inner garments. Sometimes they used hemp for sack cloth.

The woollen shirt Bjørn wore was one of his favourites but had faded from repeated washing and some of the old stains were permanent. It had small ragged holes front and back.

Bjørn picked at it. "Can't you fix this one?"

"What we can do is bury it in the bog." Valdís said waspishly. "You have two others that you could wear. You're an embarrassment to the women of the house, wearing that."

"The others are tight across the shoulders."

"That is because you kept them in storage while you grew," Sigríd said and sniffed with disgust. "If yor had of told oss there was a problem, we would have let them out."

"I was saving my better clothes for later and now they don't fit." Bjørn complained. "I work on a farm enn yor wifr don't dress mik; so yor need feel neinn embarrassment."

"It would be better if we did dress ðú." Sigríd frowned with womanly disgust. "If another woman saw ðú she would think badly of oss women, not yor. Anyway, yor shouldn't be listening in, this is women's talk."

"It's about me."

"Just stop listening, but one day that shirt will disappear." Sigríd chuckled.

The men turned back to teaching Edmund while they carved and fixed tools. Hervor concentrated on her spinning. She would dye the new kyrtill for Bjørn madder (red), she thought. She smiled to herself, imagining him in a smart new woollen shirt.

The rhythmic work began to sooth her, her hands working quickly and expertly. She began to hum softly and go into the secret place inside herself that every elf could visit. The men were talking softly amongst themselves but Hervor had no problem hearing.

"So a man's fate is cast by the *nornir* (fates) before his birth?" She interrupted to ask Olaf.

"Not just men, but women, trees and animals; even the Gods." Olaf agreed. "When a warrior fights in battle, whether he lives or dies is already decided. So there's no point in running, no matter what the odds are, all you can do is stand and fight bravely. And you were not supposed to hear that, missy. It is men's talk."

"You had no problem listening to us, and Hervor has these." Sigríd giggled and lightly touched Hervor's elfin ears. Hervor looked down and gave Sigríd a shy smile.

"So fate can't be changed." She asked.

"Not much," Olaf agreed. "There are three great nornir: *Urðr* (weird), Verðandi, and Skuld. They determine the main weave of fate which determines all major events, like death. Urðr is fate from the past and is the most powerful of all three. Verðandi is fate from the present and Skuld is fate from the future. It *is* possible to change fate. It changes not only our fate but the fate of those connected to us, so we can't do that in major ways, at least not the likes of you and me."

Hervor knew that to the Norse, fate is seen as a thread. Norn, the name for a weaver of fate came from the Norse word for 'twine' as in 'twining' fate, and the Norse word for magic (seiðr) meant 'cord' for much the same reason.

Apart from the three great *nornir* (norns) there were lesser nornir who could also influence fate especially at birth. Some of them were malevolent.

Norse magic is mainly practiced by women. For a man to practice it is seen as womanly because it involves a sort of weaving and trickery, not manly fighting. While it has its own shamanistic rites and incantations the highest form of Norse magic is focused on trying to understand or change the threads of fate. Female practitioners of this type of seiðr carry a distaff in their ceremonies and are called *vølvur* (wand carriers).

"How can events in the future change the past? How can the present change the past?" Hervor asked.

"Because all three are connected in a cycle of course," Olaf said, frowning with irritation.

"So, from the moment I was born, I was meant to come here." She said. "How I will die is already decided."

"Yes, now if you will excuse us ..."

"So if yor face death, you must do so bravely." Bjørn said, resuming the lesson for Edmund and trying to ignore the interruption. "If yor fight bravely and skilfully yor may be chosen to join Óðinn in *Valhøll* (Valhalla, 'hall of the slain') or join his wife *Frigg* (Freya) on the *Fólkvangr* (army field)."

"Excuse me," Hervor piped up again. "Do you mean to say your Gods are building up armies? Why, are they planning to fight each other?"

"Of course not!" Olaf replied, scowling. "Óðinn and Frigg are husband and wife. They are the rulers of Ásgarðr. Though Frigg is of the Vanir and Óðinn is of the Æsir. Those two groups of gods did fight a great war, but that was at the beginning of time." He waved his hand dismissively. "They are preparing for

Ragnarøk (twilight of the Gods). It is the final battle with the Jøtnar, before the world is remade. Frigg, Óðinn, Þórr and many other Gods and creatures will be killed. Only two humans survive. It ends a bit like the first war of the Gods, in a truce."

"If the outcome is already decided," Hervor asked slowly. "And they will all die with not a lot achieved, why are they still collecting their armies? Do you know how crazy that sounds? Are even your Norse Gods mad?"

Sigríd and Valdís were having trouble keeping straight faces.

"None of that matters!" Olaf growled irritably. "You just don't understand. We must fight to the last breath, facing our foes. It is the battle that is important, that is the Norse way."

"Hervor," Bjørn interrupted to explain it a different way. "If a great enemy was attacking your home, your family and friends and all that you have pledged to protect, would yor not fight even if yor knew ðú would lose?"

Hervor nodded, tears came to her eyes at the thought and she rested her spinning on her lap. "When I saw those daimôns, I knew what was going to happen. No one can fight a daimôn and no one knows that better than an elf." She shuddered at the memory. "And yet I ran *towards* the fight. I expected to die and yet I ran. Bjørn saved my life three times that day: once from his own men, once from myself and once from the Illvættir. I was too angry to thank him for that."

And I still am.

Bjørn put the leather he was mending aside. "From the moment I saw you Hervor I loved you, even in the midst of battle. I loved your courage and your beauty took my breath away. They say there is a Goddess that shoots arrows into the hearts of mortal men to make them fall in love. I think that must be ðú."

He gave her such a look it made her feel hot and dizzy. Blood rushed to her face and tears came to her eyes. She had to turn away.

"I wish someone would say that to me," Sigríd said loudly, nudging Hervor and shooting her husband a disdainful glare.

"The leg," Hervor whispered back. "I shot him in the leg, not the heart."

"Our men do a lot of poetry," Sigríd explained. "It's mainly about old fights or insulting one another just before the next one. I think they should do more love poetry, don't you?"

* * *

Finmark, Upplænd region.

It was the cold time before dawn when Nilse woke with a terrible cry. He sat bolt upright, panting, and flung his blanket aside. The three elves woke in an instant, reaching for their bows. The fire had burnt down to a few faint embers but it gave enough light for the elves.

"What in the Goddess's mercy is wrong?" Jossur asked as he warily scanned the inside of the lavvu. He already had an arrow knocked.

"Sorry to wake you like that. I dreamt of something terrible."

Nilse lent forward and rubbed his hands through his grey hair while Gyrd fed some small branches to the fire.

"The farm where Hervor and the children are will be attacked soon by many men. Konungr Alrik has broken with the Illvættir and will offer an alliance to the Elf Jarl. This I have seen. A great invasion fleet will sail for Farsund, this I have also long seen.

"Líðandi lies between Vest-Vágar and Vest–Fold. I now believe our common enemies will attack Líðandi first, and they will be there very soon."

"Can Líðandi resist a raid?" Dómarr asked.

"It is only a small fishing village, a couple of hundred men, women and children. There are more people scattered throughout the hinterlands: foresters and farmers, but they are all living their life in peace. They have no idea what is coming for them. I have no way of sending them a warning. Unless we can get there in time, they won't have a chance. The Illvættir will know exactly where Hervor and the children are and who protects them. As soon as they take Líðandi, they will send a large war band straight there to kill them. They will be outnumbered and totally unprepared. I saw Hervor running but she was exhausted and wounded. That man who had been protecting her was lying, wounded on the ground, covered with blood.

"Hervor and the children are in terrible danger. We will have to hurry, like we have never hurried before."

* * *

Dwarves in Ālfheimr

The dwarves struggled to beach their ship near the abandoned elf village. They should not have attempted the crossing, they were too few and they were still too weak. Fortunately their luck had held and they had been carried on fair winds over calm seas.

They stumbled up to the grave barrow that dominated the ruins of the old stockade and fell to their knees, heads bowed in a prayer not only for the elf dead but for the dwarves they had lost.

Finally, Sindri stood up.

"How long will you keep us waiting?" He called out to the trees.

A single elf warrior stepped out from behind a bush. He had his bow slung across his shoulder which was a good sign, but there would be more bowmen in hiding; they would be nervous and ready to shoot.

"My name is Nibelung," The elf bowed and waited.

"We have travelled a long way to meet your Jarl."

Nibelung said nothing, he simply waited.

"We have brought a weapon that can be used to fight daimôns."

* * *

Olaf's farm

The barn had stalls for up to two dozen cattle if needed. It was a lot, but Olaf supplied a lot of dairy products to the fisher folk and breeding stock to nearby farms. He was also putting metal and livestock aside for Bjørn to set up his own farm, should he wish.

Norse cattle, like their horses and dogs, were small, not much over four feet high at the shoulder but very stocky. He had two bulls he kept for breeding. Three cows had already delivered and all but four of the others were heavy with calf, in time to deliver for spring. He had brought six in-doors, judging their time was soon.

Hervor's tasks were simple enough; mucking out the stalls, storing the manure for fertilizer, checking the animals under Olaf's watchful eye and feeding them with extra grain so they would bear sturdy calves. She didn't mind the work, even heavy work would make her strong for the fighting with staves, but today it felt no effort at all, and the time had a strange way of passing, as if stopping and starting and jumping about.

She sensed someone watching her and turned around to see him standing in one of the empty stalls, amongst fresh clean straw. For some reason she didn't wonder at it. Nor did she wonder that he was bare-chested. She looked at his muscular chest and shoulders covered with golden hairs and took a deep breath.

He was so gorgeous.

She had no thought that her love for her slave master was forbidden. She felt herself getting lost in his light blue eyes, his curly golden hair, his thick beard and his strong lean face. It felt like even seeing him here had stolen the breath from her lungs. She desperately wanted to run her fingers through his hair and over his chest. She wished he would take her in his arms.

And then he smiled at her and her legs felt weak.

"Hello Bjørn," her voice cracked.

He gave his cocky smile, the one she hated so much, but this time she couldn't help but smile back. He moved closer and his fingers brushed her hair back from her face. Her skin tingled where he touched it.

"Don't," she whispered.

"Don't?" his eyebrow arched in query.

He knows I'm lying!

He knows I want him!

He reached for the shoulder strap of her dress and she just stood there, trembling, as he lifted it over her shoulder. She wriggled her arm free, her heart was thundering as he reached for the other side. The dress dropped to the floor and that's when she realised she was naked underneath.

"You're so beautiful." He whispered hoarsely. "Even when I first saw you, I wondered how a woman could look so beautiful."

"Please," she said, but all fight had gone out of her. She was helpless before him.

His hand traced the air before her body. She was filled with a yearning she had never felt before and her body leaned towards him.

"Do þú want me to touch yor?" He asked.

"Yes." She whispered it, her voice hoarse. It was all she could say.

Trembling, she took one of his hands and lifted it to her breast. She gasped at the feel of his coarse hands, her nipples becoming erect. She felt his strong arms fold around her as her lips reached hungrily for his. She slid her leg between his and pressed her naked body against him.

"It's time to get up," Inka said.

What was Inka doing here? Hervor tried to shut her eyes and dive back into the dream.

Inka grabbed her blanket and tugged.

Eventually Freya joined in on Inka's side.

Cursing, she tossed her blanket at the stupid, annoying pair. They retreated to the other side of the fire place, poking their tongues out and making faces at her. She felt like chasing them and hitting their heads together.

Inka had set up a lamp for them to see by. Hervor realised she wasn't naked as she had dreamt. She was wearing a simple woollen nightgown and using her hand as a pillow on the wooden bench.

"You're normally more pleasant than this in the morning," Inka said. "Didn't you sleep well?"

"Let's just get started," Hervor growled. "That Bjørn always gets up so accursed early and he is always hungry straight off."

* * *

The moon painted the world with silver: the snow, trees and clouds.

As Bjørn walked towards a clearing he saw a lynx in the branches of a tree, clad in its silver winter coat. It was just sitting there, watching him, its eyes shining in the moonlight.

Hervor ran past him, laughing; her long red hair flying behind her. She wore a light dress and was bare foot in the snow; her steps so light she hardly left a trail. As she ran up to the lynx it didn't stir.

"Careful Hervor!" He cried out in alarm.

"Oh Bjørn, the lynx would never hurt me, I am an elf!"

"Hervor," He called to her. "Could you ever love me?"

She ran back to him. He marvelled at her red hair, green eyes and face pale with its dusting of freckles, but when he tried to grab her she ducked away laughing.

"Silly human! What does your heart say?"

He noticed she was burdened by a small girl child, was it Brenda? The child turned to face him and he saw she had strawberry blond hair but was otherwise an exact copy of Hervor. Their two elf faces shone silver in the moonlight.

"Why Bjørn, here is our daughter! There is no need to ask if I love you!"

* * *

No sooner had Hervor mentioned Bjørn than he leapt up, and took his shirt off.

He began stretching and grunted as his muscles flexed and rippled and joints cracked. Hervor couldn't tear her eyes away. She was having visions of those strong arms holding her.

He splashed some water on his face and chest and slipped his woollen shirt back on. He saw Hervor squatting there, watching him while she coaxed the embers of last night's fire back into life and remembered the dream of their child.

"Góðan Morgan," He said cheerfully.

"Góðan Morgan, Lord." Inka said, smiling back at the big Norseman.

"Góðan Morgan, Uncle." Freya chimed in, smiling at her foster uncle.

"Your breakfast isn't ready," Hervor flushed, scowling at him. "You give us no time at all."

"*Arliga* mik (I'm early)." Bjørn apologised.

He left to relieve himself outside. When he returned, instead of annoying Hervor, he grabbed a piece of stale bread and peered hopefully into the ceramic pot at the edge of the fire pit. There was some ancient stew in there, so he poked tentatively at a layer of white fat with black dots all over. Underneath was brown liquid and an unappetising gluggy mass of congealed lamb and vegetables at the bottom. It gave off a funny smell.

"For the sake of all your Gods, don't eat that!" Hervor snapped at him. "It's there to take to the pigs. Can't you wait a moment like any normal person would? I can give you skyr with fresh bread and eggs and I'm making fish and onions this morning."

"I wasn't complaining." Bjørn said meekly.

He whispered to Inka. "Why is Hervor in such a bad mood?"

"I don't know," Inka said, "she woke up like this. Mayhap she didn't sleep well."

"Do alfir wifs (women) have bad times of their moon, just like human wifs do?"

"I suppose so," Inka considered. "Do you think that might be the problem?"

"Why are you asking me?" Bjørn said. "You're an alfr and you're a female."

"Bjørn, I'm only seven years old. Do you know how young that is for an elf?"

"I can hear you talking about me," Hervor growled brandishing a wooden spoon.

"Damn alfr hearing." Bjørn muttered.

* * *

Horse riding with Bjørn

It was so frustrating! He could never catch Hervor free!

He had her practicing quarter staff and he loved the joy and excitement of something they shared. A vision came to him of her pretty face flushed with exercise, her eyes twinkling as she laughed. But what he really wanted was some quiet time alone with her.

After they had kissed each other, he wanted to kiss her again. How could he woo her when she was so busy all the time?

Bjørn's mouth set in a firm line as he thought about what to do. He got everything ready first and then he went in search of Hervor. He found her weeding a patch that Valdís had wanted to plant.

"Hervor, yor always verk!"

I'm a slave, I'm supposed to work, Hervor thought, but she kept this to herself.

"I don't tire easily," she said instead, giving Bjørn a serene smile. "When we elves do repetitive work we go into a place inside ourselves, where we feel close to the Great Mother, perhaps it is part of our little magic. Then we don't feel tired."

That didn't seem to satisfy Bjørn, she noticed his accent thickening.

"Yor need to relax *sumr timi* (some time). Soon *ver* (we) will be ploughing and planting for the *vor* (spring) and then ver *nauðr* yor (we need you), já?"

"Spring wheat, that's nothing," she giggled.

Bjørn should have known that Olaf was only experimenting with spring wheat. The main planting was barley in the autumn, sometime after harvest time. The seed lay dormant under the snow till the sun warmed it and the melt-water moistened it, ready for the spring growing season.

"We will need to move the animals to the high pasture and you are good with animals, we villr need yor then, já." Bjørn added. "Yor need to get some time away from the *staðr* (steading) before then to relax!"

"Þakka, Bjørn, but that is not needed. I went foraging for Olaf only the other day."

"I vanta yor to go riding viðr *mik* (with me)! There is something I want to show yor."

"Neinn Bjørn, but takka, I planned to weed the onion patch. Onions don't have a lot of roots so they need to be kept free of weeds."

"STUBBORN ALFR!" He shouted, colouring. "YOR ART COMING VIÐR *MIK*!"

"NO I'M NOT! I'M TOO BUSY!"

Bjørn's voice softened, "please, Hervor."

He fixed her with those blue eyes of his.

"Oh Alright," Hervor said through gritted teeth.

It was out of her mouth even before she had a chance to think about it.

Well, he did ask nicely and Bjørn, being Bjørn, wasn't going to give up anyway, so she may as well agree.

Then Bjørn was all smiles and excitement as he led her back to the house. She was surprised to find he had already put padded riding blankets and carry bags on Askr and Embla.

She felt a touch of panic at the thought of being alone with Bjørn. On a thin excuse she ducked into the house searching frantically for Valdís. All she could find was Sigríd tidying up after breakfast.

"Sigríd, Bjørn wants to take me riding!"

"I know. I helped him pack a picnic." Sigríd gave her a smirk, "have a nice time."

"You don't understand. It will be just the two of us!"

"Just the two of you? Really?" Sigríd looked like she was struggling to keep a straight face. "You know you can trust Bjørn not to do anything you don't want him to. So what have to fear?"

"But..."

Hervor couldn't think of an answer to that, it wasn't Bjørn she was afraid of, it was herself.

She left, her shoulders slumped in defeat.

She had not ridden before so he gave her Embla, the mare, and had to show her how to sit a horse. Bareback was better for serious riding; sheepskins or blankets could slip, but the skins were easier on rider and horse and they would only be doing gentle riding.

Fjord horses were not all that fast when they carried full grown men like Bjørn anyway, but they were muscular and very strong for their size and good in difficult terrain.

He led her up the hill behind the steading and then they swung west, parallel to the ridge. Despite her nervousness she had to admit riding was pleasant ... and it was very pleasant being with Bjørn. Some of his excitement began to rub off on her.

The first stop wasn't far, a small green wooded area just above the farm. They hopped off and tied their ponies to graze while Bjørn led her to a clearing and waited, watching her.

She stood, entranced.

"It is some sort of *berg* (barrow, mound)." He said.

Hervor said nothing for a moment.

Before her in a clearing lay a great earth mound standing six feet high and thirty paces across. It was faced with large hand cut stones but the work was unusually neat and close fitting. It was covered by grass and flowers on top but here and there stone peeped through. Any rooms and passageways inside the mound must be capped by great slabs of stone, hidden by the detritus of time.

The ground in front gently sloped down to the front and base, shaded by the mound and surrounding trees. From this there was a step down to a dark entrance leading somewhere inside the mound, lined with fitted stones on the floor and walls, with a massive stone lintel where it entered. The stones in the shade were covered in moss and ferns grew out of small cracks. Off to one side a small mossy rivulet of moisture dribbled from half way down all the way to the base.

There were three standing stones in a line, three metres high, carved in geometric designs and covered with moss: one to the right and in front of the tunnel entrance, one on the top of the mound near the centre and one at the rear. A cheeky Siberian Jay flew onto the standing stone on the top of the mound and hoped around, looking at them curiously. It called its thin high call, as if asking them what they were doing here.

It was old, she could see that at a glance, before Bjørn's people came, likely before the elves, and it had a strange and powerful aura she had never felt the like of before. She had a vision of the people who had built and used this place, but distant, as if seeing something at the bottom of murky water; it was so long ago.

"This is not your ancestors'." Hervor said, knelling by the entrance. "Have you been inside?"

"No, it's dark in there and there is a feeling that it wouldn't be right to do so."

"It wouldn't be. I really wish you had shown this to me before, Bjørn. The children will want to come here to pray."

"I have been trying to get you here," Bjørn said with a twisted grin. "Olaf thought it was an old grave."

"It was an outdoor temple." Hervor whispered. "Only the priestesses entered the mound. The people worshipped at the standing stones, each for a different ceremony. They follow an old line of power. Two people have been buried here; Nynniaw, a great leader and his wife Genovefa. She was their greatest priestess."

Bjørn turned to her, "How do you know such things?"

"Shh," she said, turning her head to the side as if listening.

Then she gave him a small smile. "In case you haven't noticed it Bjørn, I am an elf. They are bidding me welcome, they haven't met an elf before." She said. "They want to know what happened to their people. There was a cold period and their people left, never to return."

"It seems sad, missing them like that."

"It's the curse of the dead. The soul moves on to the next life but it leaves a residue, like an echo living in the sad shadows of memories. I'm surprised they are still so strong after all this time." Her voice lightened. "They like you and the other humans on Olaf's farm. They think of you as their new people."

"We can come back later," He said. "There is something else I must show you."

"Not yet."

She knelt before the entrance and took a deep breath and the pure notes of her singing filled the air. He couldn't understand the words, but it was so beautiful it brought tears to his eyes. Finally, she turned to follow him, her own eyes moist.

"Takka Bjørn, this is a rich place of old magic. Where are you taking me now?"

"I want to show you Líðandi."

"But we saw that when we arrived."

He didn't reply to her, just gave her another of his superior smiles. After a short while they seemed to be riding the wrong way.

"Bjørn, we seem to be heading west. Líðandi is south."

"Is it now?" He gave her a smirk.

Knowing she would get no further explanation, she contented herself with following. It was only a short way. He led her to a high rocky plateau painted in patches by lichen: green, grey, orange, yellow, grey-green and brown. The layers of rock tilted up slightly to form a ledge which jutted well out over an abyss. The cliff had been undercut by the glaciers in the past.

To their right a stream bubbled in a rush to fall to the river far below. Out by the sea was Líðandi, a few dull yellow dots showing thatch roofs, tiny at this distance.

"Oh, Bjørn, it's so lovely," she cried.

She hurried to tie her horse and ran as light as the breeze, to the tip of the ledge. "Look, I can see a waterfall!" She called back to him, leaning way out. "Come and see."

"Hervor!" His voice was shrill. "You be careful!"

"It falls in two columns."

"Já, in the morning you can see a rainbow."

He wanted to join her but his muscles had gone to jelly; his testicles were in free fall. "Hervor, you be careful."

"Don't be silly, elves don't fall so easily!" She laughed back. She bent out again and looked straight down. "Look at the drop!"

Bjørn couldn't breathe. When he came here on his own with no one to see, he inched his way to the ledge, if others were around he tried to pretend he wasn't afraid.

Hervor looked up to see his pale face, his forehead dotted with sweat and a look of anguish on his face.

"Don't you like heights, Bjørn?"

* * *

Bjørn set up a picnic for them by the side of the stream on a grassy patch back from the abyss.

"The stream flows better now in the *vor* (spring)." He explained as he spread out a blanket and set out unleavened bread, cheese, smoked fish, apples and brown goat's cheese. "I'm glad you could see it now."

"Ah you brought Gjetost!" Hervor exclaimed with delight.

Gjetost ('yay-tost', meaning 'goat's cheese') is made by boiling goat's-whey till the sugar caramelized. It was brown creamy cheese but tasted like elvish fudge and was one of Hervor's favourites. Her mouth was watering at the smell. "I'm surprised Olaf would part with any of it without a fight."

"He did when he knew it was for *you*. You're a favourite of his, you know." Bjørn laughed. "But you can't have any till we have eaten. It's for desert."

He set out two cups and a small pottery flask of dandelion wine.

"No thanks," Hervor said automatically.

"The wine is for me," Bjørn told her but he rinsed the cup in the stream and offered her some water.

Then he sat near her. He was not touching her but for Hervor waiting there nervously, it felt like his body was giving off heat like the afternoon sun on her back. While he was distracted, she grabbed a bit of the Gjetost that had broken off and snuck it into her mouth. Her eyes closed for a moment in bliss.

"I made something for you," Bjørn said, trying to appear casual.

Hervor gave him a shy smile. She couldn't reply because she was still pretending there was nothing in her mouth.

He passed her a small package wrapped in leather. It was a small exquisitely carved wooden horse on a leather thong. She hadn't seen him carve it so he must have made it in secret.

"Bjørn, it's beautiful." She said, her voice hoarse.

She slipped the leather cord over her head. She didn't know how to thank him, should she give him another kiss? She waited a minute, feeling awkward.

"Do you wish for me to serve you?" She asked.

"No," Bjørn replied.

He broke off some ordinary cheese and bread and offered it to her instead. Their hands brushed and every instinct Hervor had screamed *danger, danger*! Her heart began to race, she felt flushed. She felt warm and tingly, especially in her breasts and between her legs. She knew she had to resist him!

She told herself she was strong enough ... but it was a lie.

"This is the most beautiful place I know," he murmured, his voice was low and sexy. He took her slender hand in his. She realised she was trembling. "And you are the most beautiful woman I have ever known. I wanted to share it with you."

It was such a lovely thing to say that it brought tears to her eyes. She moved her other hand up to touch his beard. He was beautiful too, but not like an elf. He was big and strong and gentle and kind and wonderful. He radiated body heat and a male smell. Then he smiled at her, without any conscious thought she found herself leaning closer to kiss him.

Thoughts of resisting her love for him had fled. Her treacherous lips and arms had taken control again! She couldn't stop them.

And she didn't want to.

* * *

Finmark, Central Norge

They had descended from the high plateau and were entering the southern part of the back country. They had to detour to avoid an isolated farm and were hurrying past a path to forester's hut. They were too far south now for Nilse's far-sight to work but still had a long way to go. All Nilse and the elves could do now was pray ... and hurry.

* * *

Ālfheimr, Brynjar

Brynjar saw Báfurr limping after him, so he leaned against an oak tree and studied the deserted harbour while the dwarf caught up. The rain had finally gone and the skies had cleared. The water was a deep blue, reflecting the few clouds and the hills. Soon he would leave Ālfheimr, he wondered if he would ever see it again.

When Báfurr greeted him he gave him a friendly nod, and waited.

"My Lord, they tell me you are thinking of using the armour."

Brynjar nodded silently, glancing back over the water in thought. He hadn't decided yet, but neither had he rejected it out of hand, and that was upsetting quite a few people.

"Have nothing to do with it, it is cursed!" Báfurr said. "It cost me one of my boats and most of my crew. If I had not given my oath I would have cast it overboard."

"I am truly sorry for what you have lost, dwarf. And I am grateful for what you have done, we all are. But it wasn't a curse that you ran into; it was the same enemy that did this to us." He gestured back towards the village.

"Maybe, maybe not, but that thing is evil." Báfurr insisted.

"Yes, it is evil." Brynjar took a slow deep breath. "There was a time when we elves were many and great and our cities were filled with wonders."

He paused again for a long time. "You tell us there was a weapon to fight daimôns back then but we were never given it. No elf now living has seen our old cities but I remember *this* place and my people, and I remember what was done to us."

He looked towards the great barrow, the grave of all the elves that died that day.

"If we had been given a chance, most of our people would be alive today. Do you have any idea what it is like to see your people slaughtered, to lose everything and have your people hiding in the shadows, one step from extinction? They are my people, dwarf! I was supposed to protect them. That is a greater evil than jumping at shadows."

Báfurr flinched at the insult. "But, aren't you afraid?"

"What, because it is a monstrous thing that wishes to take my soul?" Brynjar turned to him, his face expressionless. "I have argued with all the people that love me until I'm hoarse. I'm sure I don't want to talk to you about it as well but, if you must know, it terrifies me. What you have brought is already mentioned in prophecy, I wonder if I will be given any real choice when it comes to it. Maybe my fate is already sealed."

With that, he turned and walked away.

Chapter 11: Journey to the High Pasture

Olaf's farm

Once Olaf got his cattle, sheep and goats up to the high pasture he would let them roam free. Still, someone needed to stay up there to keep an eye out for predators, especially with the new lambs and kids. Since he came back from the last of the king's big wars Þórsteinn (Thor's stone) liked being on his own. He had always refused to say what had happened. But the high pasture over summer, with only the occasional visitor checking on him suited him fine.

Hervor, with her ability with animals, offered to help him take the animals up, but it would mean she would be returning on her own. Most of the others were now used to Hervor's foraging the nearby woods and bringing back what she called 'the Mother's bounty' for them. She would be one night on her own, which didn't worry them, but it clearly worried Bjørn.

Every time the topic was brought up (like now while Hervor and Valdís were making breakfast for everyone) he made it very clear that he was coming and he would accept no argument. *Was Bjørn going to become over protective now that he knows I am in love with him?* Hervor wondered.

Yvla had run away and something in the wilderness had killed her, so Hervor understood part of his anxiety but ... silly human, she thought, I have no intention of running away and I will be fine for one night! My name is Hervor, not Yvla, and I'm not human. I'm not as helpless in the wilderness as you might think.

But she had a more immediate problem, and shared it with him as he was finishing the last of his breakfast.

"Bjørn, if I have to protect the lambs and small kids from wolverines, lynxes and golden eagles a quarter staff is useless. I will need some sort of projectile weapon. If you would allow me, I suppose I could make a long-bow from ash or wych-elm, but I've never tried to do that before, so it won't be very good."

"Isn't yew best?" Bjørn asked, putting his plate aside.

"It is," Hervor agreed. "It is slow growing which makes it dense and that is perfect, but it has to be worked with the outer sap wood and the inner heart wood in just the right layers in the bow stave … and of course it's poisonous, so it's really only for experts. Anyway I'm not even sure if I'm allowed to have a bow. I could become a slinger, I suppose."

Bjørn seemed to consider this for a while.

"I have a better idea." He said. "Let's see if ef þú can use these."

He stood up to lift one of the benches. After digging around a little he brought out half a dozen throwing spears wrapped in cloth.

"Bjørn, they have copper tips!" Hervor's eyes sparkled as she gave him an excited smile.

Ah, my beautiful shield maiden, excited over weapons, Bjørn thought.

"What's this?" Hervor asked. She had a strange piece of wood, curved with a lip at one end and a handle underneath.

"It's a spear launcher."

He could see her mouth moving silently as she studied it. Human archery could not match what elves could do for speed and range, but a well thrown spear had more stopping power in battle. Some throwing spears had a leather thong to improve range and power but a spear launcher would be even better.

He grabbed her other hand and tugged her outside. They hurried to set up two bails of straw, one on top of the other near the wood shed.

"I thought þrællr were not allowed to touch weapons."

"Most menn will not like it, já" Bjørn agreed, "but they can't say much if I order it for a good reason."

He tied a small piece of cloth in the middle of the top bail. With his first caste, he missed. The spear hung high up in the bottom bail.

"I thought you Norse only used spears for war." Hervor said, as he passed it to her for her turn.

"Neinn," Bjørn insisted. "Sometimes *ver* (we) hunt and fiskr with a *spjør*."

Hervor felt the balance of the small spears. She practiced a few casting movements and then tossed one up in the air and caught it. Then she turned to the spear launcher and practiced flicking it with her wrist.

She placed the spear in the launcher and cautiously moved it back and forwards. Satisfied, she stretched her arm back and effortlessly flicked the spear with an overhand caste. It landed inches from the centre of the target. Grinning she ran back a few paces and then ran and launched, hitting the target exactly in the centre.

"I won't ask you, because you will only say you haven't used these before." Bjørn looked at the grinning elf.

"I haven't ... honestly Bjørn!"

He watched her playing with a spear and the launcher.

"I'm not too sure giving þú these was a good idea."

Hervor looked embarrassed, "I was aiming at your father, not you."

"Aren't þú going to give me my spears back now?"

Hervor put her arms around his neck and kissed him slowly on the lips. Then she broke away smiling.

"Now they are minn." She said giggling.

For a moment Bjørn looked a little flustered. "You're not going to hit me again, are you?"

She gave him a cheeky grin, "We'll just have to see about that won't we?"

She ran over to the barn with her loot before he could change his mind. As she was wrapping the spears up with some cloth she realised that Bjørn had wanted her to take them.

She had kissed him for nothing!

And she didn't mind at all.

* * *

Journey to the High Pasture

Þórsteinn had his own pony, *Léttfeti* (light foot). She was too old for him to ride but she was good company and could carry most of his supplies.

Bjørn had insisted he come with them, much to Þórsteinn and Hervor's amusement. It didn't escape Hervor that it would be just the two of them returning alone. She couldn't help a small wicked smile at the thought of getting her handsome Norse man all to herself for one night.

Bjørn brought out three packs made out of hide stitched to hazel-wood frames. After filling them with supplies he tied a woollen blanket wrapped in hide at the top of each. They could be used as cloaks or for sleeping. Then he got them to hang leather and woven pouches containing food, water and tools from their belts and packs.

Not all of it was supplies for Þórsteinn. It may be excessive for a round trip of three days but the men of the farm had a lot of respect for the weather changes in the high country, even in spring.

Hervor was very good at fire starting but both Bjørn and Þórsteinn carried small sacks of woven birch-bark with live embers made out of dried black-rot from birch, all stored in wheat. In other pouches they had dried mushrooms and other kindling. A fire was necessary for comfort and cooking; in a winter storm it might be the difference between life and death.

In their hands they carried fire-hardened ash staves. Hervor had a sling she had been practicing with and a small pouch of carefully selected river stones at her belt. Léttfeti would carry the rest of their weapons and supplies.

She felt her heart was a bird taking flight on the clear spring morning as she waited with her handsome man. Her new family (as she thought of them now) was waiting outside the langhús to wish them good bye.

Olaf's young dogs: Fenrir, Hati and Skøll were lying on their bellies, waiting to start. Old *Garmr* (rag) would be left at home, so he was tied up. He was whining piteously, his heart completely broken, until Brenda walked over to hug him, and talk to him and tell him why they both couldn't go.

"We should take the cattle first and make another trip for the sheep and goats just like last year." Bjørn said. "Fenrir! Hati! Skøll! *Upp hunder!*" He called.

The dogs whined and looked up at him, but didn't move.

"Way boy! Way boy, go!" He sang pointing at the cattle.

They still didn't move.

"What's wrong with the dogs?"

"They have more sense than some people, I think." Þórsteinn laughed.

He turned to Hervor. "Shall we go?"

Hervor's musical voice rang out in a single elvish command and they felt a faint surge of 'little magic' in the air around them. The cattle began to slowly follow one another up the path and then the sheep and goats followed in crowded bunches, milling and pushing at each other. Finally the three dogs got up to trot leisurely after them.

Hervor saw Bjørn staring at her.

"Ready?" She asked and nodded invitingly to the trail.

The children were laughing at him but were more restrained, the adults could hardly stand. Þórsteinn had collapsed to his knees using his staff to keep himself up, Olaf and Sigríd had fallen to the ground with mirth.

Hervor said nothing more about it, but for some time Þórsteinn would mutter "Upp hunder!" to himself and burst out laughing.

After a while, Hervor let Þórsteinn take the lead and she dropped back to walk side by side with Bjørn, by which time he was more than ready to forgive her.

There was something companionable about hiking the hills together, much of it in friendly silence. Bjørn would sneak a glance from time to time at Hervor and he realised she was doing the same to him. Sometimes their eyes met and they would exchange a secret smile. That evening the three camped under the stars, but with Þórsteinn along Hervor and Bjørn didn't do anything more than keep smiling at each other.

They were almost at the high pasture the next day when Hervor called a halt. She carefully laid her quarter staff down and approached a stand of trees. A sleek black animal looking a lot like a bear cub trotted out from the foliage and squatted a little way from her.

When he saw it, Bjørn gasped. "Hervor, that's a wolverine!"

He ran to get his bow. Þórsteinn tried to make a grab for him.

"Bjørn, don't be a fool!"

Bjørn ran back with an arrow nocked but Hervor herself stepped in his way. He couldn't get a clear shot ... and then the carnivore was gone.

Hervor had never seen him so angry.

"What did you think you were doing? It could have savaged you."

Hervor stood up to him, a slender red haired elf facing off a big angry Norse man.

"Do you have to kill everything? She is a mother with two *kits* (cubs). I was warning her to leave the lambs and kids alone or we would hunt her down."

"Did she agree?" Bjørn sputtered, incredulous.

"Er ... no." Hervor admitted.

"Then why didn't you let me kill her?"

"Bjørn, she had come to talk!"

That evening in the small cottage that was up at the high pasture Þórsteinn gave him a peace of his mind. "You are a bloody fool, Bjørn Alriksson, have you forgotten everything you learnt about animals of the forest?"

It only made Bjørn feel angrier (and even more misunderstood).

His heart had almost stopped when he saw Hervor in danger.

"It was a wolverine, it could have attacked her."

Þórsteinn took a slow breath. "And she is an alfr and they were talking; you showed no respect by going for that weapon. You can accept a lot of things about her, why not this?"

Because I couldn't stand it if she was hurt! Bjørn felt like saying.

While Þórsteinn said no more about it, Hervor wouldn't talk to him, and it wasn't any better the next morning when they set out to return. By the time the shadows were lengthening she still hadn't said a word all day. Bjørn was surprised just how much looking at her cold, silent, angry face made him feel anxious. She was obviously much better at silence than he was; he didn't know if it was because she was an elf, or a woman, or a bit of both.

But why *should* he feel anxious and guilty? He was only trying to protect her.

He finally indicated a small stream, "we should camp."

Hervor shrugged silently and turned towards it. She lay her pack down and gathered dead branches to build a fire. She still hadn't said anything.

He offered to get more wood and fill their waterskins; not that he really had to ask her, he was just making conversation. She didn't respond, just busied herself cooking for both of them. He had the impression she could keep this up for days, maybe weeks.

"Hervor?"

No answer, but she did look at him, waiting for what he would say next.

"I don't think you knew how much danger you were in." he tried.

Wolverines were not much bigger than a dog but they were all teeth, speed and sinew. He had seen one take down a young buck deer.

Hervor said nothing in reply to that, she just scowled.

I knew the wolverine wasn't going to attack.

Bjørn sighed, "I don't want you to do anything silly like that again."

"Silly?" The word hung in the air between them. "So you think I'm silly, do you?"

Bjørn's mouth moved as he searched for something to say that would convince her.

"Just don't do that sort of thing again."

As he said it, he knew it was the wrong thing to say but he couldn't take it back.

"You think you can just *command* me, because I am supposed to be your Þræll? No matter how stupid you are."

"No, I ..." Because I love you, if anything happened to you, I couldn't stand it.

But he didn't say it; he was beginning to feel his own anger. Here he was trying to protect her and she was making him feel like he did something wrong. She even called him stupid.

Hervor almost threw his food at him and ate with her back facing towards him. He stared at her beautiful red hair that he loved so much, her slender shoulders. She was so desirable but unobtainable; she may as well be on the other side of the moon.

Finally she went to sleep with her icy back turned to him.

For a while he lay, watching her, and then he sighed and rolled over. Sleep was a long time in coming.

Even the first day back they hardly said a word to each other. It wasn't till the morning after that Bjørn felt calmed down enough to want to talk to her. She was mucking out the stables but only yelled at him to go away and threw a shovel of manure over his feet.

Chapter 12: The Battle for Líðandi

Olaf's farm, early summer, making hay

In the north lands with the shorter growing season hay could only be harvested twice a year: in the early summer and in the autumn. To minimise the need for hay, surplus animals were slaughtered in the late autumn and the meat was stored, but a well-run farm still needs a lot of hay and Olaf, being Olaf, was very fussy with his hay.

"There is really only one time to cut hay." He explained to Hervor as everyone trudged up to the meadow he had reserved for hay making. "Before it dries out and starts to go to seed. That gives you two weeks if you want to get it at its best."

"Two weeks?" Hervor said in surprise.

"Two weeks," Olaf repeated. "Later than that you get more bulk, but it will be poor quality."

Everyone had to join in, barring little Brenda. The adults would hack at the stalks of grass with short hand-held sickles while the children would follow behind to begin the process of raking it out to dry. Olaf had a few of the older sickles with obsidian and flint glued on to bone but most of his sickles had copper blades and wooden handles. Hervor followed what the humans did and chose one of the copper ones and sharpened it.

As she studied the sickle, she realised it would rely on the muscles of her arms to cut the grass while the weight of her upper body would be borne by her back as she was bent over. There was no way to get the rhythm of her whole body into the grass cutting like an elf would like to do.

Elves harvested grain but did a lot more foraging. They didn't make hay anywhere near as much as the Norse famers did. Their sheep and cattle were often left to find the grass lying under the snow in winter. It didn't seem the best thing to do, so Hervor wondered why the elves didn't do what the Norse did.

She was about to find out.

They formed a line with each adult six paces apart. It was a hot dry summer's day, good for harvesting dry hay but the sun baked down mercilessly and soon Hervor was hot and sticky.

In hardly more than half an hour her back felt as if it was on fire from bending and her arms and shoulders felt as if she had been pounded and pounded till they were bruised.

She watched in dismay how fast and strong the humans were with the back-breaking work. Even Edmund was already well in front of her. She bit her lip, wiped the sweat from her brow, blew loose hair away from her face (no time to tie it up) and grimly set herself to work even harder, ignoring the pain.

Her blade came loose from the handle and she had to stop and rebind it. The copper needed re-sharpening, which she did as quickly as her tired arms would allow her. She was already a long way behind.

She was strong for an elf maid but relied on speed, balance and dexterity for some of her apparent strength and endurance. She had no hope of matching humans for this sort of work.

The field was fenced off by a turf wall and when Olaf finished his row he walked back to see how the others were doing. He found Hervor puffing away, her face as red as a tomato, grubby and dripping with sweat ... and even further behind the others.

"Have a rest, girl."

Hervor shook her head, panting. "Neinn, I have to catch up."

"You're doing your best, but I think alfir are not as good at some work that humans can do well enough. With all the rest of the things you can do, there is no shame in it."

Hervor looked at him, her jaw clenched stubbornly. "But —"

"Rest for a while girl!" Olaf laughed. "Go on, just do as you're told."

* * *

If hay was stacked while it was still fresh and moist, it would rot. Sometimes it could even generate enough heat to start smouldering deep inside, the wet hay on the outside keeping the heat in.

The next step was not so bad for Hervor; spreading out the hay to dry and turning it over with a fire-hardened rake. She made sure she did a little extra each day to make up for her failure at mowing. The others called out for her to stop, that she didn't need to, but she just pretended to be a deaf elf.

As soon as the grass was dry enough she went out with Olaf and the children to make small stacks.

The last step was to build a proper full sized hay stack and Olaf had promised he would show her how it was done. He did it on a bed of branches for ventilation and heaped the hay around a tall central pole. Then he raked the outside to form a water-proof effect, a bit like a thatched roof.

Today she was out raking with Olaf. She was day-dreaming as she worked. She thought one day Bjørn might want a farm of his own and she hoped that an elf like her could make a good farmer's wife.

She no longer cared if he called her his þræll or not, she knew she would follow Bjørn to the end of the world if need be.

Things were still cool between them and she felt sad about that. That night alone with him, the one she had looked forward to so much, had been totally ruined. He used to drive her crazy the way he pursued her and wouldn't let her be, but now he seemed to be avoiding her ever since she threw manure over his favourite moccasins and leggings.

She didn't know what to do. She tried to make him his favourite breakfast ... and he thanked her. She tried to talk to him and he replied briefly and politely ... and still he stayed away. Just because she had screamed at him that she hated him and would never love him and wanted him to stop bothering her. Surely he must know she didn't mean it.

She just couldn't bring herself to apologise about the wolverine. She knew he was only worried about her and he had special reasons to fear losing another woman in his life, but she was shocked by just how angry and worried he had been. An elf wouldn't react that way. It felt like he didn't trust her and she really needed him to trust her. She couldn't help being an elf.

She had asked Valdís and Sigríd what to do but they just said to give it time, but still it felt like her heart was smouldering just like the hay stack Olaf told her about.

She jerked out of her reverie as she saw a large group of men in the distance on foot. She put her hands to her mouth and gave a penetrating whistle. People began spilling out of the langhús, the adults grabbing weapons. Hervor lifted the thrusting spear Þórsteinn had given her when they parted. She always kept it handy now. She would never make the same mistake she made at Álfheimr, leaving all her weapons back at the house.

Olaf appeared at her side with a shield and spear, a war club tucked into his waist band. "What is it þú see, sharp eyes?"

Hervor smiled at the compliment.

"A small *gangr* (group of travellers) of ten Norse, all on foot, they have leather armour and are armed with spears and shields. They seem to be in no hurry, their shields are slung on their backs and they are coming up the main track."

"Likely it be friends then, but it doesn't hurt to *vørðr (ward, guard).*"

"I think the pair in front might be Torgny and Sveinn, Bjørn's brothers."

"*Vørðr yðvarr tunga* (ward your tongue) around them girl. That is Bjørn's family and Torgny is the future Konungr."

"Já, Bjørn's family, the menn who wanted to rape me."

They went down to the langhús to wait, Hervor leaning on her spear, as Torgny and Sveinn approached with their escort of eight warriors. Bjørn was jogging down from an upper meadow.

"Góðan dag, Velkominir," Olaf said formally as everyone bowed to the guests.

"Are we to be *mæta við a þræll beran* (met with a thra-ell bearing) weapons?" Sveinn asked, sneering. He had already warned Bjørn about his female þræll getting above her station.

"Hervor is obeying our orders." Olaf said, keeping his voice mild.

"She is like a dotter to us." Valdís added, moving closer and giving the visitors an unfriendly stare. "And she works as if she were *tvau* (two)."

"Your alfir seem to have stayed loyal, then. Most of the other wretches have repaid our kindness by running away." Torgny said. "Perhaps yor would allow me to make a purchase."

"None of them are for sale." Bjørn said quietly as he joined the others.

"Come broðir what would yor say to a modest *stadhr* (farm, steading) of your own in exchange for the alfr wif?"

Hervor whistled faintly, it was an unprecedented offer, was he even serious?

Bjørn shook his head angrily. He took a grip of Hervor's shoulder with one hand and pulled Brenda to him with the other. The other children were being held by the adults as if to guard them against a threat.

"Ah, I see þú have tasted her then, broðir. Was she sweet?" Torgny reached into a bag and pulled out a wooden tablet carved with runes.

He spoke more formally. "I have orders from our faðir for you to turn your elves over to mik. Ver are to offer an alliance to the elf Jarl, and if he agrees all remaining prisoners will be returned to him." He winked at Hervor. "Don't worry; I will look after them for yor till then."

"I have already set them free." Bjørn said, meeting his brother's gaze levelly. "I plan to adopt the bairnr and marry Hervor, if she will have me."

"The people of this hús will bear witness to that." Olaf said quickly.

Valdis and Sigríd also gave quick nods, trying to look earnest.

Hervor looked at him in shock, tears came to her eyes. "Bjørn," she whispered, overwhelmed.

It is a foolish, desperate lie, she thought, meant to protect her from his brothers. But he had turned down a farm for her and he still loved her! She placed her hand over his as he clutched her closer.

"All you will get in Bjørn is a barefoot beggar with the arse shining out of his trousers." Torgny shook his head as if in sorrow. "You would have done better as my þræll."

Hervor shuddered.

Bjørn had spoken for her, so any further insults were crossing the line of propriety. It was Olaf who replied.

"I don't care if you are the Erling (heir) or not, boy, this is my stadhr and yor heyra your broðir. Keep your *flyta* (insults) to yourself. Bjørn has enough to start his own farm and he will always have a home here: if you have neinn *meiri* (more) business, then gan on your way."

Torgny coloured. He would remember this, but then he had given the old man little choice. He would get no respect if he tolerated insults to those under his roof.

"Apologies *forn* (old, from former times)." He sneered, his accent thickening. "I do hafa business with dyrr broðir minn. We *kenna* (see, know) that the *seiðmaðr* and his witch-wif are allied with the wifly menn af Vest-Fold and Grener too. Þeir hafa brought two more of their foul kyn."

Two more Illvættir!

"They will kill us all." Hervor moaned.

"Broðir *telja* yðarr (tell your) *wif* (woman) nar to interrupt when menn spraki!"

"Þagða (silence)!" Bjørn shot her a warning glance.

"Hervor, now yor are a free-woman soon to be a systir, I would ask yor to help oss search *yðvarr* kyn to make peace. It is in the interest of both our peoples."

"I will go if Bjorn and Harald can come, if they chose it." She said. "My people will need to gather food and supplies so they will be close to Ālfheimr. They will be wary and in a sorry state, but they won't attack if I go with you."

"Takka then." Torgny said with a forced smile. "We have received beggarly welcome at this hús so we will call yðvarr crew and send þeim her."

Olaf coloured but said nothing as Torgny signalled to his men and left, heading north.

"Bjørn, did you mean what you said." Valdís asked.

"Já," Bjørn said. "Hervor, will you marry me?"

Hervor looked at him with eyes shining. She opened her mouth and took a deep breath.

"Stop!" Valdís said and quickly reached across to put a hand over Hervor's mouth.

She turned to Bjørn. "You'll get neinn reply until you free her properly. And don't expect her to pay for the celebration."

Hervor looked terribly disappointed but all she could do was to give Bjørn a little shrug of helplessness.

* * *

Olaf's farm, gathering the hay

The very next day Olaf took the cart and the two horses to gather the hay from the temporary stacks. He wanted to have his main stack done before Harald, Bjørn and Hervor left for Ālfheimr.

Hervor was greatly relieved that things between her and Bjørn were better now but she had mixed feelings about going home. Her parents and little sister were dead, as were so many of her people. Maybe she would find her brothers alive and maybe a few others, but it would be a sad meeting. It would be good to see them, but it would also break her heart to see what had happened to her people and her home.

And no matter what she did, she would be a traitor. If she didn't turn her back on these humans she would be a traitor to her people. If she did, she would be a traitor to her human family ... and her heart.

Bjørn and Harald went to cut branches for the pallet and the centre of the stack while Hervor went with Olaf, Edmund and the children to rake and pitch hay. It was warm and sunny and Brenda set herself up in the shade to play with her doll. Hervor, Olaf and Edmund had delivered the first load of hay and they were half way through loading the second lot when Hervor stopped and shaded her eyes.

"That's strange."

"What sweetling?" Olaf asked, resting his weight on his pitch fork.

"Oh," Hervor laughed, "I must have imagined it." She pointed, "I thought I saw a flash of light in the forest way over there. There it is again! Like the sun shining on copper, but there is no road there."

Olaf turned to Edmund. "Edmund, take the children and hide them in the woods."

A feeling of utter dread washed over Hervor.

"I can fight!" Edmund protested.

"Já but can you follow orders, fool? Now lad! I need you to keep them safe!"

Hervor had been thinking of Álfheimr. Someone was coming that way, they were bearing weapons and they weren't using the road. They weren't friends ... and there were a lot of them.

Would they come and kill her human family now, like they had killed her elvish family?

No! No! Dear Goddess, no! She turned and ran.

At first, Olaf thought she was running away. Then he realised, she was making for the ridge. He saw her kneeling, lighting the signal fire they always kept there. She was quick! Within moments a thin trail of smoke rose from the tinder and then she was blowing on it and adding more leaves.

As he struggled to release the horses from the cart, Hervor passed him, running flat out to the langhús. She hadn't whistled. She would use the signal horn so Bjørn and Harald would be sure to hear it at the same time as their enemies. It was only a small hope but maybe their enemies hadn't seen Olaf and Hervor or weren't sure they had been spotted yet. If so, they needed any small advantage they could get.

He glanced back to the signal fire, it was soaked in pine resin and she had dumped green branches on top. A thick column of smoke was already rising high into the sky but if their enemies hadn't seen it yet, they would soon enough. They had very little time before sounding the alarm.

Olaf was half way back home when the women came spilling out, carrying bows, shields and leather vests for the men. Hervor followed, she had swapped her thrusting spear for throwing spears and grabbed the signal horn. She put the horn to her lips and it gave a long low blast that echoed out across the valley. Much later, another horn replied, faint in the distance.

Thirty armed men broke cover and started jogging across the lower meadow, all need for concealment gone. Olaf looked at them with dismay, how could three men and three women stand up to thirty warriors? They couldn't, and he was slower than he had been. If only Þórsteinn was still here.

He was almost back at the house when Hervor ran up to him; she wasn't even out of breath yet.

"Bjørn and Harald are coming. Use the old woodshed. I'm going to challenge them."

"Don't," Olaf gasped, but she was gone, running like the wind.

She stood on a small rise, tall, slender and proud. The heavy set men facing her paused in a group as her clear, silvery voice rang out across the valley. "Who are you men to come sneaking onto my lord's land? Put down your weapons if you wish to come in peace."

"So," their leader replied. He had a fur vest for protection but most of his men were in woollen homespun. "Olaf sends a wif to challenge a group of warriors, perhaps he is a wif himself. Minn nafn is Gifli of Grener. All yor need to kenna is that I koma to kill yor alfir und your menn."

"Well Gifli, son of no man, I am an alfr as you can see. Do you need so many men to kill one wif or mayhap you haven't brought enough, because none of you are real menn!"

Gifli smiled at the exchange of insults, he'd never had them from a single woman standing up to a full war band before. The elves had lost very badly at Ālfheimr. Perhaps their much vaunted inhuman fighting abilities were a myth.

He nodded to the man next to him, the man did a running throw and cast a spear. Hervor didn't flinch. He had done her the honour of the ancient challenge; the spear sailed over her head.

Her reply was fast, faster than any of the men had ever seen. Their spearman grunted, bent over, as her throwing spear took him in the stomach.

With a roar his men raised their shields. "Die witch!" they screamed as they charged.

Bjørn and Harald had arrived at the long term wood storage shed and helped Olaf boost Sigríd and Valdís with their bows onto the roof. The homestead was half way up a rise; it had a turf wall around it, with gates and stiles. The shed stood hard against the downhill corner and had a pig pen on the other side so it could only be approached from the front. It was a good choice; it was the most defensible spot on the whole stadhr.

"Ho!" Olaf slapped Bjørn on the shoulder. "Now they will learn how an elf can run, já Bjørn?"

Bjørn didn't reply, he was watching in frozen horror as one man short of thirty screaming warriors chased the woman he loved.

Hervor ran up the hill, keeping just in front of their enemies. They had stone battle axes or clubs in their belts, most had long thrusting spears topped with copper and they had unslung their shields, so were more burdened than she was. She was playing for time, trying to tire the men. Olaf's neighbours would come as fast as they could; he was a good neighbour. But Bjørn couldn't see how they could make it in time to help.

Hervor started running away from the langhús but this time only half the war band followed her, the other half split off and made straight for the main steading. They would be hoping to deal with the other adults and find the elf children.

She led her group of fourteen enemies in a wide loop around a rocky outcrop and ran lightly through a patch of bog. It looked solid but there was only one easy route through. Her pursuers tried to fan out and there was cursing and grunts as some of them found themselves knee deep in mud. Hervor's head appeared behind the rocky outcrop. There was only one archer, for a moment distracted, and she raised her launcher and cast almost in one motion. He 'oomphed' and fell into the mud, a spear in his chest ... and then she was gone. There were two casters of spears left and then it would only be thrusting spears and stone axes against her throwing spears.

Her remaining enemies were well scattered now, which was what she wanted. It would be easier to pick targets and she could come at isolated warriors. But it was also very dangerous; she had to watch all directions at once and when she changed direction the lagging ones could take shortcuts to outflank her.

She had hoped that the warriors with throwing spears would be less burdened and out in front, but one had got mired in the bog. The other was one of the men puffing up the slope just behind her. As she paused to look back, he cast at her.

She had to dodge a thrown spear and cast in return, almost in the one movement. She missed his torso but he screamed a curse as she hit him in the groin. Was she getting tired, was she too hard pressed, or was she just too scared?

One of the men had slung his shield over his back so he could run faster, Hervor spun her body in an arc and the throwing spear took him in abdomen. Eleven left, but she was down to two throwing spears and was beginning to tire.

If only she had a heavy war-bow. Wait on, there was a bow ... in the bog ... could she get it? ... No, that would be a silly thing to try.

More of the men were slinging their shields on their backs, so they could run faster. Hervor decided to make one of those closest to her to pay for that. She spun and cast, but she almost cut it too close. The first of the men were almost on top of her.

She had to dodge past and run to the tree line, but they had cut her off from the house and most of the open meadow. If she got penned by these men, it would be all over.

Another warrior had taken a short cut and appeared near her side; she ducked around his spear thrust and rammed her shorter spear into his chest. She followed him all the way down to pull her spear out of his body; her hands slippery with his blood.

It took too long. She cried out, as much in shock as pain, as someone behind speared her in the back. Fortunately it struck a glancing blow on a rib, more painful than deep.

The men were closing in now. Ignoring the pain, she dodged past two men, casting her last spear over arm at the man who had speared her. All she had now was her belt knife and a sling, but in the distance she had seen a dead body; it was the first man with the throwing spears!

She ran like she had never run before, chased by eight men. The men were tiring but as she reached the dead Norseman her sides were heaving, her legs and chest were burning and she was drenched in sweat.

All he had was a small shield, a belt knife, a single handed club on a leather thong and three bone tipped throwing spears with thongs attached. She ignored his shield, she didn't really know how to use one and it would only slow her. She tucked the knife and then the club in her waist band, the club was not a good weapon for an elf maiden but she would make do. The bone tipped throwing spears had leather thongs. They were tricky to use, not as well balanced as the copper ones and had special points that would break off in the wound.

Let's hope I can use them properly this time, she thought, as the men closed in on her. If she was to reach the wood shed she would have to find a way to get past the remaining men.

* * *

Bjørn watched Hervor almost get mobbed but then he had problems of his own, fifteen of them and coming fast. Valdís's vision was not as sharp as it used to be and she didn't bother to fire yet. They were packed together, so Sigríd risked a long shot. A man screamed and fell and the men behind him stumbled over him. They paused to help the wounded man but he staggered up and waved them on. The attackers slowed now as they ran with their shields raised high.

Bjørn and Harald ran along the wall to where they thought the men would likely scale it. They couldn't defend the wall, but maybe they could pick off one or two of the early ones over.

Between them and the woodshed, one of the attackers dropped to boost two of his friends over the wall. Sigríd shot one in the back and Bjørn managed to hit the other in the shoulder as he and Harald ran flying past back to the temporary safety of the shed.

"We only have a dozen left for us," Olaf called cheerfully as they barrelled in to join him.

A dozen against three with two women on the roof, Bjørn thought.

The woodshed was large; part workshop with wooden planks, firewood and off cuts stacked in one half. There was no window but it had a raised skylight/smoke hole and an internal ladder leading up to it. Olaf had worked furiously to erect a barricade of wood and scattered logs all over the ground and the three men turned a work bench on its side and then clambered behind it.

Still three men against twelve, they were unlikely to last long. Their enemy formed up in a shield wall against the women archers and moved awkwardly in a scrum towards the shed.

"Sigríd says our girl has killed two more," Valdís called down, "she slipped past them and collected more throwing spears. She is on her way here but she looks completely done in."

"She should get away," Bjørn said.

"She won't," Olaf grinned, "not while we are in danger. Bjørn, Þú have to marry that girl."

"I'd like to," Bjørn said.

If we can survive this.

The raiders arrived in a wedge, stumbling over the piles of wood. Harald and Bjørn had slammed the flimsy woodshed door and wedged blocks against it. The Grener men simply began chopping at it and ramming it with their shoulders while shouting insults and keeping their shields up against the archers on the roof.

Bjørn and Harald used their spears two handed to stab through the gaps in the door as it splintered. Then they were in a fight for their lives.

* * *

Hervor had never felt so tired in her life. She may be an elf, and elves love to run, but she had run the length and breadth of the open meadow four times and had been forced to put on an extra burst of speed twice ... and she was wounded.

She ignored the pain and her exhaustion. Her human friends were sure to die if she didn't help them, though in truth she didn't feel like she had much left to give. A sprint was beyond her but even the six men behind her who were still uninjured could barely stand, let alone stumble after her.

Just as she had arrived near the wall, her heart stopped. She could hear the sound of horses. It was too soon for it to be their neighbours, so it had to be more enemies.

The children had lost one family and now they were about to lose another.

She hoped Edmund and Þórsteinn could look after them because there was nothing else she could do. The rest of them were going to die here.

She saw Valdís and Sigríd frantically looking for openings but half of their enemies were already crowded into the wood shed. When she saw Bjørn grappling hand to hand with a great giant of a man, all weariness melted away. She was going to die but she would die defending her friends!

She gave an elvish war cry and threw her last throwing spear and grabbed the club from her waist band.

"Hervor!" a familiar voice shouted behind her before she could rush forward.

"Dómarr!" She cried in shocked recognition, spinning around.

So that's who was on the horses!

She had to point out who not to shoot, but with three elf bowmen shooting at the unprotected rear of the enemy, it was soon over.

"Dómarr, what are you doing here?"

"We can talk later. You are injured; we will take care of the rest of these humans."

Then she saw Bjørn slumped against a post, blood all over him.

"Bjørn!" She screamed as she ran to his side. "Neinn! Neinn! Neinn!"

As she pulled at his vest to expose his wounds his hands grabbed hers, surprisingly strong despite his wounds.

"Don't Hervor, it's too bad." He was pale and panting.

"Bjørn, I'm sorry for everything." She said through her tears. "Please don't die, I love you."

"Hervor, kiss me one last time in case I die." He whispered it weakly, his eyes struggling to stay open.

She knelt next to him and kissed him again and again, desperately, on the lips, on the face, on the chest, on his hair. Her tears were wetting his face and beard ... until she felt his mouth smiling.

"You bastard!" She pushed back to see he was laughing at her.

"It's not minn bloð, not all of it, anyway."

Now she really wanted to hit him. Then she couldn't help it; she started to giggle and couldn't stop. He laughed a little and then he winced.

"I hate you!" She said weakly. She carefully hit him lightly on his chest, well away from his wound. "I don't love you at all. I'm probably hurt worse than you are."

"Hervor, are you hurt?" He tried to sit up and winced again and dropped back.

"A little, but more exhausted than anything. I have never felt so tired in all my life." She lay her head carefully on his chest. Some of their neighbours began arriving then. With the elvish bowmen, they were making quick work of the few surviving Grener men.

"How many did you kill or injure," Bjørn asked.

"I had an open meadow and they only had thrusting spears. Adalwolf always said I did better in the open. It's probably because I run so well. A lot of elves fight better if they can run or hide."

Hervor found she was talking too much for an elf.

Bjørn frowned, "but how many?"

She flushed with embarrassment.

"Er, ten," she answered, "but some of those were only injured, Bjørn. Adalwolf said I was one of the best he had trained."

Not much of a lie. For her age and sex he had thought she was the best there ever was.

Bjørn whistled faintly. "Ver (we) could neinn hafa faced alfir in a fair fight, could *ver* (we)?"

"This was different, but neinn Bjørn, you could not." She reached over to kiss his face again and looked at him with concern. "You're not upset with me, are you?"

She was a better warrior than he was. After the episode of the wolverine she didn't want a full dose of wounded male pride to be the next problem for her to deal with.

"Hervor, how could I be upset? I love you, and I'm proud of you. Would you marry me, but as my free wife?"

"I will marry you, Bjørn." Tears began running down her cheeks as she kissed him again. "But of the elves that came, one is Dómarr, the elf whose ring I carry. I think he has come all the way from his home in the north to take me home. He'll be back in a moment, and I don't know what to say to him."

* * *

Hervor stood and waited when she saw Dómarr walking back to her. His face looked like thunder and his eyes were aflame with rage.

She felt waves of shame wash over her and bowed her head.

"I saw you kiss that human!" He spat.

Hervor tried to reach for him, but he threw her hand aside.

"The bodies of your parents, your little sister and all of your friends; they are barely cold in their graves, Hervor! Did you even love them?"

His words cut her worse than a weapon, she felt herself shrinking inside.

"These ones rescued more elves than they killed, Dómarr. They want to make peace and help us."

"We are tottering on the edge of an abyss because of them." He shouted, trembling with rage. Elves rarely got this angry. "You have betrayed me. You have betrayed our people. When I leave you will come with me and turn your back on these humans. I warn you though, it will be a long time before you are forgiven."

"No."

"No?" He hissed and grabbed her. She thought he would hit her then.

Valdís and Sigríd moved quickly closer.

"Dómarr, please, I never meant to hurt you. You are the first man I ever loved."

"But not the last; Hervor, did it have to be with a human? A Norseman? Give me the ring!"

It felt like he had slapped her. She wore the ring on a leather cord and kept it close to her heart. With trembling fingers she reached for it and pulled it over her head. Tears blurred her vision. He snatched at it and stalked away.

Jossur made to follow but Nilse grabbed his hand.

"Let me go. I need to talk to him anyway."

Dómarr had walked past the pig pen and was staring sightlessly at the farm house; the other men were giving him space.

"You know I can't stay." Nilse reminded him. "I must leave for Farsund tonight itself to warn their king. They are going to attack there very soon, and it will be in force."

"I will go with you, and from there I will go north." Dómarr said. "There is nothing for me here. I have lost the only woman I ever loved."

"To lose something you must first have it; I tried to warn you, though I knew you would still want to come. Hervor's fate was written a thousand years ago and it never lay with you."

"A fate written thousands of years ago? I don't know what you mean, but if you thought that why did you come here at all?" Dómarr asked. "Surely it wasn't just for me and my empty quest."

"Not empty, I didn't know it before but your destiny was to rescue these people for the love you bear Hervor. Now I must talk with Hervor myself and then I will be ready to leave. Please do not let anger spoil a life time's friendship."

"Nothing you can say will make me feel any different towards her."

"Then I will give you a second warning, one on your honour you mustn't repeat. A shadow lies over many who are gathered here."

Dómarr looked at him, in shock, "is her human going to die?"

"Bjørn will not die so young."

"Hervor?" He grabbed the human seer's arm. "Are you telling me that Hervor is going to die?"

"Yes, she is going to die. She has the mark upon her. I can see it. Now let me talk to her first and then you can say good bye, if you wish."

Dómarr stood for a moment staring sightlessly ahead as Nilse walked away.

He had said that nothing Nilse could say would make any difference to his anger towards her. But Hervor was going to die and it was his last chance to say goodbye. Death, for an elf was not the end, but did he want to part with her in anger?

She didn't know it, but she was not going to live amongst the humans, and suddenly, there was no reason to be angry with her and no reason to envy Bjørn. It was going to be even harder for Bjørn. He had only had Hervor in his life briefly, and he would lose her just when he thought he had won her.

Memories of Hervor over the years flooded back to him as his love for her had deepened. A few made him smile, despite his sadness. He still loved her, after all, and he had memories that Bjørn would never have. He looked again for his anger at her and Bjørn and his jealousy of Bjørn, but all he could find in his heart was sorrow, and pity for them.

* * *

The Sami noaidi had asked to talk to her on her own. Hervor was puzzled but followed him to where they would not be overheard.

"Hervor? My name is Nilse and I have travelled a long way to talk to you."

"Me?" Hervor laughed self-consciously.

"Did you know the dwarves have brought artefacts to Álfheimr, weapons to kill daimôns? To use them you need to wear special armour. It was designed for your brother, Brynjar, to wear."

"At last!" She breathed a silent prayer of relief. "Why, Brynjar must be Hjørvard! It was said that he would be given weapons to fight the daimôns."

"There is a cost. The armour will trap and drain the soul of any who dares use it."

Hervor blanched, "then that it is only a cruel joke! Even one eternal soul is too high a price. My kin should flee, I will stay with Bjørn."

"More than two dozen dwarves have already died to bring these things to the elves. One has sacrificed her immortal soul."

"The dwarves did all that?" Hervor was in shock. "The old debt is cancelled then. Yet I will tell my brother to have nothing to do with it."

"The Illvættir will keep coming. They will destroy the elves and any who have helped them, this I have seen. Where they can't send daimôns they will send humans in great numbers and worse than that, two of those who are hunting you have great power beyond summoning daimôns. The North will not save you."

Tears came to Hervor's eyes. "Then we will fight. These Norse have taught me that much. To the Norse, even the Gods die. An eternal soul does *not* die but all other things must. It seems that we elves will end too, but when that day comes we will die facing our enemies with a curse on our lips."

"That is your answer then."

"It is, if my brother was here in front of me I would tell him to have nothing to do with it."

"Hervor, the armour may not work for your brother. A Dwarf Prince was meant to sacrifice his soul to tame it but he was murdered because of it. It was his daughter who tamed it in the end."

Hervor looked at him steadily. "I am sad for both of them then, to sacrifice so much. But they created a horror and only evil can come of it. Now it will only cause pain, even if we don't use it. I wish they had never brought it."

"Hervor you are embarking on a dark and difficult journey. If you will permit it, I would pray for you."

Hervor offered him a puzzled smile and nodded.

He bowed and walked away, leaving her with her thoughts.

Later, she saw Dómarr coming to talk to her, walking stiffly, leading his horse. Nilse and Dómarr's friends were already mounted.

"Hervor, please forgive my rash words."

She looked at him in shock and relief. Tears came to her eyes. What had gotten into him to make him change his mind?

"Dómarr these are my people too, now." She put her hand on his sleeve. He didn't remove it. "What choice did I have? I was prepared to die but I had to protect the children. Those I thought of as enemies only gave us love and kindness."

"I don't understand these humans after all the terrible things they did to us."

"Nor, in truth, do I," she admitted with a small smile. "Sometimes they seem so crazy it's hard to believe they are even related to us, and yet I have come to love them. You have ridden all this way, surely you can stay for a while?"

"I rode here to bring freedom to the woman I love, but I find there is no place for me at your side. I will always love you and I wish you only love and happiness."

She moved forward and kissed him on the lips. "And I will always love you Dómarr."

"But not enough." He replied.

At that, he mounted his horse and, followed by his friends, rode out of her life.

* * *

It was not much later. Valdís had just finished wrapping a linen bandage around Hervor's back when Sveinn and Torgny and their men jogged up to the steading.

"I just heard about what you did, *systir*." Sveinn watched admiringly as she turned her back on them and quickly shrugged back into her dress. "I am glad you are joining my family. You are better than any broðir, I think."

"I wish minn broðir let me buy yor while I could." Torgny laughed. "Now I could never afford the price, I warrant."

As they went to talk to the other men, Hervor whispered to Valdís.

"Did you just hear Torgny and Sveinn being civil to me?"

"It's quite a turnaround, I'm sure." Valdis admitted. "I don't like them much either but they are Bjorn's brothers and yor are his betrothed. Besides, yor have earnt their respect and more."

* * *

It was the morning of the day after the battle for the farm and Hervor had been shooed out of the house by Valdís. She grumbled that she was fine to do some work but Valdís only gave her a piece of her mind.

"Are yor indeed Hervor? That wound is still seeping. Yor are just as bad as one of my menn! Now do as your told, gan outside and rest in the sun."

She found Bjørn and Olaf sitting outside, both looking a little sheepish. Bjørn was pale and in pain, Olaf had his right arm in a sling.

"You too?" Olaf laughed. "I tried to tell her I could work with one arm but once she is in one of those moods it is best not to argue with her. In truth every muscle and bone in my body aches and I feel like I'm ninety years old."

He gave them both a grin. "We did it. We beat them."

Hervor didn't know quite what to say to that, the way he said it. She was overjoyed they were still alive of course, but the Norse men saw fighting as some sort of lethal game. It was something she could never understand. She was saved from replying by Bjørn's brother, Sveinn and three Vest-Agdir men riding up. They looked very grim.

"It's as we thought," He said. "They have taken Líðandi and they hafa maybe two hundred more menn left and one of those cursed witch-menn. So far the hinterland is ours."

"Amma!" Hervor moaned. She would never forget the old lady and the women of Líðandi who had been so kind to her when she so badly needed it. "Please tell they are alright."

"Only a dozen escaped, menn and wifr. I don't know the fate of the rest, but I suspect it went poorly for the menn." Sveinn shook his head. "They have our canoes, so we are cut off and can't send messages out. We can raise maybe another fifty men and a few women who can fight. Are you able?"

"I am."

"Bjørn?"

Bjørn tried to sit up straight and look alert. The effect was spoiled when he was caught by a sharp spasm of pain. Hervor shot him a look of disdain. "Neinn, but he will say he is."

"Do any of yor have any ideas?"

"I know how to send a message to my people and Nilse. He is a noaidi on his way to your father at Farsund."

* * *

The ancient temple near Olaf's farm

Later that morning Harald led Hervor, Sveinn, Torgny and two others on the short hike to the temple just above the farm. Hervor decided to take all the children (and Freya as an honorary elf). Valdís insisted Bjørn and Olaf were not up to travelling.

While Hervor's heart was aching with worry for the fisher folk of Líðandi she almost burst out laughing when she saw that it was Sveinn who was carrying Brenda. He was smiling at the little elf and she looked very contented and comfortable in his arms.

"Yesterday the dog tripped me while I was running." Her eyes were wide as she told him her big news. "My knee was *bleeding*." She told him with emphasis.

"*Amma* (Grandma) Valdís had to clean it with water and bandage it! I wasn't allowed to run or play *the whole day*."

"Now that was a terrible shame, darling." Sveinn said, looking suitably sympathetic.

"Amma Valdís made this dress for me."

"And yor sure look pretty in it."

"I know."

She looked so smug it set Sveinn to laughing and Brenda giggled along with him. It broke some of the tension in the group.

Hervor stopped listening as she concentrated on trying to show she wasn't in pain. Her back was stiff and hurt more today than at the time she was wounded. Valdís said it was because she should be resting it, but she wasn't so sure.

She had retrieved the long bow from the bog before the water got to it. All she had to do was dry it and restring it. None of the arrows had gotten wet and there were spare arrow heads, tools, a pot of glue and spare tendon in a small pack.

It was not nearly as powerful as her old war bow, more like a strong hunting bow, but with her injury that was just as well.

It was still mid-morning when they found the clearing in the forest and the ancient temple. The elf children gasped when they saw it and Brenda wriggled to get down from Sveinn's arms.

Harald talked quietly, explaining to the other humans about the temple and grave site, while the elf children, Freya and Hervor filed in. They sat and joined their hands in a circle around the lower standing stone. As they started to sing, a light blue light began to fill the clearing, reflected on their faces.

Later, Freya told what she saw and heard. "As the light filled the clearing, I felt a power swirling through me. They were singing in elvish and it was so beautiful, but somehow I understood the words and I could sing it too."

'By Tiw the guiding star we sailed
Through heavens ablaze with light
It steered a never failing course
Guiding our ships both day and night.
The Goddess of a thousand names

Smiled at us in happy greeting
Ever beautiful, wondrously blessed
She called us to that happy meeting
Our voices were raised in joyous prayer.
Our souls were alive with joy
As laughter and singing filled the air.'

"For a moment I was afraid, deadly afraid. I had touched something fey, and knew I could never be the same again. I was no longer a simple farm girl and now was part fey myself, but then I felt the love of my elf friends and tears at the beauty that surrounded me.

"A shining figure with long golden hair and a flowing white dress stepped out of the grave. She spoke into our minds. 'Welcome alfir and welcome Freya, little elf-friend. Do not be afraid, Freya for you are to become a great priestess and you will be our special gift to your people.' She turned to Hervor. It seemed they talked for a long time but none of the rest of us heard what was said."

As the singing finished, Hervor came out of her trance.

"This place will get stronger every time we visit, and Genovefa said she will teach the children, Freya as well. She has agreed to send a message of warning to all she can reach. She can protect all of us from the enemy's far sight, at least while we are in Líðandi and not too close to one of the Illvættir. There is more and it concerns us all but especially the elves. Nilse had already told me part of it." She paused, looking pale and frightened. "Eight halflings and one ship have come to Álfheimr. It is all that is left of thirty dwarves and two ships that travelled over land and rivers from the other end of the world."

"By Þórr's hammer," Olaf said. "Is it even possible? We carry small boats covered with hide or small canoes, but who ever thought to carry a great ship?"

"Their ships are light and they have carts and winches. They are a small people but very strong and have great magic to pass unseen and carry heavy loads. They were attacked before they reached the sea and that was where they lost most of their men and one of their ships. They brought armour and weapons for my brother to kill daimôns, but the armour drinks the soul of any who dares wear it. Genovefa warned me not to have anything to do with it, but I had already decided that."

"Leave that foul *seiðr* alone." Sveinn agreed.

"Did she tell you anything about Líðandi?" Torgny asked.

"They killed all the men and the half grown boys that they could catch; the women, girls and young children are still alive."

Torgny spat out a curse. Sveinn coloured and began tossing the head of his axe in his hands with jerky movements.

"They know the raiding party they sent to kill us failed. Fifty men have just set out to Olaf's farm on foot, they know our numbers are few and we have had no chance to gather more."

"Well, little sister," Torgny smiled down at her with a look of fondness she found just a little unsettling. "The more I know about you, the more I like you. It only saves us the trouble of looking for them."

* * *

On the way to Olaf's farm, Rudolf

Hróðólfr (Rudolf, 'famous wolf') strode along the dirt road as if he already owned it. His older brother Hallbjørn had been appointed Yfirmathur of Líðandi, Konungr Anathon's newest acquisition. Now, at last, Hallbjørn had put him in charge of his own war-band.

Some of the other leaders made fun of Rudolf, saying he wasn't smart; even Gifli, though Gifli wasn't as bad as the others. No one would say it to his face though. Rudolf may not be as smart as some, but he was bigger than most and he was the best at fighting.

He could beat anyone in wrestling on land or the special Norse wrestling waist deep in the water. At boxing his fists had pounded many a strong man into submission and few could match him with a weapon in his hands.

Gifli had been Hallbjørn's favourite until now. He had promised Gifli Olaf's farm but Gifli had made a mess of things and got himself killed. Not that Rudolf minded that, the farm would be his now and it was one of the best farms in all Vest-Agdir.

All he had to do was to kill the men, one alfr wif and four alfr bairnr. He would have no trouble killing the men or the alfr maid. She fought like a hero and he really wanted the chance to kill her himself.

He didn't like the idea of killing the children, though. Even for a farm, he didn't want to kill children. He liked children, children didn't make fun of him and there was no honour in killing children.

He had offered a reward to any of his men who killed an alfr of any age. He thought that was rather clever, maybe it would all happen before he needed to see the little children or see them being killed.

That witch-man had done that trick with water and they watched all the mistakes Gifli had made. It had made Rudolf laugh at how he split up his forces and chased the alfr bitch across the meadows. That was the funniest part.

She wasn't supposed to have weapons but she did. Alfir were very dangerous, he could see that now, but there was only one alfr left now and she was wounded.

Rudolf wouldn't make the same mistakes as Gifli. No, he would come by the main road and capture the farm first. He would keep his men together and they would fight like real men, not running all over the place.

When he saw nine men waiting for him off to the side he burst out laughing. They waited across a mown field with hay stacked on either side of it, hard up against a turf wall. They couldn't be attacked from the rear or the side; but they couldn't escape easily either.

"Torgny! I heard we trapped you and your brothers here. Is this all the men you have?"

"This is all I need, Rudolf." Torgny replied as his men formed a shield wall. "We killed the other men your broðir sent and now we will kill yor."

"No yor won't, Þú (thou) will die like a rat in a trap!"

Five to one odds, Rudolf didn't bother to form his men up. With a great cry he scrambled over the turf wall into the paddock and charged, his men following like a mob. Just as Rudolf reached Torgny, Sveinn and his men burst out of the hay to one side and Hervor and two spear casters appeared on the other side.

The Vest Agdir men were still outnumbered two to one, but all of Torgny's men were battle hardened húskarlar and Sveinn's were veterans from the hinterland. The Grener men were out of formation and outflanked. Hervor was wickedly effective with a bow firing into the enemy's unprotected rear.

Just before he died Rudolf led the remainder of his men in an attempt to break through the ring of shields that surrounded them. He injured three men, two men badly, and killed a fourth even after he was already wounded. It was Torgny who killed him, though he said he could never have fought him if he wasn't already exhausted and wounded.

They buried the Grener men in a mass grave but in respect they raised a cairn for Rudolf and buried him with his shield and weapons. The next step was Líðandi and Hervor wondered how Torgny was going to manage that.

* * *

Líðandi, early the next morning, the Illvættir

"That's him," Hervor whispered.

Even Torgny could have picked the Illvættir. He was tall, six foot, with golden silky hair but, unlike an elf, he had a thin beard. He wore a white woollen cloak and gown, belted at the waist and bordered by gold thread. The only weapon he carried was a bronze belt knife. It seemed he had been given a small cottage to himself.

"He looks like an alfr," Sveinn murmured. "Can he see in the dark and fight like an alfr?"

"He can do none of those things," Hervor said. "All his power is in his magic but in that he is unimaginably powerful."

"Then," Torgny whispered, "We had better not give him a chance to use it."

* * *

Liðandi late that same morning, Amma

Amma couldn't remember feeling so tired.

She had been working since first light and all she had had was water.

"I'm too old for this," She muttered to herself.

The other women tried to help her in secret and give her the easier jobs but Hallbjørn, who called himself the Yfirmathur, delighted in ordering her around. He had cut her hair and made her wear a leather collar like an animal and he called her his 'drudge'.

Now he had sent her to wash all his húskarlar's clothes. She wearily carried the first sack past a pit house and one of the smoke houses to the well and dumped it on a large boulder the women of the village used for the purpose. Then she lowered the bucket into the well. A slender woman moved quickly to her side and pulled the bucket up with swift, strong movements. She wore a hood pulled over her hair and ears.

"They don't want me getting any help." Amma reminded the woman, and then she realised she didn't recognise her. She was a stranger.

"I'm sure they won't like the help that I intend to bring you, Amma."

"Hervor!" Amma hissed in surprise. She only just stopped herself from looking around to see if someone was watching. "Þú (thou) shouldn't be here, they are looking for yor."

"I'm the only woman we had at short notice," Hervor smiled. "Now, do you have any wine or mead hidden?"

"What do you ... Oh!" Amma realised suddenly. "Yes we have a great store of wine in a nearby pond."

"I think it would make a nice present for some thirsty Grener men tonight, don't you? Tell them that the women of Líðandi have decided to surrender to their new masters, and make sure your prettiest women are *very* friendly; in fact, all your women. Whatever it takes, I want as many of them as you can manage drunk. Don't tell your women the real reason, though some will guess."

"They came one morning, the sun at their back." Amma sighed. "We tried to fight, both men and women, but there were too many of them and none of us were great fighters. They killed our men and older boys and laughed as they did it."

"And now they will die."

"Hervor, I don't know why but they sent a large number of men to kill you and when they didn't return they sent more."

Hervor smiled, without any humour. "You should know that elves are not easy to kill, and I have Bjørn and his brothers to help me. We'll see you late middle watch. Try to make sure any of the women are back in their own quarters by then but the fewer you tell, the more of us will live. Now tell me where everyone will be sleeping."

* * *

The Battle for Líðandi

The sea shushed softly, the half-moon shone silvery on the water. The stars were faint, though only a few small clouds could be seen, dark and touched with silver. There had been a large outdoor fire but it had burnt down in the night, allowing the shadows to move back in.

One man was pacing outside the second largest house, a dark shadow. The women and remaining children were crowded in there. Most of the Grener were quartered in the langhús and four other houses. By this time they would be sleeping heavily, helped by as much wine as they could drink. Torgny heard the nearby call of an owl and he smiled as Hervor rose out of the darkness.

"As long as you don't expect me to make bird calls," he chuckled softly.

He saw her teeth flash in the gloom.

She pointed out where the guards were hidden and Torgny nodded to three waiting men. To Hervor it sounded like they were stomping and kicking through dry leaves but apparently to the other humans this was moving quietly, because no alarm was raised.

Once all the guards were dead, they quickly and quietly brought the women and children out. Many of the younger women whispered that they wanted to stay and help. Torgny had brought plenty of spare weapons captured from the dead Grener men. They would make very poor reserves, but it would be better than no reserves at all.

Amma refused to run with the other older women and young children.

"I'm too old and too short to run." She said. "Besides these bastards killed my people and I want to watch them die."

She stared Torgny down. Eventually he nodded.

"Give us a few moments Amma and we will try to kill them for you, but keep out of our way."

The rest they hoped would be easy. Some men put fresh brands on the fire. Most of the Norse houses had a single narrow door and no windows, relying on the smoke hole and the central fire for light. Torgny's men piled straw and sticks around the doors. A large log was carefully wedged against the door of the langhús to stop it opening outwards. It was a favourite Norse trick, come at your enemy at night and burn them alive in their house.

Around the door of the house with the sorcerer they formed a smaller pile. They didn't want him trapped inside; he would only summon his daimôn. They wanted him to stumble outside, confused and bewildered from waking to fire and smoke.

Two of their best bowmen waited in front and two casters of throwing spears stood on either side. They gathered ice from the ice house and three of the women who couldn't use weapons took a bucket of ice slush each just in case they had to fight his daimôn. Hervor's job was to wait alone by the side of the door and shoot him in the back.

Everyone signalled that they were ready and half a dozen warriors collected the brands from the fire, concentrating on the langhús.

Perhaps they had made noise or one of their enemies had a sixth sense. There were loud shouts as enemy warriors came charging out of one of the smaller houses. Hervor could hear the fighting and screaming. She knew things were going far wrong but she ignored it.

She waited, motionless in the shadows, with an arrow knocked, and tried to avoid looking at any fires and spoiling her night vision. If they did nothing else tonight, they had to kill the sorcerer.

With a great cry the blond Illvættir burst out of the hut and charged through the smoking pine leaves. Almost simultaneously he was hit by two arrows from the front but they bounced off a shimmering magical shield. He flicked a ball of fire at the archers, just as the two spear throwers cast.

BANG! An orange daimôn in the shape of a wolf appeared and ran at one of the spearmen. The women began frantically pelting it with ice and it paused, just as Hervor fired at the back of the sorcerer. Her arrow bounced off. She drew an arrow and fired again in almost a single movement just as his daimôn was banished. His shield flickered in that instant and her second arrow struck his back, not at full power but enough to make him drop his magical shield.

He turned to look at her as her third arrow hit him in the side. He spun to run and got hit in the front by a throwing spear. He fell on to his side, moving feebly, and finally was still. Only one of the four men in front of him was left alive. He ran over and slit the sorcerer's throat.

"He's dead," he shouted unnecessarily.

Hervor hardly paused; she ran to one of the dead archers and took a spare quiver of arrows. Their plans were falling apart.

Maybe thirty Grener men had managed to escape two of the burning houses and were battling the Vest Agdir attackers. Torgny only had fifty men and women plus the untrained volunteer women from the village to fight them and prevent any more from escaping.

Some men from the langhús had climbed out of the smoke hole, which was now billowing with dense smoke. Screams, pounding and coughing could be heard from inside but it was getting weaker.

The fires were ruining Hervor's elvish night vision and she didn't know who was who. She shot two men who leapt off the roof of the langhús. There was a small knot of women huddled behind shields being attacked by three men with battle axes. She shot two and the last man spun around and charged at her. She managed to kill him when he was only two feet from her.

Her eyes followed a trail of bodies to find Torgny fighting against two men. She shot one in the back and the other glanced quickly at her just as Torgny hit him with his axe over his head.

"Takka, little systir." He shouted and waved.

"I don't know who is who." She wailed, running over to him.

"Not him!" He said, causing her to lower her bow and then he ducked a throwing spear. Hervor spun and shot in one motion. "Yes him."

The battle was turning in favour of Torgny's men and Hervor was running out of targets. She shot the last man hiding on the langhús roof: with an anguished cry he pitched forward to the ground below. Then it was just the Vest Agdir men and women and a half a dozen Grener men that were wounded. Torgny had to stop Hervor and the other women from killing them out of hand.

"Where is Sveinn?" she shouted to him.

Torgny looked at her with a bleak expression.

"My broðir is dead."

Tears came to her eyes then, all she could do was shake her head.

Amma limped up, a dazed look on her face. She hugged the old lady to her.

"We have won," Hervor whispered to her softly.

They had won, yes, but Amma's home and her people were all but destroyed.

A few of Líðandi's men had been away at the time of the attack but it was mostly women, some girls and younger children left. Even some of their women had already been killed earlier and they had lost more in tonight's fighting. Of the people of the hills that answered the call; few enough would be returning home.

And it was not over. Unless they were defeated at Farsund, Grener men would come again and again.

"What will you do now?" Hervor asked her softly.

"Just let me mourn, Hervor." Amma said. "Tomorrow is soon enough to decide what comes next."

Harald came searching for her.

"Hervor, I can't find Edmund. We got separated in the fighting and now I can't find him anywhere."

Not Edmund!

They called and searched, checking faces of living and dead in the flickering light. Their eyes were stinging in the choking smoke, the air was filled with the crackle and roar of fire and moans of the wounded.

They finally found his body lying amongst the dead reserves where Sveinn had fallen. Sveinn had led them into the fight when it looked like the Agdir men would lose. It had been enough to turn the battle, but the reserves had not been good fighters and the cost to them had been high.

The young boy had been stabbed in the chest but it was the only mark on him. He looked at peace, and so very young. Hervor fell to her knees beside his body to kiss him while Harald knelt, motionless, on the other side.

Torgny seemed to be everywhere; organising, encouraging and giving kind words. They put out the fire in two of the huts. In the second one the fire had got into the thatch but the dense thatch was only smouldering. Removing it and putting out the fire was a dangerous job, with two men climbing on the roof to strip it while others stood by with water and dirt to stop it flaring as they broke it up and brought it down.

The other fires were still burning uncontrolled. Sometime in the night the roof of the langhús collapsed, burying the greater number of enemy dead inside.

Hervor felt numb with exhaustion, and sick at heart. Her old wound was on fire. When she could no longer drag one foot in front of the other, she simply lay down where she was and fell into a dreamless sleep.

Bjørn and Olaf came the next day. Olaf was driving, his arm in a sling. Bjørn still looked pale and in pain. To Hervor they looked like they had already heard about Edmund and Sveinn. She watched Torgny walk up to him and wondered what he would say. Would he tease them for missing the fight? Instead he reached out his hand to Olaf.

"Olaf I'm tryggr sorry. Edmund died a true maðr."

Olaf took his hand and nodded wordlessly. Hervor realised, that despite what she had thought of Bjørn's brother before, he was growing into the role of heir to his father, a true prince at a time his father's kingdom was under serious threat.

"Bjørn I'm glad you are with mik, tonight ver must say good bye to our broðir und all the fallen."

"Will there be neinn burial?" Bjørn asked.

"No broðir," Torgny shook his head grimly. "Ver are at war."

They chose one of the enemy war canoes with a sail rigged. Sveinn was placed holding the steering oar lashed into position. The other oars were shipped but the other dead men and women were arranged on the benches, even some of the Grener dead. Weapons, shields and personal goods were placed and the great canoe was provisioned for a long voyage. It was soaked in pine resin and when it was dark, the people gathered on the shore with torches and the canoe was towed out onto the bay.

Everyone shared a mug of ale to toast the dead, even the older girls and the Grener captives well enough to drink. Finally the sail was raised, and secured and kindling was lit. The sails filled, and the great canoe started to move slowly. The resin caught fire with a 'whomp!' the blaze reached up in to the heavens, being fanned by a light breeze and reflecting on the faces of those watching on the shore. Hervor stood next to Bjørn, holding his arm tightly, her voice raised in a haunting elvish melody as the dead of Líðandi sailed their final journey in a ball of fire.

* * *

Arrival at Farsund

Torgny ordered the remaining Líðandi men to stay to help the women and children go into hiding; some to the hinterland and some to secret bays and estuaries. The surviving Grener men agreed to peace. The worst of the Grener men had been killed in the fighting and those that were left were young, second and third sons, with no prospects of inheritance or marriage. In the way of defeated Norse warriors, rather than returning home in disgrace they accepted the better prospects being offered by joining their former enemies.

Torgny, Bjørn, Hervor, Harald and the few of Torgny's remaining húskarlar who were fit to travel left the next morning, before any more Grener re-enforcements could arrive and trap them once again.

As their canoe approached Farsund it was met well out to sea by three fast Vest-Agdir war canoes, about sixty warriors, and they were escorted into the main harbour. The town seemed in chaos, every able bodied man had been summoned to its defence. They were erecting earth works and palisade fences in addition to what the town had before. It seemed like there were tents everywhere and Norse warriors engaged in mock combat, working with the fortifications, sitting around and gambling or just swaggering about. They all wore red armbands and some had an 'F' stitched onto the front and back of their kyrtills. It was too many men from too many places for everyone to recognise each other by sight.

The harbour was jammed with great canoes: patrolling the waters, unloading men and supplies and evacuating women and children, some heading for the hinterland, most heading deeper into the sound.

As their canoe beached Bjørn stumbled into the water to help Hervor out. He had to clutch to the side of the rocking canoe till his pain subsided.

"Don't be ridiculous," Hervor scowled in disgust. She leapt past him to land lightly onto the beach. Torgny smothered a grin as Hervor ignored his brother's attempts to help her.

"Come Bjørn," he had to grab him by both the shoulders to help him out of the water. "Let's find Faðir."

There was an elf waiting for them, "we haven't been here long, my lords, but our seiðmaðr has already told the Konungr that you were coming. Your father is in discussion with our Jarl and their advisors."

"Nibelung!" Hervor went running to hug him.

Despite everything, she was soon making squeals of delight to be followed by heavy sighs as Nibelung told her who had survived, and who had not. She stopped and stepped back when she saw her brother Brynjar marching towards her, his face in a scowl.

"I heard you have joined yourself with a Norse human!" Brynjar said, his voice dangerous.

"I love him, brother." Hervor said quietly defiant, all her doubts had been washed away.

She took a deep breath, gathering herself for the storm, but to her surprise it didn't come. Instead, a look of anguish passed over his face.

"It wasn't them." She said softly. "They came to raid us, not destroy us."

"And that's supposed to make me feel better, is it?" Brynjar gave her a tired smile; but it was only a ghost of his old smile. "They only meant to steal from us and enslave my sister and so I should forgive them, should I?"

He wasn't acting at all as he should; she expected to have a terrible war with him. That's how an elvish brother *should* act to his sister falling in love with a human, especially a former enemy.

He would forgive her in the end, Úlfr might not, but Brynjar always would.

First Dómarr and now him, what was going on?

To see him like this tugged at her heart: so worn down, defeated and worried ... they were facing annihilation, but his courage would not fail. No, this must be something even worse.

Then, with an icy stab of fear, she knew what it was.

"The armour, Brynjar, please tell me you're not thinking of using it."

Brynjar tried to make his voice sound light. "It seems that the dwarves have finally honoured their promise, even if they are seven hundred years late. All that we need now is the man who is Hjørvard returned. Naturally if you are looking for a great hero of the ages, well here I am." He gave her a twisted grin and a mock bow.

"The worst part for me is that I am about to be trapped for eternity with a bearded lady."

"Noo!" Hervor grabbed him by the shoulders as if to shake him. "For our Goddess and for the love I bear you, please don't do this."

He shrugged her off, pretending to laugh. "Don't worry about me little sister; you know how brave and strong I am. Did you know that at the start of the wizard wars the dwarves had a weapon ready for us, but they were infiltrated by the Illvættir?"

Her look was enough.

The smile dropped from his face. "Hákon says we will face three daimôns this time and two human armies. What do you think they will do to this place?"

She looked around the human village and could see it burning.

"If we can't stop them this place will be Álfheimr all over again and your Norse men are the only thing that stands in the way of them hunting us elves to extinction. Nilse and Hákon both say that. This is our only chance, Hervor. As soon as I knew that we were coming here, I knew I would wear the armour."

"When the Illvættir took a forbidden power, it turned them to evil."

"I'm too stupid to become evil." Brynjar laughed more genuinely now. "Once I put on the armour I will be fuse with the Princess and the armour itself to create a new being and the new being will sleep when it is not needed."

"You will lose who you are then."

"I will become part of something new, the greatest hero this world will ever see. That is not a bad legacy. It is good enough for someone like me, I think."

She looked deeply into his eyes, he was frightened. She could tell that. But nothing she could say would change his mind. He would do this to save their people.

"Show me the armour." She said, her voice flat.

She gave him a light punch on the arm, to try to lighten the mood.

"Oh by the way Brynjar, dwarf women don't have beards."

"That's a relief."

"They are quite stout though ... and short, but you know that."

Nilse and Sindri were outside talking softly and followed them in.

"I'm not sure what would happen if an elf other than Prince Brynjar touched it, Lady Hervor, but please be careful." Sindri warned her.

They had laid the armour on a low table with its shield and spear nearby. There were slits for the eyes and holes for the ears and a thin split below the nasal bridge. It looked empty yet she knew it was aware of her as soon as she entered the small hut; it was angry, and watchful.

A dwarf had bound herself to that *thing,* at the cost of her immortal soul. She must have had her own reasons. She must have hated the Illvættir for what they had done to her family, but she didn't have to do something like that!

No, she had done it for the elves, Hervor realised, and now it required an elf to complete the spell, a dwarf couldn't do it anymore. If Hervor's brother didn't bind himself to the armour, her sacrifice would be in vain. Hervor didn't know what to say in the face of such a terrible sacrifice.

"It was supposed to be her father, but he was murdered by the King." Sindri said.

"There is no guarantee that the daughter has been able to make it work." Nilse reminded them.

"Yes," Sindri admitted, his face bleak, "so many dead and it might all come to nothing."

"Well, there is only one way to find out," Brynjar said taking a deep breath and giving them a weak grin. "But we don't know how long it will last, so we have to wait till the last possible moment. Hell of a battle plan of course. We must be ready to fight three daimôns on our own if it fails."

Hervor knelt beside the armour.

"Your Princess was named Dís, wasn't she?"

"Dís?" Sindri dropped down beside her. "Can you hear her?"

Hervor waited a while, "It is very faint but it seems as if she is whispering inside my head. She says she is sorry. She says she loves you."

"No one else has been able to hear her," Sindri said. "How is it that you can?"

Suddenly it was all too much, the evil, the dreadful sacrifices, Hervor couldn't breathe.

"Sorry," She staggered up and stumbled blindly to the door. She had to get out of there or she would go mad.

Nilse followed. "Are you all right?"

She didn't bother to answer, why did humans ask such stupid questions?

They walked along the shore in silence, watching the Norse unload their great canoes while Hervor struggled to calm herself.

"There is something you are not saying." Nilse said softly.

She looked at the human next to her. Maybe he wasn't so stupid after all.

"Dís spoke to me, but you had already told me, something has gone wrong with the armour." She took a deep breath, "If the armour doesn't work for my brother, I will have to try it."

"I thought you wanted nothing to do with it."

"Brynjar is right, what choice is there?" Her expression was bleak. "What the Illvættir is doing to us, it has to end."

"Will you tell Bjørn?"

"He will only try to stop me. I have finally found Bjørn and we will be given what? Maybe a handful of days? I'm not going to waste them in useless arguments. What do *you* think I should do?" She asked bitterly.

"Should I pray that the brother whom I love dearly is chosen rather than me? Should I run away and leave all this behind? I don't think I will be given the chance to even say good bye. Bjørn has already lost so much, I guess we all have. I fear it will kill him if I leave him too."

When Bjørn was finished with his father's war council, he came in search of her. It felt so good to have his strong arms around her, to taste his kisses. She really needed him now.

"We can sneak into the barn," she suggested. "Knut would see we were not disturbed. You're not too wounded are you?"

"I'm not *that* wounded." He gave her a cheeky smile.

Just a few days, is that all we will have?

Hervor put her hand in his and pulled him along.

Chapter 13: The Death of Hervor

Off the Southern Coast of Norge (Norway)

That elf girl, the one with red silky hair, had begun to appear in Brice's dreams almost every night. Sometimes in dreams that were not dreams and sometimes simply in dreams.

He could see her working on the farm and he could see her fighting the Norse. She was magnificent! Her fate must be linked to his, but how?

He had seen her kill Fáelán. Maybe that was the reason, but that didn't seem right. He had a feeling that she was more significant than that.

And then she and the children had disappeared from the dreams that were not dreams and also from his far sight. There was no trace of any magic concealing them ... so they had been killed by the Grener men. He was surprised how sad it made him feel.

He had known it was more than their entwined fates. In the daylight hours he often found his thoughts turning to her: her beauty, her long legs and the graceful way she moved. He knew he had been infatuated by her. He wondered what it would be like to be her lover, to have her lying naked in his arms.

It was not too surprising he might become infatuated with an elf. He and Silver had grown up amongst elves, most of the svartálfar his age had, even Aranwen. Most of Brice's friends had been elves including his best friend, Morcant. As a child he had felt closer to Morcant's parents than his own.

The svartálfar had been very few and the elves had been many. They had built great cities together and for a long while their union had kept them both safe from the Illvættir, the enemy that Brice had finally joined. But the Illvættir didn't die like the svartálfar did and slowly, very slowly, their numbers increased.

He was one of the ones assigned to destroy the city of his birth. It had been the home of all his memories but it made sense. He knew where the people would hide or try to flee to. Illvættir didn't build anything like cities, but with their daimôns helping they were very good at destroying them.

He knew he should feel guilty about what he had done: the city of his birth, the Free Svartálfar; after all they had been his own people once. He should feel guilty about the elves; what he had already done to them and what he was going to do to them now.

And yet he couldn't feel it.

Maybe it was the sickness of his soul, telling him a lie; telling him that it had to be done, that he had no choice. Telling him it was them that were evil, not him; telling him that they deserved it.

No, all he could feel was a deep and abiding sense of loss.

While he and the other Illvættir destroyed the world around them, all he could feel was such a selfish thing, a feeling of loss! And it would only get worse as it all wound down ... as they drove themselves and everyone around them into extinction.

Brice shook himself mentally and tried to focus on what they were doing now. The death of a single elf and it had sent him into a melancholy spiral, a feeling that was becoming more and more familiar to him.

They were making their way to Farsund, but something was shrouding it from his far sight. Máedóc would have noticed, but had he realised it was not the usual elvish or human magic? It was something completely new to Brice. Could it be dwarves?

He had no intention of telling Máedóc. Let him walk into a trap, if there was a trap. Brice would be careful. He really should tell Aranwen and wondered why he didn't. Why was he increasingly thinking of what he had with Aranwen as something that was belonging in the past, or soon would be?

He forced himself to think of what happened at Líðandi and he smothered a smile. Now that was something better to think about! Fáelán was dead in exchange for one elf maiden and four young children! Máedóc had lost his lover and most faithful and powerful ally, and now the only way for him to preserve his own reputation was to emphasise just how dangerous this mission was.

Brice's reputation was not only restored, it was enhanced. After all, he had destroyed the last elf stronghold and killed most of the elves there. That one of the Illvættir died in the battle or a few elves escaped was no longer surprising. From being an early target for many members of the council when the Illvættir finally turned on one another, he was starting to be seen as useful again. All he had to do was to refrain from openly gloating.

He made sure he was completely solicitous, a perfect lieutenant; while secretly hoping something would happen to Máedóc next ... even if he had to organise it himself.

Máedóc would not trust him of course, that was not the way of the Illvættir.

* * *

Máedóc sat, staring sightlessly at the coast as it passed.

Had it really been three thousand years?

The memories of the first few years with Fáelán were still fresh, despite all that time. They hadn't joined the Illvættir back then. They were happy, with a wide circle of friends and so much in love and lust. Both of them were promising sorcerers and the future seemed bright.

But it hadn't been enough for Máedóc. With a daimôn to command, he could have so much power he would be like a God.

During the war and the time after, hunting down the enemy survivors, Máedóc and Fáelán had discovered a new thrilling talent that they had. Most of their fellow Illvættir used daimôns for the more dangerous svartálfar and they used their allied humans to kill small groups of elves and any opposing human forces.

With their daimôns Máedóc and Fáelán had already killed many tens of thousands. Now, working together they could hunt down and kill most surviving enemy humans, elves and even svartálfar using only their own powers. Without using daimôns or anyone else.

By themselves they killed hundreds: men, women and children and the thrill of it was indescribable. Nothing could compare to the individual chase; the hunting down and killing of the most dangerous and clever of all prey, a member of one of the various races of man.

No wild animal could even come close. And if it looked like it was going wrong they could always command their daimôns to help them.

In the last moments their quarry begged, raged or cursed, some tried to flee or fight or protect their loved ones. In the end nothing did them any good; nothing saved them. And the final killing was just so delightfully erotic. It had never failed to fire the lust Máedóc and Fáelán felt for each other.

They both knew that one day they would turn against each other. In a way hunting each other down would be a delicious end to their friendship, but they had expected many hundreds of years and many more hunts before that day came.

In the end Fáelán had been killed by a single elf and she too was gone, killed by the Grener men. He would have liked to be the one that killed her; it would have made him feel better. But he would have his revenge on all of the remaining elves instead, and any that dared shelter them. Two years, he thought, two years and the elves would be finished.

He was second only to Áedán in power. He didn't need his daimôn to track and kill elves and they would find no sanctuary in the north. As he thought about it he realised that without Fáelán it would be a hollow victory.

He was surprised at how alone he felt. All their old friends were gone now and for millennia he had despised the idea of making new friends, or he thought he had. When he killed the last of the elves he would feel even more alone.

He would turn against his fellow Illvættir then, but without Fáelán the thrill of killing was gone. He wondered how he would kill Áedán if they both lived that long. Even with Fáelán helping, it was always going to be hard.

With all he had gained, all the power, he knew that the bonding with a daimôn was not worth what he had lost. And it was getting worse. Yet he would go on, there was no choice now.

He was riding in the royal canoe with Ragnar, the king's húskarlar, Brice, Aranwen and eighty Norse warriors. Brice had shown no signs of gloating over Fáelán's death but he was probably hiding it. Aranwen seemed genuinely sorry. It seemed that Aranwen hadn't been poisoned by whatever had affected the rest of the Illvættir ... or else she was clever, dangerously clever.

He tried to turn his mind back to the task at hand. Now was time to fulfil the bargain with Ragnar and help him take Farsund. The Vest-Agdir men were the last real obstacle to eliminating the elves.

Something there was blocking his far sight. It had to be elves, waiting there for him. They would be ready for the daimôns this time, but he had a simple plan and it would make all the difference...

* * *

The Battle for Farsund

When Hervor heard the distant signal horn the memories of her home and those last few moments came flooding back. This was the last chance for the elves. If Farsund fell, even the North would not be safe.

She reached for Bjørn's hand and they stood hand in hand, holding their breath, waiting in fear for the first sight of their enemies. She somehow knew it would be their last day together.

If the Norse were right, her fate, Bjørn's fate and the fate of all of her people—elvish and human—had already been decided. All she could do was face it with courage.

She was an elf, courage was never a problem, but this would break her heart. She squeezed her eyes shut as tears ran down her cheeks. All she wanted was peace. All she wanted was to be Bjørn's wife. All she wanted was to raise the children they had been given and bear him more, living on a farm of their own, with Olaf as a neighbour.

But she knew deep inside that whether they won or lost, she would not be given that chance. Her dreams were ashes. It was Hákon who had warned her. If she were needed this day, fate would call for her to lose all that she held most dear.

"Bjørn," she whispered. "You are my true love, you know that. If anything happens to either one of us, I want the other to promise that one day they will love and marry again."

"And who would I love and marry, if not you?" Bjørn laughed.

"Please, Bjørn. It will ease my mind."

He looked at her and realised she was serious.

"I will try, Hervor but you must promise to be careful."

"No Bjørn," Tears filled her eyes. "Neither one of us can be careful, not today."

Torgny and his men launched their boats. He had his own men and three dozen elf warriors with him, the very best from the surviving elf army, and the finest of the Sami archers. He would try to prevent a landing so the enemy couldn't bring their daimôns into play.

When Hervor saw the number of the enemy canoes, she gasped. It was greater than what the elves had faced. Konungr Alrik had a few giant warships, clinker built, and he had the largest individual fleet, but it looked like it was about to be overwhelmed.

But Torgny knew what he was about. He sunk fishing boats laden with rocks and debris at either end of the harbour to narrow the entrance. He removed any sails as a fire hazard and then formed his giant ships up; lashing them together to form a solid wall guarding the entrance to the harbour. Smaller canoes were tied in front, filled with lumber, oars, yards and ropes to obstruct any attempt to storm the floating fortress.

It still left him a score of canoes outside the harbour to harry any ships that tried for a landing deeper into the sound.

The enemy war canoes charged in but they were low in the water and their men had to man the paddles too. Torgny and his men could run across from one ship to another, shooting down into the enemy canoes and concentrating their fire on one canoe at a time.

As Hervor and Bjørn watched, a few of the attackers made it onto the small canoes but they became tangled in ropes and obstacles and exposed to fire from above. Their superior numbers were doing them no good. The sea was stained red and body after body rocked gently in the smaller waves and rose and fell in the swell. Men's screams and shouts filled the air, while enemy canoes with their cargo of the dead drifted like ghost ships.

The weakness of the plan was that the enemy could bypass the harbour and land further into the sound and Torgny didn't have the ships to prevent it. As soon as Hervor saw this happening she shook herself free of Bjørn and grabbed two spare quivers of arrows and set off at a run. Alrik had fortified the next beach with a wooden palisade behind earth works. The enemy had to either go further into the sound, which would prevent them co-ordinating with the rest of the attack, or they had to storm that beach.

Soon wave after wave of men were leaping off their canoes and wading waist deep through the water to the beach. The defenders sent a hail of throwing spears at them. The air was filled with shouting, war cries and the screams of the wounded. But it was a relatively small guard facing the main force. Some attackers discarded their spears and ran to attack the palisade, shields held high.

The fighting was intense around the gates. The attackers had already cut down a tall tree to make a ram and a couple of dozen of them were making a run with it at the gates. Many of the beleaguered defenders were already out of throwing spears and were throwing rocks and lumps of wood down at them.

A line of enemy archers and spear throwers appeared to cover the men carrying the ram and even Hervor had to take cover from a hail of arrows as the gates shivered from the first impact.

The men with the ram backed back and came running at the gate a second time. Hervor was still forced to crouch on the crude walkway; the attackers were peppering the wood she was hiding behind with arrows and throwing spears. The only thing they couldn't stop was some defenders throwing rocks blindly over the gate.

The gate wasn't built to take this sort of punishment. On the second strike it bulged inwards, the brackets holding the beam already loosening. Hervor bobbed up for a quick look to see the men with the ram running for the gate the third time. Attackers and defenders alike seemed to be holding their breath.

With an explosive 'crack' the brackets holding the bar were wrenched from their mounts and the door was thrown wide. Defenders and attackers alike crowded in to face each other across the gap. Hervor fired arrow after arrow at the tightly packed attackers but eventually the enemy began appearing amongst the small knot of defenders. They had found a second way in! The Vest-Agdir had left the wall undefended. The enemy had made a breech, which they were rapidly widening.

"Retreat!" the Farsund yfirmathur in charge screamed, but the retreat became a rout as a horde of screaming Norsemen chased the rapidly dwindling survivors to the next layer of defences, an earthen wall. Hervor ran over the top of it, with the enemy on her heels, she tossed her last spare quiver away and turned to fire, but the enemy were already washing over the second line of defenders as if it wasn't there.

It was time to flee to the town gates.

She scrambled through the gates only just in time and ran for the steps of the walkway to join the other archers and spear casters up there. The retreating defenders behind her had already disappeared under a milling crowd of enemies.

She chanced a quick glance at the harbour.

They were losing it too. The attackers had set fire to the first layer of Torgny's fleet with pine resin. It had been beyond the ability of the defenders to douse the flames and now many of the smaller Farsund ships were burning ferociously and had been cast adrift. Some of the giant ships had drawn back intact but the fighting around them was fierce. Torgny had dealt a mighty blow to the combined fleets of his father's their enemies, but the wall of ships was broken. She wondered where he was in all the smoke and fire and battle for their few remaining ships.

BANG! BANG! BANG!

Her attention was jerked back to the gates, the ones she had just run through. Three daimôns snapped into the world just outside. The Illvættir must be somewhere in the second beach landing!

Alrik's men were waiting with buckets of ice but only one of the daimôns, the one in the shape of a huge black panther, was attacking. The other two: a giant red wolf and an orange dragon were defending it, sending daimôn blasts and jets of flame at any human throwing ice or water bombs.

A moan of horror escaped Hervor's lips.

There was no answer to this.

Where was Brynjar? He was needed now!

She leapt off the palisade, as the black daimôn played a jet of fire along it. Ducking low, she ran for the cottage where her brother and the dwarves were supposed to be waiting.

"What's happening?" She demanded as she burst in. "If you are still going to do this, we need you now!"

Brynjar was naked, kneeling by the armour. His hand was slick with blood from pounding on it. He couldn't get in.

"It's a trick; we have been betrayed by the dwarves again!"

"It is no trick!" Sindri shouted at him. "Good people died to bring this thing to you!"

A large group of dwarves, humans and elves were arguing and it was getting louder and louder.

"Wait!" Her voice cut through it all. "Let me try. I'm the other heir to the prince. Everyone get out but my brother, I'm not getting undressed before you all. Out! There is no time!"

Brynjar stared at her in horror. "No Hervor, not you! I was ready."

She began to take her clothes off and passed him the charm that Bjørn had given her. "Tell Bjørn I love him, all I wanted for was to be his wife."

She was about to reach over to touch the armour when Bjørn burst in to cling to her, his arms wrapped around her.

"Bjørn, I love you with all my heart. I will always love you, but this is something I must do to save both our peoples."

"Hervor, please no!" He held her as tightly as his wounds would allow. "Please don't leave me."

"Bjørn my darling, I have no choice. Please love the children and say good bye to them for me."

"Hervor, we will raise them together!"

She twisted away and hit him as hard as she dared over his wound.

He collapsed to his knees and bent over in agony. She kissed him on his cheek for the last time. "I'm sorry, my love."

She dropped to kneel before the armour. As she stretched out her hand it passed through the armour and her anguished scream ripped through the air.

* * *

Hervor felt the cold anger wash over her like a great wave.

She was already up and moving towards the door.

"Wait, Dís! Let me take control. You can't just charge into a battle unprepared."

"We have to hurry!" The dwarf princess seemed to be in her head. "They are destroying the village."

"I'm the warrior, not you!" Hervor tasted Dís's need for vengeance and understood it, but it was making her act stupidly.

She was rapidly absorbing knowledge of how to work the armour as her mind merged with Dís' and the cold implacable monster they had both joined. While they were fusing into a single being, there was no time for her to change her way of thinking. She still thought of herself as Hervor receiving messages from the other two, much of it unspoken.

Bjørn lay where he had fallen, a broken man, but there was no turning back, no time to grieve and no time to spare to comfort him. There was a cluster of people outside the cottage door.

"Keep well away from me." She shouted. Her voice now harsh and guttural.

In the back ground she heard people speaking around her.

"I thought it wasn't working." She heard someone say. "Which man has managed to bind with the armour?"

It was Nilse who answered him, "It is Hjørvard. It is the man who never was."

"It was supposed to be me." She heard her brother say.

"I don't think that was ever true, Brynjar. Gudmund's prophecy is only an echo of an earlier one and to me it is clear enough, it wasn't meant to be a man at all. I think this was Hervor's fate before she was even born." Nilse replied. "I'm sorry but you have lost her. She has become part of something new."

She put it all behind her and turned her mind to what she now had to do.

The being that was called Hjørvard ran effortlessly up a small rise to look out. For the moment it allowed the part of it that had been Hervor to be in control. She hefted the shield that two strong men could not lift and raised the heavy spear. What she saw was a disaster.

It had only been moments and only one daimôn had attacked but already the town's main stockade was on fire. Most of the fortifications had been blasted away. The dead seemed everywhere. The great ships of the Vest-Agdir were burning furiously in the harbour. The enemy was hanging back out of the daimôns' way for the moment but once they attacked there could be no hope.

One of the daimôns became aware of her. The one that had mimicked the form of a giant panther came bounding across the beach. Its eyes blazed and a blast of power and fire shot out towards her. She stepped back and leant into the shield as the fire swirled around her.

"Ugh!" She grunted.

"Throw the spear!" Dís screamed.

She didn't need to tell her. Hervor threw the spear, putting all her skill and new strength into it.

It sailed through the air with a whirring noise and passed straight through the daimôn and followed an arc that circled back around her. She raised her hand and it flew back into her grip.

Now that's handy!

The daimôn and Hervor stood eyeing each other for an instant.

A pall of darkness began to issue out of the daimôn's wound, and then a great explosion flung her back. She landed with her knees bent, crouched behind her shield. Where the daimôn had stood there was a faint figure made of smoke. It formed a cloud, rising up into the air and getting darker and stronger as it began to fly, faster and faster back to where Máedóc was hidden.

For she had killed a daimôn and all incredible power was now hers, but first it would claim Máedóc and the vast energy contained in his immortal soul.

The two other daimôns paused for a moment as a mighty roaring storm hit the area where Máedóc was, boiling, black and crackling with power. It sucked men and debris into the air, spinning faster and faster. It had taken up every bit of power from the daimôn and Máedóc's soul. And now it would deliver itself to its new master ... if it didn't destroy her first.

It started slowly, picking up speed. When it reached Hervor, it exploded over her with a mighty clap of power, destructive, deafening and blinding. The Vest-Agdir men screamed in horror and dismay. Surely nothing could survive that power. But when the smoke cleared and they could see again, there was Hjørvard, still standing, shining like the sun.

Hervor raised her hand and a bolt of pure power swept masses of enemies away.

The two remaining daimôns turned to face this new threat.

"Is there any way to call them back?" Aranwen shouted to Brice.

"No, they are commanded to attack anything that attacked that other daimôn. We can't control them now. We have to wait till they run out of the energy they brought when we summoned them, if they last that long."

Brice had seen her from a distance, firing her arrows, as he crouched in the boat. It was the same elf girl and she wasn't dead! He didn't know why, but for a moment he was filled with a wild fantasy of standing beside her, fighting for her rather than against her. He wondered how it would have been if he had this with Silver.

Once they summoned their daimôns and commanded them there had been little for them to do but to watch and keep out of the way. He caught sight of her again running for the hut and when this monster had emerged he knew.

It was her, and her name was vengeance.

His daimôn was still shaped like a dragon. It sprang high in the air and began to wing towards her.

Hervor waited, motionless. When the daimôn was closer, she tossed her spear and held out her hand for it to return. The daimôn crashed to the ground followed by a mighty explosion, killing hundreds of the Vest-Fold warriors.

Brice pushed Aranwen away from him, "RUN!"

She looked at him, perplexed and then he saw dawning comprehension in her grey eyes. She grabbed for him and clung to him with surprising strength.

"What are you doing?"

"I love you, Brice," she said. "I will always love you. I don't want to live without you."

"But it is your soul, Aranwen! I'm not worth it! Surely you wouldn't lose your soul to be with me only for a moment?"

She smiled at him. Tears were in her eyes as their lips met.

A black cloud descended on them, sucking everything into the air.

Epilogue

"The end is all. Even now high on the headland Hel stands and waits. Life fades, and I must fall and face my own end, not in misery and mourning but with a man´s heart." The Sonatorrek, Egil Skallagrimsson (translation by H. Pálsson and P. Edwards)

Bjørn led his small escort on foot across the stream that ran below the langhús. He moved slowly as if he had aged. He could see them waiting for him: Sigríd, Valdís and Olaf, clutching the children. In his memories he saw Hervor standing there waiting for him too, smiling for him, but he would never see her again.

Brenda spied him and broke free. Even though she was tiny she ran as only an elf could.

It felt like something deep inside himself was dead and yet he could still feel his face crease into a smile. He lifted her up and hugged her for a long time; his tears wetting her hair. Somehow hugging little Brenda gave him the strength he needed. He turned to climb the last few steps to where the others waited.

If the children stayed he would find a way to go on. He had promised himself that. He would be a true father to them. He wouldn't do what his own father did in the years after Yvla left ... and yet it hurt so much!

For a moment he felt some of the anger he had always held for his father melt away, was this what it had been like for him?

Sigríd saw that one of the men was leading a live pig.

So they have come to make a sacrifice to the fallen.

"Where's Harald?" her voice was hollow. "I have buried three children and now I have only the one. Where is my man?"

Bjørn shook his head "I'm sorry Sigríd. He was a great man, a mighty fighter and the best ever of friends. We have come to raise an altar and make a *blót* (blood sacrifice) for our fallen: Edmund, Harald and Hervor."

"She is dead then," Sigríd said.

Bjørn pulled out the ivory charm from around his neck and kissed it, his eyes filling again with tears.

"She is no more." He nodded, looking grim. "She sacrificed her soul and very existence to save us all. She has joined with the dwarf princess and a monster to make Hjørvard, the greatest hero this world will ever see. After Hjørvard destroyed the Illvættir it was filled with the power of two of their three daimôns and two of their souls. It was shining so bright it was hard to look at it. Then it turned on our human enemies, destroying many until they fled in panic.

"When that was over, its fire went out and it simply lay down where it stood. Nilse tells us Hervor is gone. I knocked on that thing till my hands were bleeding and broken. I and her brother and others called till our voices were hoarse, but we received no reply.

"The thing that is Hjørvard will travel with the alfir to Hatti and whatever is left of Hervor will go with it."

"The elves are leaving?"

"Yes, their Jarl has called them and all but very few of the southern ones will go. The kynder can go if that is their wish."

"Nooo!" A chorus of moans came from the humans and the elves alike.

"We want to stay!" Brenda told him loudly as she clung to his neck.

"Don't ask us to give them up as well!" Sigríd shouted, wiping tears savagely from her cheeks.

"I had to offer, though my heart would break again and again if they left." Bjørn said. "If you agree, Sigríd, I will name you their mother and I will stand as their father both in law and in my heart. I would also like to foster Freya if you both allow. I will be staying at the farm as much as I can, but will have trips to Farsund and duties I cannot neglect. Torgny died on our faðir's ships in the final battle, and I am the new Erling now. The war is over, both sides have taken too many casualties, but my father and I will continue the alliance with the Sami and any elves that remain."

"Then they will all be our children Bjørn, and Freya's brothers and sisters. She is half alfir already." Sigríd said.

"Losing Hervor hurts, hurts more than I thought possible, but for the children and for everyone else I will go on. I must be grateful for the little time I had with her."

Sigríd, Valdís and Olaf pulled the children, their children, tightly in their arms.

* * *

This is my own version of the legend of Hjørvard, the greatest hero of the elves. It is based on a little known version, with me filling some of the holes.

All versions agree in most of the major details right up to the battle for Farsund. In all of them Brynjar has a sister whose fighting ability had earned her the nickname of Hjørvard. In most versions this is seen as little more than a curious coincidence.

In all of them Hervor does not return from that final battle. In the older and better known versions she is killed and it is her brother Brynjar who fuses with the armour and the dwarf Princess.

Thousands of years later, when Ælward wrote his prophecy, he referred to Hjørvard by the epithet 'the man who never was'. It was assumed that this was because Brynjar was not Hjørvard wearing the armour, as many had expected to happen; Brynjar's soul fused with the armour and the dwarf princess to produce a new being, called Hjørvard. So Hjørvard was not a man at all.

This lesser known version gives a far simpler explanation for 'the man who never was', that Hervor wore the armour. If this is so, Brynjar never travelled with his brother and the rest of the Southern Elves to Anatolē, he remained in Norge. Perhaps he was unable to face what had happened to his beloved sister.

* * *

"The Paladin Chronicles" series by Neil Port takes up the story many millennia later.

www.ingramcontent.com/pod-product-compliance
Lightning Source LLC
Chambersburg PA
CBHW062116170626
46813CB00002B/469